PRAISE

'A wry, dark tale of accidental murders, *The Beresford* is a gripping novel laced with humour and cutting character insight and is a thrill from start to finish. As with all of Carver's brilliant work, expect the unexpected!' Sarah Pinborough

'Curses on Will Carver for writing yet another ridiculously addictive book' S J Watson

'Equal parts enthralling and appalling ... quite unlike anything I've read in a very long while. Perhaps only the late and much-missed Iain Banks has that same deadpan humour and playfulness around such awful misadventures' James Oswald

'Absolutely stunning ... a masterclass in character, intrigue and storytelling' Chris McDonald

'A masterfully macabre tale! Will Carver never disappoints, but this is a whole new level of creepy magnificence, and I didn't want the book to end. Don't ring the doorbell but DO read this – now!' Louise Mumford

'Reminiscent of *The Shining*, *The Beresford* is a creepy and perfectly crafted novel tinged with dark humour and malice. Read with the lights on' Victoria Selman

'I stepped into the imagination of Will Carver and closed the door behind me. The darkness was unending, and I let it swallow me whole' Matt Wesolowski

'Magnificently, compulsively chilling' Margaret Kirk

'*The Beresford* is Will Carver at the peak of his powers! ... Fans of Chuck Palahniuk in his prime will adore Carver; he is utterly brilliant' Christopher Hooley

'Another great novel written in true, unconventional, Will Carver style. I love an author who isn't afraid to take risks ... great characterisation, quirky in the best way possible, definitely original' Catherine McCarthy

'Creepy and bril

'This was intense, brilliant, horrific, humorous and everything in between. I ADORED it' Liz Loves Books

'Slick, stylish, has a very modern feel to it, and includes plenty of black humour ... a sharply crafted and delectable slice of entertaining darkness' The Tattooed Book Geek

'This is such an original, chilling and compelling read. I've said it before, but I'll say it again, no writer writes like Will Carver ... If you're a fan of his books, then you will love *The Beresford*. It is so good. Highly, highly recommended' Hooked from Page One

'There is a twisted, madcap logic to it all that kept me hooked right to the very last page' Jen Med's Book Reviews

'Alright, yeah' Mark Lowes

'Bloody and brutal and darkly funny and acidic and mind-boggling and thought-provoking in a way that only a Will Carver novel is' From Belgium with Booklove

'I have come to expect unique, shocking and more than a little bit out-there when reading a Will Carver, and *The Beresford* is no different' Karen's Reads

'Disturbing, cynical, darkly funny ... nobody does fiendishly twisted better than Will Carver!' Hair Past a Freckle

'You can't put this down, even if you want to. Fantastic in every sense by a first-class author who you can't get enough of. Unforgettable' Bookmark That

'Another addictively twisted creation that burrows under your skin and leaves you reeling ... This literary thriller will grasp you by the throat, hold your nerves and increased heart rate prisoner as the storyline unravels, the atmosphere becoming suffocating as the layers build' The Reading Closet

'Will Carver has outdone himself. Again ... This book will keep you enthralled ... Every chapter got better and better. Will knows how to draw a character so well that you feel you're related to them. And boy are there some characters here' Mrs Loves To Read

'Arguably the most original crime novel published this year' *Independent*

'Cements Carver as one of the most exciting authors in Britain. After this, he'll have his own cult following' *Daily Express*

'True enough to impart to the reader the thrill of genuine discomfort, presented with the chilly conviction of Simenon's most unflinching *romans dues* and just as horribly addictive' *Telegraph*

'Carver weaves these strands together for an unsettling but compelling mixture of the banal, the horrific and, at times, the near-comic, wrong-footing the reader at every turn' *Guardian*

'Carver examines in cool but involved prose the agenda of the global suicide cult behind the deaths. Not for readers of delicate sensibilities' *Financial Times*

'Unlike anything else you'll read this year' *Heat*

'Utterly mesmerising' *Crime Monthly*

'Beautiful, gripping and disturbing in equal measure, a postcard from the razor's edge of the connected world we live in' Kevin Wignall

'A novel so dark and creepy Stephen King will be jealous he didn't think of it first' Michael Wood

'A taut, highly original novel from one of the most underrated crime writers out there' Simon Kernick

'Beautifully written, smart, dark and disturbing – and so original. The whole thing feels like a shot of adrenaline' Steve Mosby

'Possibly the most interesting and original writer in the crime-fiction genre ... His best to date – dark, slick, gripping and impossible to put down. You'll be sucked in from the first page' Luca Veste

'A genuinely creepy thriller ... completely enthralled' Margaret B Madden

'A pitch-dark, highly original, thrilling novel. If you're a fan of *Fight Club*, you'll love this' Tom Wood

'A twisted, devious thriller' Nick Quantrill

ABOUT THE AUTHOR

Will Carver is the international bestselling author of the January David series and the critically acclaimed, mind-blowingly original Detective Pace series, which includes *Good Samaritans* (2018), *Nothing Important Happened Today* (2019) and *Hinton Hollow Death Trip* (2020), all of which were ebook bestsellers and selected as books of the year in the mainstream international press. *Nothing Important Happened Today* was longlisted for both the Goldsboro Books Glass Bell Award 2020 and the Theakston's Old Peculier Crime Novel of the Year Award. *Hinton Hollow Death Trip* was longlisted for the *Guardian's* Not the Booker Prize. Will spent his early years in Germany, but returned to the UK at age eleven, when his sporting career took off. He turned down a professional rugby contract to study theatre and television at King Alfred's, Winchester, where he set up a successful theatre company. He currently runs his own fitness and nutrition company, and lives in Reading with his children. Follow Will on Twitter @will_carver.

THE BERESFORD

WILL CARVER

ORENDA
BOOKS

Orenda Books
16 Carson Road
West Dulwich
London SE21 8HU
www.orendabooks.co.uk

ISBN 978-1-913193-81-2
eISBN 978-1-913193-82-9

Typeset in Garamond by typesetter.org.uk

Printed and bound by CPI Group (UK) Ltd, Croydon CR0 4YY

For sales and distribution, please contact info@orendabooks.co.uk

For the hell of it.

*'Some people never go crazy.
What truly horrible lives they must live.'*
                                        —Charles Bukowski

OBITUARY

Jordan Irving, famed screenwriter, director, race-relations activist and philanthropist was discovered dead at his home in the early hours of the morning. Authorities suggest that the influential young filmmaker had taken his own life.

No note was found, though the situation is not being treated as suspicious.

Irving sprung up from nowhere to gain critical acclaim and commercial success with his first screenplay, *South of Heaven*, after working as a runner and location scout on several independent features.

He joins an illustrious list of performers and artists who were taken on the upswing of their careers at the tender age of twenty-seven. Known widely for his clean lifestyle, Irving did not fall into the usual traps of substance abuse or alcoholism, though he did struggle with his mental health.

He was a notably warm collaborator and passionate auteur, but those close to him have commented that he was increasingly tormented towards the end of his life, believing that he was not deserving of his success.

A hard worker, Irving never rested on his laurels. In his short career, he wrote nine screenplays and was due to direct his third feature, following armfuls of awards in both categories. A catalogue of work that any filmmaker working in the industry for twenty years would be pleased with. It is a stark reminder that this gifted storyteller leaves behind a legacy that is so much more than the hidden desperation of his life and brutality of his untimely death.

PART ONE

ONE

Your daughter brings home Abe Schwartz and you're pleased. Not for her.

This guy won't last. He's not dangerous or charismatic. He's not on any of the sports teams. He doesn't ride a motorcycle or wear a leather jacket.

He's scrawny and academic and polite. He's average. He's normal. He's nice. What he lacks in charisma, he can't make up for with enthusiasm.

Yes. Your daughter brings home Abe Schwartz and you're pleased. For you.

She drinks too much at a party, and Abe Schwartz is going to put her safely into a cab and walk her back to her doorstep; he's not even thinking about how he will get home. Maybe he's not drinking so he can drive her back himself. That's the kind of thing he'd do.

Abe probably doesn't like parties, anyway, because other people make him feel anxious and uncomfortable.

Your kid is never going to fall off the back of Abe's bike at 90mph and shatter her skull or fracture her pelvis. Don't worry.

And that pelvis won't be moving into a position to squeeze out a child anytime soon because Abe will double-bag his penis if things get that far, or he'll shoot a load into his pants. He doesn't have your daughter bent over in an alley behind the club. That Schwartz guy isn't knocking anybody up. He's a safe bet.

Here's the thing: no parent had to think this. Nobody had to feel pleased for themselves about Abe Schwartz because Abe never dated in school.

By the time he hit university, though, that whole 'geek' thing was really taking off.

He got laid. He wore a condom. Just the one. And he didn't come in his pants.

And he did go to parties and drink and he tried the softer drugs, and he liked them. He still does, occasionally. But he never rode a motorcycle and he never let a girlfriend make her own way home whether she was drunk or not. He fucked in a bed, never outside, and only twice on the floor.

Then he did what was expected of him, which was graduate and obtain a job that he never really wanted, he doesn't really care about but cannot leave because he has to buy food and pay rent. And he doesn't want to starve. And he doesn't want to get evicted.

That's Abe.

And that brings us up to date.

Abe Schwartz lives in a one-bed furnished flat. An apartment building called The Beresford. The bell rings and he's the one opening the front door to a stranger.

Before that, he's dragging a dead body into his room, mopping up blood and asking himself, *What the hell just happened?*

TWO

Like so many, Blair Conroy was on that long road to the middle. She'd always had good grades, not the best, but high enough to excel without drawing any attention to herself. She was athletic. A distance runner. Fast enough to be competitive – she worked hard – but not enough to have the consistency that a champion requires. She was beautiful in that not-really-trying way and popular without being a bitch to those deemed (by others) to be on a lower social rung.

Blair was always going to do just fine and nobody begrudged her that prospect.

Her parents were the well-meaning, God-fearing type. But pleasant with it. They'd been married forever. Not passionately in love but not merely existing in the same house. There was a love there, a tenderness, boring as it looked to Blair.

She loved them dearly but it was not what she wanted for herself.

They wanted their daughter to excel, to accomplish more in life than they ever had. They were ready for her to leave – as long as she didn't go so far away that visiting was made difficult.

'The Beresford,' her mother had chirped, 'sounds very posh.'

The rent was low, it was available for immediate occupancy, and there was no need to commit to a lengthy contract. Blair didn't have the heart to say that she'd only seen pictures and spoken with the landlady on the phone.

She just wanted out of that small-town life, that tiny-world mentality. She wanted the city and noise and thrum of culture and vibrancy of characters. She'd even told herself she wanted jazz, though she definitely did not.

It annoyed her that she agreed with her mother but the old woman was right, The Beresford sounded like a great place to live. The best thing about it was that Blair had paid an insignificant deposit, so all she had to do now was pack her bags and she was gone.

Goodbye, town meetings and church on Sunday and cooing at

the year-three dance recitals. So long, baking for the school fete and carolling with the neighbours at Christmas. Fuck you, bridge night and babysitting for the McDowell brats and the goddamned farmer's market.

See you never, mother.

Blair's father hardly spoke as he helped to carry the box of books and few bags of clothing to the car.

'You're sure that's everything you need, darling?' That's all he said, his eyes screwed up in disbelief and concern.

'Yes, Dad. The place is furnished. You can come and see once I'm settled.'

He nodded, wanting to believe her.

'And you've packed your Bible, of course,' her mother chirped in. It wasn't aggressive. More of a friendly nudge towards the Lord.

'Dad carried my box of books.' Blair's way of not lying to her mother.

Farewell, scripture study group and creepy Father Cahill and Mary Miller's too-weak tea with too-dry pastries. See you later, CreationFest and the 'unmissable' Christian rock concert.

Screw you, Jesus.

It was a tearful but brave goodbye – Blair's mother was tearful, her father was brave. Blair didn't want to look in the rearview mirror, her focus was on what lay ahead. She was getting out of that town where she thought she had never belonged, her future started now. But she couldn't stop herself from glancing. She'd waited as long as she could but there they were, her parents, waiting in the same spot until she disappeared from view, and for a moment Blair felt sad enough to ease her foot off the accelerator.

Just over an hour later and she's walking up the steps to her new home and ringing the bell. Within ten seconds, the door is opened by a man, thin, late twenties/early thirties – and he's out of breath.

THREE

The Beresford was old. The kind of building you don't expect to see near a modern city. A hulking edifice that seems to appear only in sepia photographs or black-and-white newsreel footage. The building had been noteworthy on occasion. In the twenties, it had been home to several writers and artists before they moved on to Paris. In the seventies, it is rumoured that a notorious serial killer had stayed there for almost a month after a murderous spree, avoiding capture. None of this was ever substantiated. Ten years later, a couple fell from one of the top-floor windows.

Look back another hundred years you'll find a hundred more stories like that. A mafia wedding reception, business conventions, celebrity affairs. And there's another hundred stories you won't find anywhere.

New Year's Eve, 1982. A woman went missing from one of the upper-floor apartments. She was found two days later, frozen and naked on the roof. Nobody could understand how she got up there unnoticed. The cause of death was seemingly an overdose. It was unclear whether it was accidental or not, but suspicions were roused and The Beresford came under some scrutiny.

It changed after that.

The top eight floors remained the same as they always had been. But a new entrance was built around the side of the building to access the lift that would take residents to the upper levels. An antique, art deco design with iron doors you have to shut yourself. The kind you would expect to find in a jazz-age hotel, complete with its own operator.

The third floor was cordoned off for functions, conventions and other events. This was also accessible from the new side entrance.

That left the first two floors. No lift. The original entrance to The Beresford – a discreet doorway that opened into a large communal area. Five apartments. Two up the grand, white stone staircase and three at ground level, including one occupied by The Beresford's owner and keeper, Mrs May.

She had seen it all. The stories everybody had heard and embellished and mythologised, and the ones that had never left the walls of The Beresford, much like the old lady herself.

The exterior of The Beresford altered over the years. Originally renaissance revival in its architectural style, gothic archways were introduced at ground level. The facade was updated in the mid-twentieth century and the high gables and balconies suggested more German renaissance, while the interior high ceilings felt Victorian. The hodge-podge nature of its styling reflected in the multi-culture of its residents over time.

The Beresford was old. It was grand. It evolved with the people who inhabited its rooms and apartments. It was dark and elephantine and it breathed with its people. Paint peeled and there were cracks in places. It was bricks and mortar and plaster and wood. And it was alive.

FOUR

Flat two is Abe's place. The entrance is tucked beneath the stairs, which is fine for Abe now, because it means he doesn't have to summon strength he does not possess to haul a body up to the first floor. Until today, Abe has hated that he has to sleep at street level; it never felt safe to him.

This is the first person Abe has killed. And it was an accident, he thinks. Though the two black marks beneath the dead man's Adam's apple suggest it was not. Surely he could have stopped pushing against his windpipe. He could have let him live. Maybe just knocked him out.

Abe panics and checks the body over.

Not breathing. Definitely dead.

He takes his phone from his pocket and opens his internet browser.

He types 'serial killer body disposal' and hits the search button.

> 'Following each murder, Nilsen would observe a ritual in which he bathed and dressed the victim's **body**, which he retained for extended periods of time, before dissecting and **disposing** of the remains by burning on a bonfire or flushing down a lavatory.'

Jesus Christ. Not that. Bathing with them?

Abe Schwartz throws up onto the floor next to the dead guy from flat three.

He tries again.

'How to get rid of a dead body.'

Search.

Something about Greeks and Romans cremating bodies. Blah blah. He scrolls.

People also ask: can you keep a body at home? The dropdown suggests that this is possible but involves putting embalming fluid into the bloodstream to delay decay. Abe isn't even sure what he will use to clear up his own vomit. This looks like too much.

He scrolls.

'Ten Ways To Get Rid of a Dead Body (If You Absolutely Have To).'

Click.

First things first, you have to destroy the teeth, finger/toe prints and the DNA. Abe Schwartz did not learn to ride a bike until he was a teenager, and now he has to pull somebody's teeth from their skull. Abe Schwartz, whose two main hobbies are reading and masturbating, has to find a tool that will allow him to cut through bone so that he can remove the twenty digits that are easy identifiers of the man who no longer lives at number three.

He's sweating. He looks at the body, then the door, then back at his phone screen.

Options include:

BURIAL. Too risky.

BURYING A DECOY. So, burying the body ten feet into the ground then burying something four feet above it. Like a dog. But then he'd have to buy a dog and kill it. And what about the digging? Ten feet? Abe's biceps start to ache if he takes more than three minutes to whack one out.

REUSE A GRAVE. Preferably a recent one. Dig it up and throw your body underneath. Abe was tired just thinking about all this digging.

A sound outside. Abe Schwartz holds his sick breath. Probably Mrs May skulking around in the foyer near the stairs. He'd got rid of the blood, there was only a small patch. He was sure he'd cleaned it up well enough.

The body was going to have to stay in his room until he knew what do with it. Abe put his phone on the bed, grabbed the former resident of number three beneath the armpits and dragged him towards the bathroom. The floor was tiled and would be easier to clean. He took a deep breath and hauled the body over the edge of the bath tub. The head and arms were flopped inside while the legs were still on the outside.

Then the front doorbell rang.

It couldn't be the police. Not now. Already? Surely not.

Abe Schwartz gave himself a quick look in the mirror and ran his fingers through his hair. He wiped his face and mouth on a towel that was hanging over the door and he went back into the foyer. He had to act normal.

The old landlady was nowhere to be seen. He would open the door. Make it look like nothing important had happened that day.

Through the window he saw a young woman. Similar age to himself, maybe younger. WASPy. He opened the door, still breathing hard.

'Hello, can I help you?'

Act normal.

'Hi, er, yes. I'm Blair Conroy. I'm here to see Mrs May.' She waited. Abe looked at her. A moment of silence. 'I'm supposed to be moving in today.'

FIVE

Mrs May would joke that she was so old, she knew Jesus the first time around.

'I'm hanging in for the second coming because he still owes me money.'

It was her icebreaker with every new tenant at The Beresford. Everyone found her charming and Blair was no exception to that rule.

'So, number two is over there beneath the stairs. That's Abe, who you met briefly when he let you in. He's kind of quiet and bookish but a very sweet and reliable boy. You're upstairs in number five, which is above me. You're not a tap dancer or anything, are you?' Mrs May smiled.

'Oh, no. Nothing like that.' Blair smiled back.

'Well, the room next to you is empty at the moment and the kid in the one next to mine is hardly ever around. I can't think of his name off the top of my head.'

The rates were reasonable for the space you got at The Beresford, and the deposit was so low that, often, tenants would move out or move on without a word and not care about forfeiting the money. The place had something of a turnaround. You could forgive Mrs May for not remembering everyone's names, but she blamed her forgetfulness or her age, of course.

She handed Blair the key to flat five.

'That's it?'

'That's it. The place is clean and ready to go. I can have a chat with Abe and get him to help you with any boxes you have if you'd like. I'm sure he'd help.'

Good old Abe. Chivalrous Abe. Predictable Abe. Always there to lend a hand.

'I'm sure I'll be fine.' Blair wasn't sure how accepting help would fit in with her new independent lifestyle.

'Nonsense. Why don't you go up and take a look around, and I'll have a word.'

Blair nodded, gripped the keys to her new home tightly in her right hand and made her way up the stairs. Halfway up she turned back to see Mrs May tottering back to her own place. She must have been in her eighties but her movement was more sprightly than you'd expect.

With the key pushed halfway into the lock, Blair Conroy took a deep breath before forcing it all the way in, turning and opening up to her new life.

Mrs May was right, the place was spotless. The long corridor led into a large kitchen, complete with central island, which had double doors that could open the space out into the living area. There was a coffee machine, wine rack, bowl of lemons and vase of daffodils to dress the white room and give it a splash of colour.

Care and attention had been paid to keep the space neutral in order to appeal to any new resident while illustrating the impact one's own colour preferences could have. This was not something that was offered 'upstairs'.

The lounge had a huge bookcase that was only half filled. Plenty of room for the two boxes of literature that Blair had brought with her. Parquet flooring and wooden cladding on the bottom half of the wall made it darker than the white painted wood on the hallway walls. But it was somehow more comforting. And warmer, even when the open fire was not yet roaring. There was nothing she could do about the floral fabric sofas but there was plenty of scope to make the space her own.

She remembered her promise to send a text when she arrived safely, so she took a seat and fulfilled that obligation. Her parents would respond to her within the minute. Blair took that minute to sit back and take in the space that was her lounge. Through the window she could see the light was beginning to disappear from the day and she still hadn't unpacked her car.

Just a minute to breathe. To take it all in.

Her phone vibrated. Proud parents. They were going out for dinner. They wanted pictures of the place once she was unpacked.

Hello, constant stream of questions from afar. Good day, irritating video calls filled with tech-idiot muting and awkward pauses. Greetings, awkward interrogations concerning the whereabouts of local churches and bible groups.

Blair was looking forward to a few things in that first week: preparing her own meals, leaving the bedroom door open while she got dressed, leaving the bedroom door open while she masturbated but, mostly, it was the lie-in she was going to have on Sunday – every Sunday – by not going to church.

Another buzz.

Another message.

We love you, sweetie.

Blair Conroy was glad to be away from the mediocrity of her hometown. The residents were humble and modest and ultimately caring, and it pissed her off. She knew they weren't bad but she had always felt outside of it all. And she understood that her parents were not. They were firmly rooted in the pleasantness of everything. Part of her wanted to switch her phone off and ignore them, but they hadn't done anything wrong. They had looked after her from birth until about two hours ago when she drove away from dependence.

She sent back two kisses.

Then she turned her phone off.

Below her non tap-dancing feet, she felt the vibration of music from Mrs May's place but couldn't make it out. Classical. Maybe whale song. Panpipes?

There was no need to think about that, she had to get the things out of her car before it got dark.

Welcome, first night alone.

SIX

BURNING. Logistically difficult and there's also the smell of dead flesh.

Abe was back in his room and scrolling through his options.

Dissolving in acid. This seemed like the least amount of work. No digging. No bonfire. And all the bath tubs at The Beresford were cast iron, which could hold the acid without eroding. On further investigation, it seemed as though there was no need to surreptitiously purchase industrial-sized barrels of hydrochloric or hydrofluoric acid, because most drain cleaners are corrosive enough to dissolve human hair and skin and, in the right quantities, reduce bone to something brittle enough to be ground into a dust.

Abe Schwartz, who tried to do right his entire life, who lived on the peripheries, who was quiet and kind and thoughtful, had his first seriously dark thought.

He would experiment.

The removal of fingerprints was key, he recalled. Fingers are small. He would use the secateurs that Mrs May pruned her roses with to cut off the fingers – maybe the toes, too. He would obtain the drain unblocker from the cleaning products cupboard, fill the sink and place the twenty digits in overnight. At the very least, it would remove the skin, therefore the fingerprints, and give him an indication of how well this plan might work on the rest of the body.

If it didn't work, then he'd have to rent a woodchopper or feed it to some local pigs or take it out to sea or cook the flesh and eat it himself. He sniggered at that and didn't know why.

Abe looked down at his former neighbour, the vomit still on the floor next to him, and he wanted to say sorry. He wanted to say, 'This isn't me.'

Not once did he think to call the police and explain what had happened, that it was an accident. Neither did he contemplate phoning his parents and getting the family lawyer involved. He'd probably get off with a moment of madness.

Instead, the likeable Abe Schwartz was panicking and considering how best to cover up his stupid mistake. He was deliberating between burning, burying, melting and eating.

And then there was another knock at his door.

He hadn't given Blair Conroy a second thought.

SEVEN

It wasn't the new girl, it was Mrs May.

'Oh, hello, Abe. Thanks for letting in the new tenant.'

'That's not a problem, Mrs May.' Abe was keeping his door ajar enough to fit his face through the gap, and nothing else. He was already paranoid about the smell, though his old neighbour had only been dead for an hour. 'Is there something I can help you with?'

'If you have a spare moment, Ms Conroy has a couple of heavier boxes in her car. She's a young, modern woman and wants to do it all herself, but I think it might make her feel more welcome if you could give her a hand ... if you're free...' She let it hang in the air.

Abe looked inside at a dead man.

'Sure, I mean, I was just reading, anyway. How long do I have? Enough time to finish this chapter?' He was surprised at how easily the lies were rolling off his tongue.

'She's just gone to settle in and look around, so you've got ten minutes, I'm sure.' She didn't blink.

The newly minted killer of men gave the old lady a nod and a goodbye before she trundled back to her own flat.

Once inside, Mrs May flicked her music on. It wasn't panpipes. It was the flute. She pottered around, humming along, not really doing anything. She took her teacup from the dining table, poured away the cold remnants of her last brew and shook her head at the pattern of the tea leaves before placing it into the sink.

Her place was the same layout as Blair's. She poured herself a glass of iced tea from the fridge and walked along the corridor to the living room as though mimicking Blair's footsteps above.

She fluffed some pillows. Then, when Blair sat down to text her parents, Mrs May sat down to sip at her drink. When a door closed upstairs, the old landlady put on her gardening gloves, grabbed her secateurs and made her way out to the roses that didn't need pruning.

EIGHT

He went by one name: Sythe. He'd chosen it himself because it means passionate and creative. Mrs May had not forgotten the name of the man in flat number three when she talked Blair through the list of tenants, she just couldn't bring herself to say his stupid, made-up name. Because, like most people who met Sythe, she thought he was a dick.

He would sign his paintings with that idiotic label, too. And over-wealthy, undereducated dilettantes would lap it up like they'd discovered the next Banksy.

Aidan Gallagher had left home, dropped the accent and reinvented himself as an Irish American expressionist painter. Like so many who arrived at The Beresford, he'd been an outsider in the world he'd been brought up in. He was escaping.

Mrs May's place was supposed to be a halfway house, but Sythe had entrenched himself so deeply in this new persona that he'd ended up craving the poor artist's life, even though his earnings had increased exponentially.

Flat three had become his studio. There were canvasses leaning against the walls of the hallway, and the furniture that is provided to every flat had been pushed into the corner and piled up to make way for the easels and trays of acrylics.

He seemed to emerge on the art scene from nowhere. There was an interest in some of his larger, more expressive pieces, but it was an exhibition showcasing one of his portraits that garnered the most interest. A small canvas of a striking black woman was framed on the wall. Her right eye was crying a fluorescent orange tear, which streaked down her cheek and over the frame before trickling down the wall and ending in a small puddle on the gallery floor.

That's when he made a splash. In the art world, at least. In that city. At that time.

And it had made him even more unbearable.

Mrs May didn't care. As long as the rooms were filled, she was content. It didn't matter who anybody was or why they were there. She never asked why they had to leave, she never followed up if they moved on without a word. The rooms were never empty for long.

As soon as somebody was out, somebody else came in.

That's how The Beresford worked.

Sythe played his music loudly. He would get angry with his work. He would shout at his paintings. He would scream as he put his foot through another canvas or snapped a frame. Mrs May had allowed him some space in the modest, communal garden. A corner for his metal can where he could burn the work that had upset him so much. At least once a week, Sythe was out there setting fire to wood and material, watching it burn as the smoke caused his eyes to water.

He was creative and he was passionate. That part of this character he created was true. He was expressive – maybe even talented – but he was most certainly a dick and, in the end, being an expressive dick is what got him killed.

NINE

Blair took the keys, left the flat and went back downstairs. On the bottom step she could see the ruffled brown hair of the man who had let her in. There was a line of sweat running down the spine of his sensible blue shirt.

She was only a few steps down when he turned around.

He smiled.

Such a kind face.

'Blair, right?'

'Yes. And you're Abe.'

'Well, now that's out of the way again, I believe you have some boxes in your car...' Abe presented his hand, gesturing for his new neighbour to lead the way.

'If you're sure it's no trouble?' Blair wanted to do things alone, she didn't want somebody she hardly knew walking around the new home that she had not yet explored fully herself. But she could see that he was just being kind and accommodating. Awkward, but kind.

She considered herself a good judge of character, and Abe looked like the dependable lapdog type.

And Abe hadn't noticed that small-town smile. He hadn't clocked the purity and innocence. He didn't smell the sweet perfume or run his gaze over the contours of Blair's body. Because all he could think about was the dead one in his flat.

Still, he managed to pull himself together. 'No trouble at all, m'lady.'

He regretted that as soon as he had said it.

Blair led the way to the car, explaining that there really wasn't that much to help with but that she appreciated his efforts. She asked how long Abe had lived there and he told her it was almost a year, maybe more, maybe two. He noticed her accent and she told him that she was from a place about two hours north. Abe was from the other side of the city but had always lived around these parts.

'What about the other guy?' Blair asked. Abe stiffened, his lower back already in discomfort from the weight of the books.

'What guy?' He knew what guy.

'The one in number three. What's he like? Mrs May couldn't even remember his name.' She grabbed a sports bag from the back seat, which contained most of her shoes.

'He's an artist. A painter. Bit of a recluse, you know? Keeps himself to himself.'

'Oh, very mysterious.' Blair was intrigued and Abe could tell.

'Honestly, you could be here for three months before you even catch a glimpse of him.'

He had either quashed her intrigue or piqued her interest, he couldn't tell.

Blair spotted Mrs May from the corner of her eye. She was outside the front door, wearing a pair of gardening gloves and clipping parts of a rose bush. Or pretending to.

'You think she's listening in?' Blair whispered.

Abe gave a short but genuine laugh. 'She does like to be kept abreast of everything.'

'She seems nice enough, though.'

'Oh, yes. Mrs May is a gem. Very sweet, old lady. A little eccentric at times. I mean, she's clearly not pruning anything over there, and I have heard some weird noises coming from her apartment. Some of the music she plays is so God-awful.' He added another laugh but noticed Blair balk a little. 'I'm sorry. I didn't mean to offend you.'

And she could see he meant it.

'No. No. I'm not offended. Not in the slightest. It's just that where I'm from, nobody would ever use a phrase like that, you know? God is everything to everyone. But not to me. It's okay. That's the thing I wanted to get away from.'

There was a tender moment of silent understanding between the new friends before Abe broke it by saying, 'Now can we get away from this car because this box of, I'm going to guess encyclopaedias and anvils, is starting to pull on my back.'

They walked back up the front steps, where Mrs May pretended that she hadn't noticed them outside. Some pleasantries were exchanged but Abe hurried things along to get inside with his load.

For a moment, he forgot that he was now a murderer.

It only took three trips to empty Blair's car. They stacked the boxes outside her front door and she told Abe that she could get them in herself. That way, she had accepted help but maintained her independence. She hadn't even looked at her bedroom yet.

'Thanks for your help, Abe, it was very kind of you. If you need anything in the future – a cup of sugar, help burying a body – you know where I am.' Blair laughed at herself.

It made Abe nervous and awkward. He wondered whether she really meant the last part. Then he managed to rationalise her words and excused himself so that he could cut the fingers and toes off the artist hanging over his bath tub.

TEN

That morning, there had been another of Sythe's infamous burnings in the corner of the garden. His paintings had been taking a slightly darker turn, and he wasn't comfortable with the direction he was heading. He had taken his frustrations out on a canvas, and it had fought back a little. He had snapped the frame, and the splintered wood went through the palm of his left hand, bleeding over the floor and the ruined picture.

He cursed loudly, just as he always did. Then wrapped his hand with a rag, tucked the broken masterpiece under his arm and took it outside so that he could set fire to it.

Twenty-five minutes later, there was a knock at the door, which Sythe answered.

'Is it you?' The man was angry.

'I'm sorry?'

'You. Is it you that is having a fucking bonfire in the middle of the day?' The middle-aged barrel of a man took a step closer, and Sythe, instinctively, took a step back.

Abe was reading and could hear the commotion.

'Do NOT try to come in here, sir.'

The barrel wasn't listening.

'I'm trying to eat my lunch in peace and I've got smoke coming into my house. I can't even keep my windows open in this weather because someone in this house is always burning their goddamned rubbish.' He poked a finger towards Sythe's face on the beat of the last four syllables.

'Get your finger out of my face.'

'Get your smoke out of my house.'

Abe stopped reading so he could concentrate on the argument.

'I'm sorry but who are you?' Sythe looked disgusted at the sight of the man trying to barge his way over the threshold of The Beresford.

'I'm a neighbour. I live directly behind your garden.'

'And what do you do?'

'What?' His anger gave way to confusion.

'What do you do … for a living?' Such condescension in his voice.

'What has that got to do with anything?' The anger was rising again.

'Because I am an artist. I have a process. And part of that process is editing out the works that are not fit for consumption. In simple terms, I burn the shit. I rip it apart and I set fire to it. Erasing it forever and cleansing myself of it.'

'Well, you need to be more considerate about when you do it.' The overweight neighbour seemed to think he was in a negotiation with a rational human being.

Mrs May's music seemed to get louder.

Abe came out of his flat, a hardback book in his right hand, and perched himself against the wall a little closer to the action. He didn't know why. Morbid curiosity. Perhaps he was hoping the man from over the fence would punch Sythe on the nose. That would be funny.

'You're wrong. You wouldn't understand. You probably sell insurance or something. The only thing I have to consider is my work. If I need to purge at midday or midnight, that is when I will do it.' His face was so punchable.

But the complainer was so taken back by the self-importance, it took him a moment to compose himself.

'Take this as a friendly warning: the next time smoke pours over that fence and into my house, it will be the last thing you ever fucking burn and the first thing I ever stick up your arse.' And, with that, the barrel turned and rolled back home.

Abe had to stop himself from laughing. Mrs May was still in her flat with the flute blaring.

Sythe shut the door.

'Everything alright?' Abe asked, suddenly finding himself out on the open landing between the downstairs flats.

'Mind your own business, Abe.' Lost somewhere in the moment, a little of Aidan Gallagher's accent found its way out.

Abe exhaled in disbelief. 'Jesus, I was only asking.'

Sythe's venom had a new target. He paced over to Abe Schwartz and stood close to his face, just as the neighbour had done so threateningly a few moments before.

'What's it got to do with you, eh? What do you even do all day around here? You're always reading some book or another?' It was as though he'd forgotten he was Sythe at all. Abe was hearing some Irish impersonator.

'Why are you so—?'

There wasn't time to think of the correct word before Sythe or Aidan or whoever he was pushed Abe in the shoulder.

'What the—?' Again, Abe was stuck.

'You're always skulking around, not doing anything. What are you, a spy for old Mrs May?' He pushed Abe again.

'Mrs May? What has she got to do with anything?'

Then Sythe slapped Abe around the face. Hard. It may have been residual anger from his last conversation or some kind of pent-up frustration over his artistic failings. Perhaps it was that Sythe was a dick. And he was bigger than Abe, so he thought he could push him around a bit. Sythe had thrust himself, somehow, onto this art scene and he had nobody around him to reel him in, to keep him grounded, like his family did back home in Ireland.

Maybe he thought he was invincible and could get away with anything.

He provoked Abe once more, slapping him with the inside of his bloodied hand. What he didn't expect was for Abe to lose himself so completely.

The hardback book came straight up, almost sending Sythe's nose through his skull. His eyes watered and he hurled some obscenities, but Abe was not himself. Soon, they were on the floor. Abe straddled the artist's chest. He hit the book into Sythe's face a few more times and pushed downwards with all his force so that both thumbs pressed either side of Sythe's poisonous windpipe.

There was kicking and gargling and a bloodied nose and the woodwind instrumental from the corner apartment.

Then stillness. And realisation.

The first kill is always the best.

The next time the smoke crept over the fence, it would be Abe attempting to dry out the bones of the man he had just strangled to death.

ELEVEN

'Jesus Christ!' Blair held a hand to her heart.

'I'm sorry, dear, I didn't mean to scare you.'

Mrs May raised a gloved hand towards her new tenant in apology for sneaking up on her. Blair had two boxes left to drag inside her new home. She wanted to get some books on the shelf, drink a large glass of wine and masturbate with the bedroom door wide open. It wasn't the most refined of plans but it was what she wanted to do on her first night of freedom.

'Where did Abe go? He stopped helping you?'

'It's okay, Mrs May, I asked him to leave me be. I haven't even seen all the rooms myself. He helped get the heavy things upstairs. I'm more than capable of taking things inside myself.' And she smiled that wholesome country-girl smile of hers.

'Well, if you're sure. I was going to give him a piece of my mind.'

'No, no. Please don't do that. He seems very kind and gracious. The kind of neighbour anyone would want. Really.'

Then Blair found herself in a too-long conversation with Mrs May about nothing. She was too polite to leave the old woman out in the hall but also didn't want to invite her in. All the time hoping she would go away so that Blair's freedom plans could be realised. The wine was on the side in the kitchen. Calling her.

'It's been a long day. I'm going to get these last couple of boxes in and probably turn in for the night. We can catch up again tomorrow.'

In Blair's mind, this was courteous. She was making future plans for discussion but she was busy right now. That's how they'd see it back home – what used to be home. But she was in the city now. And the look on Mrs May's face made Blair feel as though she had been too abrupt and had insulted the woman who provided her shelter (for a more than fair price).

But she couldn't hesitate. That would draw attention to her possible mistake. Blair had to ride it out. She edged into her new place, the last two boxes stacked on one another in her arms, an elderly lady in gardening gloves staring at her. Wordless.

'Goodnight Mrs May,' she tried.

Nothing.

Blair set the boxes down in the hallway, letting the door close behind her, and waited to hear feet shuffling back downstairs.

She waited some more.

Was Mrs May still waiting out there? Blair was too uncomfortable to look through the peephole. Instead, she bolted the door and pulled the chain across before honing in on the wine.

Her first glass went so quickly, she stopped thinking about the creepy landlady and managed to unpack one box of books. She drank the next large glass in the bath. Washing away her past and the scent of mediocrity.

The bathroom was at the end of the long corridor that stretched from the front door to the back of the apartment. It was the same as Abe's place, Mrs May's and the artist formerly known as Sythe's studio. Wet footprints marked the black-and-white tiles of the hallway floor where Blair had not dried herself off fully.

With the towel wrapped around her, she poured another glass in the kitchen then laid herself down on her new bed, opened the front of the towel and placed her hand between her legs.

She wasn't worried about the noise but she had closed the door.

She wasn't quite ready.

She would wake up tomorrow and make new plans.

WHAT DO YOU WANT?

It should be simple.

What music do you like?

Well, definitely not Coldplay, I can't stand them. Their first album was great but they're awful after that. And no ABBA. In fact, nothing of that ilk from around that era. Or from that part of the world. Everything in the charts is so manufactured and insipid now, too, I prefer to drive in silence these days, rather than have the radio playing.

You want to put a film on?

Not sci-fi. I'm not in the mood for that, at all. And I'm sick of all the romantic comedies coming out of Hollywood at the moment. It's the same old shit. Even the people in them look almost identical.

Hey, kids, what do you fancy for dinner tonight?

Not stir-fry. We hate stir-fry. And not that horrible pasta sauce you did the other week, either. And definitely not soup again.

What do you want to be when you grow up?

I don't want to work in an office.

*Where **do** you want to work?*

Not a big corporate. But not a start-up, either.

So, a reputable and established independent company?

Not in the city.

Saying what you don't want, what you don't like, what you don't agree with, is so much easier than the opposite. Deciding what you do want, the things that interest you, and standing for something, requires belief.

Belief in yourself.

Belief in something higher.

Not committing to something that you want – no matter how

small – does not protect you from never attaining it. It prevents you from ever starting. Leaving you to walk through this thing you call life like it's purgatory. It is your waiting room for death.

Start small.

Keep it simple.

Have a go or go to hell.

Can you say one thing that you do want?

We want to belong.

TWELVE

Abe often went out into the back garden at night, to smoke weed. The same spot where Sythe burned his awful paintings.

It was funny how the neighbour over the fence had never complained about that.

He liked his new neighbour but she really had arrived at the exact wrong time. He imagined that they could be friends. She was warm and funny. She apparently enjoyed reading, and they both seemed to have an aversion to organised religion. Marriages were built on less than that.

But he couldn't focus on new friendships right now. Not while the world's most overrated abstract expressionist corpse was starting to stink up his bathroom. He needed some time to think. And smoke. And be outside of the fear for a moment.

It was cold but Abe didn't care. The line of sweat running down his back had been widening with every trip up the stairs, carrying a new box.

He was panicking. Did the body already smell? He'd seen enough crime shows to know that bodies start to kick out fluids and odours fairly quickly. And what about Mrs May? Luckily, she hardly saw Sythe, and it was obvious that she wasn't particularly fond of him. If he wasn't around for the next week, it wouldn't be out of the ordinary. But she must have keys to all the apartments. She owns The Beresford. It's her business, her livelihood. She can't have tenants camping out and not paying their rent. What if she goes into Abe's room to drop off some mail? Very innocent and helpful of her, of course, but she'd be hit by the scent of death. And curiosity would take her further inside the depravity.

Then what? Kill Mrs May? Murder Blair, just to tie up all the loose ends?

This wasn't him.

This wasn't Abe Schwartz.

He did not want to go on a killing spree. He just wanted people to leave him alone.

Abe drew in a couple of lungs of smoke, shut his eyes for a moment and held it there before releasing it into the air. A few seconds of calm.

He was all alone. He always had been. He liked it that way. Look what happened when you got involved with other people.

A light turned on in the house behind the garden and somebody opened the window. Abe ducked down behind the fence, stubbed out his joint and held his breath. A few seconds later, he heard the window squeak closed and let out his breath.

The Beresford looked huge from his position, looming over him, rounding its back. The red bricks had turned grey and it looked somehow haunted now. The decking was uncomfortable to sit on but Abe stayed, surveying the area.

There was a clear separation between the upper and lower sections of The Beresford. The third floor, when not in use by some company for an end-of-quarter presentation and kick-off party, acted like a dark tourniquet that kept the upstairs levels from touching the section where Abe lived.

A different sound came from the higher floors. It felt edgy to Abe. Things were probably happening on those floors that he didn't want to know about. He enjoyed being out the back but, at night especially, it felt like those shadowy floors above were pressing downwards and that empty corporate space on level three was the only thing stopping him from being crushed.

Mrs May took such care of the garden. Flowers everywhere. Vegetables growing in raised beds. She had been out the front of the building earlier while Abe had been helping Blair, and he had thought she was just being nosey, trying to listen in. But he could tell that he had been wrong. Mrs May must have continued her pruning out the back of the house because there, resting on an oversized plant pot next to her roses, were her secateurs.

The old dear must have been distracted by something. She seemed a little senile and was probably always misplacing items.

The old Abe would have taken them back immediately for fear that Mrs May would start to worry.

The new Abe thought they'd be perfect for cutting off fingers and toes. All he needed now was the drain cleaner.

THIRTEEN

Mr and Mrs Conroy soaked up the hospitality of their church group that night. Their friends were sensitive. They were caring. They were the way that all Christians believe themselves to be but many rarely are. The community was their church. Not the building they frequented.

Blair had hated it because she didn't belong, not because there was anything evil or cultish or untoward. It was perfect. And, to her, there was no beauty in perfection.

No risk.

No passion.

No point.

Just how the Conroys wanted it to be. They went out for dinner with two other married-forever couples. They all had the soup starter. For main course, everybody ate meat apart from Mrs Conroy, who was vegetarian. It was the one thing that set her apart from the others at church and, as such, was the one thing Blair truly respected about her mother.

They shared two bottles of red wine between the six of them, which was more than enough to have them nudging at the barriers of propriety, but the extent of their rebellion was giggling too loudly at Mr Conroy's jokes.

It was a pleasant evening where Blair's parents got the opportunity to focus on themselves rather than the hole that had been left in their lives.

They each ordered a dessert. Mr Conroy took his usual affogato, which he had found to be the most wondrous concoction since seeing it in the movie adaptation of *The Talented Mr Ripley* – his second favourite book after the Bible. His wife had once tried to make him one at home, but it just wasn't the same as going out for dinner.

The men shook hands afterwards and kissed each other's wives goodbye on the cheek. They smiled and walked home in different directions, talking about the joy of their evenings. Not a bad word was said about another person at that table.

And then the Conroys were home.

The house already seemed bigger. They imagined an echo that wasn't there. The living room had too many seats and the upstairs had too many bedrooms. It was just them, now. A home built for three – with one guest bedroom, of course – was now occupied by only two.

'Shall we have a nightcap?' Mr Conroy suggested from, seemingly, nowhere.

'Dear, don't you think we had enough at dinner?'

'It was lovely, darling, but we would usually come home to Blair and she is not here. Things are different, so I think it could be an idea to do something we wouldn't usually do.' He had already made his way over to the drinks cabinet and was crouching down to pull out a bottle of something.

'Okay. I'll take a thimble of sherry, if you must.' She was playful.

'Then I guess I'll have a large whisky.'

Mr Conroy poured the drinks, they clinked glasses and paused. He was going to toast Blair but changed his mind. His wife wondered what he was going to say.

He kept it simple.

'To two'.

They took a sip and kissed. Nothing amorous. It wasn't going to lead anywhere just because they had the place to themselves. It was friendly understanding and cherished companionship. It was beauty in a moment. It was The Conroys.

And they turned out the lights and brushed their teeth and dressed in their night clothes and prayed and got in to bed, where they lay, back to back, looking out through separate walls and wondering what their only child was doing at that moment.

Blair's father imagined her underneath a lamp, sitting on the sofa with a large glass of red wine and a book, her feet tucked beneath her. Just like she did at home. Her old home. He smiled to himself as though it were true. But he could hear his wife breathing.

A sigh.

A whimper.

He knew that she did not want to talk about it. Not at that time of night. Not after they'd had such a wonderful evening.

Mr Conroy rolled over, draped his arm across his wife and pulled her in tightly. He kissed her on the back of the head and whispered that he loved her. And that everything would be okay. That 'she is going to be fine'. And he felt the tension in Mrs Conroy release.

And he didn't let go.

And they both fell asleep.

Emptier but hopeful.

FOURTEEN

The sound is exactly as you'd expect it to be. But the ease with which Abe clipped straight through the bones of the smaller toes was a shock. The thumbs required a real squeeze. They wouldn't come off in one cut, he had to gradually break through, but he did it. He successfully removed ten ways to identify Aidan Gallagher – or the artist formerly known as Sythe.

The instructions said to pour half the contents down the drain and wait fifteen minutes for it to start working. That's how long it takes to begin breaking things down, dissolving hair and other detritus. Then he had to flush it with warm water, apparently. And repeat if the blockage didn't go.

Abe's sink was fine. So he poured two full bottles of drain cleaner granules over the severed fingers and toes and left them for quarter of an hour before covering them in warm water.

He would let them sit until morning.

Warning: if splashed onto the eyes or skin, rinse immediately with cold water and contact your doctor. Never use a plunger on a drain where the cleaning fluid has been used. Never mix with other household cleaning products.

A part of Abe wanted to know what would happen if he threw in some bleach.

All that was left to do was wait. Wait to see if the fingerprints would dissolve overnight. Wait to know whether there was a solution to his problem that did not involve the physical exertion of digging a hole twelve feet into the ground. Somehow, Abe had to find a way of getting through the night with a digitless corpse swooning over the bath.

Stupidly, this meant the shower was out of action, as was the sink. So, despite sweating through his favourite blue shirt, Abe Schwartz could not wash his body, and the only way to clean his teeth was in the kitchen, but there were too many dirty dishes. So Abe opted to brush his teeth in his bedroom and spit the toothpaste out the side window.

The shirt went into the washing basket, as did everything else he was wearing, apart from his underwear, which is what Abe always wore to bed. And good old Abe Schwartz did something he had not done for years. He sat on his bed, closed his eyes, and he prayed.

He closed his eyes and called out to a God he had lost faith in and asked Him for forgiveness. He asked not to be found out. And he asked for the strength to do whatever was needed to put things right. He would even the slate. If he could only be allowed by whichever Lord was listening to get away with the murder of another human being.

He wasn't asking for dispensation, because Sythe was a dick, but it would not have hurt his cause if he had chosen that road.

Abe Schwartz pulled back the covers and got in. He wasn't sure he'd be able to sleep but he was going to try. Stillness and silence was all that it would take.

The Beresford was quiet. The walls were thick. You could chop somebody up in your apartment without causing a disturbance. The only thing anyone ever heard from another apartment was Mrs May's music, and you couldn't complain to the woman who owned the house you were living in.

And, while lying on his back, staring at the ceiling, Abe said another prayer in his head, asking not for forgiveness or a free pass, but to wake up in the morning and find that none of this had actually happened. Or to wake up and do the entire day over again. He could keep everything the same apart from the fight and the murder and the chopping up a body.

Abe tried his very best to hope, to assuage his usual brand of nihilism. He fell asleep eventually. Guiltier and emptier.

FIFTEEN

The day was new and everything that came before had still happened. Sythe was dead. No prayers were answered. And Blair Conroy woke up, on her own, in her own place, to no alarm. No pans were crashing around in the kitchen as her mother baked something for the church. Her father wasn't whistling or revving an engine in the garage after tinkering with the car.

The Beresford was heaven.

She had nothing planned for the day and, more importantly, nothing planned *for* her. Somehow, her parents had even managed to resist texting. They were giving her space. She imagined her father restraining her mother and it made her laugh. She was conscious of the noise at first, then realised she could do what she wanted. She could do who she wanted. She could be loud or quiet. She could sing, fuck, read. She could cook her own meals or order the most unhealthy takeaway imaginable.

Blair Conroy could change herself or become herself. Go vegan. Worship Satan. Crochet. Drink rosé wine. She could be anything and anyone. Everyone in that building could be just like Blair Conroy.

Creating themselves.

Recreating themselves.

The Beresford was a halfway house for the disenchanted and disenfranchised, whose focus was to become. To be. To discover and make their impact. The inhabitants were not necessarily the outsiders but were certainly the ones found on the periphery. The wallflowers at society's ball. You could be an Irish farm boy one minute and the toast of the city's art scene the next.

Blair knew exactly where she was from, but it was too early to know where she was heading. All she knew was that she felt invigorated and that she was, that morning, heading out for a run. Not to train for a race, it was for pleasure.

Because she wanted to.

Blair could do anything that she wanted to.

SIXTEEN

Abe Schwartz could not do anything that he wanted to do. Not yet. Not since he pulled a Charles Manson and lost himself for a moment. (We all go a little mad sometimes.)

He had slept as well as guilty men do. Soundly. Too deep to dream. And now, he was back on his phone, scrolling through articles and falling into the serial-killer rabbit hole. He made sure to set his browsing to private, which he had not done while panicking the day before when he went straight to Google and typed: 'How to get rid of a dead body.'

This was causing Abe some anxiety but he could blame one search on morbid curiosity. A follow-up on bone disposal or dissection would do more than raise an eyebrow.

He had discovered that flushing the bones whole – even the smaller ones – was a fast route to discovery. They almost always caused a pipe blockage. There'd be no need for a police investigation, any hack plumber could out you with sufficient evidence.

He found that a body could be buried in a shallow grave for a week or two and it would be easier to peel away the flesh. But that would still require digging and Abe did not want to dig.

Like all good millennials, he wanted the greatest possible outcome for the least amount of effort.

He scrolled.

Jeffrey Dahmer had the solution. The bones needed to be wrapped in a sheet and then pulverised with a sledgehammer. If you could break them into tiny fragments, you could deposit them in the toilet or drop a few in with the recycling or cut a hole in your trouser pocket and discreetly shake them onto the floor like you're trying to escape Shawshank prison. Dahmer had emptied his bone splinters into the woods behind his house.

Abe had a better idea. He could burn them in batches to make them more brittle and smash them into a powder. Then he wouldn't have to worry about even having to leave the house.

It was perfect.

He put the phone, face down, on the bed for a moment and thought.

What am I doing?

Can I really get away with this?

He could have and should have called the police immediately. He could have claimed self-defence. He could have said that the artist was temperamental and prone to aggressive mood swings. That Abe was the victim. He was attacked by Sythe. His mother's lawyer would have got him off on a technicality.

But that was gone. There was no turning back for Abe Schwartz.

Abe Schwartz, who has more books in his apartment than Blair Conroy could find in her old small-town library.

Abe Schwartz, who would help a stranger carry heavy boxes up the stairs to her new home, despite not being physically gifted and too lazy to dig a hole in the ground.

Abe Schwartz, who only got into a mess because he was concerned about his neighbour being shouted at on his own doorstep. He is no friend to gossip, and cares about the world and the people in it.

He had hoped the whole thing was a nightmare, that his day would restart and he could put things right, but he had woken up and traipsed into the bathroom to find that Sythe's fingerprints had dissolved, as had a lot of the flesh. He poked hesitantly at a big toe with the rubber end of a pencil and watched as meat separated from bone. The water was blotched with a deathly film that confirmed Abe was now in too deep to turn back.

So he left everything in the sink for another hour while he researched things on his phone and joined the Jeffrey Dahmer fan club.

Then he got changed. Brushed his teeth again. Sprayed some deodorant over his torso. Drained the bathroom sink. Rinsed the bones that remained. Placed them into a paper sandwich bag. Stuffed them into his jacket pocket. And left the apartment – double-locking the door.

Abe had scrubbed Mrs May's secateurs and placed them, not where he had found them, but in a plant pot on the front porch. The old dear wouldn't remember where she had misplaced them.

The front door opened and startled Abe. But it wasn't Mrs May or the police or the ghost of Aidan Gallagher, it was Blair, clad in lycra, phone strapped to her arm, earphones in.

She took out the left one. 'Morning, Abe. Out early.'

'Er, yes. Just going for a walk. Bit of fresh air.'

'I hear ya. It's a lovely day. Let's get it started, eh?' And she placed the earphone back into place before waving him goodbye and setting off down the street with a smile on her face.

That love of exercise was not something that Abe could understand. He watched the way Blair moved and, for a moment, forgot about the dead guy in his bathroom and the fact that the secateurs were now defunct.

He needed a saw.

SEVENTEEN

Mrs May does the same thing every morning. And she has done it since the day she bought the building known as The Beresford.

She goes straight to the bathroom and runs herself a deep, hot bath complete with bubbles that are supposed to help relax her muscles. She evacuates her bladder and leaves the taps running while she floats into the kitchen. She puts ten tablespoons of ground Colombian coffee – it's a mild, all-day bean – into her eight-cup cafetière, boils the kettle and pours it over the grains.

Then she waits.

Four minutes for the coffee to steep. Then she plunges and pours into a large mug, which she leaves on the side.

The bath continues to run.

Mrs May listens to some of her music. She does not sit down. After two songs, she knows that the bath is almost full. She undresses and lies in the water until her wrinkles have wrinkles.

She dries and dresses and returns to the kitchen, where her black coffee is now perfectly cold. Just the way she likes it in the morning. She drinks it with her two poached eggs on brown toast with more black pepper than anyone would ever need.

This is every day and it will not alter.

Mrs May remembers that she came back to her apartment the night before, wearing her gardening gloves but without her secateurs. She knows that the last place she was pruning was in the back garden, so checks outside near her favourite rose bush.

She is old and she is slow but Mrs May has all her mental faculties. She knows that she left the tool out the back. She saw both Abe and Blair leave the Beresford in the morning so cannot ask them if they have seen anything or picked them up, perhaps. She knocks on Sythe's door. No answer.

There is a cupboard in the downstairs communal area of The Beresford. Mrs May keeps it stocked with things like plant feed, tools, firewood, cleaning products, along with two brooms – one for the inside, one for outside – and a vacuum cleaner. If somebody found her pruning shears on the floor outside and it was late, this is where they would put them.

They're not in there. The only thing she notices is that the firewood needs restocking and both bottles of drain-cleaning fluid seem to have been taken. It's not a product that is used often, and when it is, it is used in small quantities. So it stands out.

She would replace everything but makes a note to check in with the residents to ensure there are no plumbing issues.

Through the window, Mrs May could see that Blair had returned from her run. She was standing on the front porch, leaning against one of the wooden beams and stretching off her thighs. Blair didn't even hear Mrs May open the front door because her headphones were still blasting out something upbeat and motivational.

'Good morning, dear.'

Blair was oblivious. Mrs May tried again. Louder.

'Good morning, dear.'

Nothing.

Mrs May moved around into Blair's line of vision.

'Ah, Mrs May,' she smiled, her face glowing with sweat and activity, 'how are you today? Lovely, isn't it?' She was still breathing a little heavily.

'Yes. It is. I see we have another early riser in the building.'

'I just felt like attacking the day.'

Blair smiled and started walking towards the door as if to go inside.

'You slept well?'

Blair stopped and turned back, that country-girl smile still draped across her flushed-from-exercise pink cheeks.

'Oh, like a baby, Mrs May. It was just perfect.'

'And you're all unpacked and settled?' Blair nodded but didn't have an opportunity to speak before Mrs May continued. 'And you've had a chance to look around? I only ask because I think I left my pruning shears out the back yesterday evening and I can't seem to find them this morning. I wondered whether you may have picked them up and put them somewhere.'

Blair's smile dropped a little at what seemed to be an accusation. She felt awkward. Didn't know what to say. Didn't know where to look. Above Mrs May's head she saw a spider's web in the corner of the porch roofing. Over her shoulder, half a mile down the street, she could see Abe walking home with a plastic bag in each hand, which she assumed were his groceries for the week. Her gaze flitted to the side to avoid the old woman's eyes and landed on the plant pot by the front door. The one Mrs May had mimed trimming while desperately trying to listen in on Blair and Abe talking at the car.

'Handheld cutters? Teal-coloured handles?'

'Ah, you *have* seen them.'

'I can see them right now.' And Blair leant down to pick up the secateurs. The ones that Mrs May was sure she had left in the back garden because she *had* left them there. These ones, the ones out the front looked exactly like hers, but a lot cleaner – scrubbed and bleached and disinfected and rinsed after chopping off the fingers and toes of her artist neighbour.

'You may not have noticed but I am quite an elderly woman.' Mrs May gave a smile that was more a plea for forgiveness than a joke.

Blair Conroy was brought up to be forgiving, to understand and empathise with the failings and faltering of others.

'An easy mistake to make when you're so busy.'

There was nothing barbed about her response. Blair had not been ravaged by city life yet. She was sweet and wholesome and fundamentally *Christian* for an atheist. And she was still riding the wave of new independence and post-exercise endorphin release. So, like everyone who ever lived at The Beresford, she was in the honeymoon period, where everything was changing and everything seemed perfect.

Mrs May was far more cynical and suspicious. She had been at The Beresford from the beginning. And, though she was certainly old, she remembered everyone who had ever lived there. She remembered the people that had stayed for years and she remembered all the ones who had left without a word.

And she remembered, without doubt, that she had left her pruning shears in the back garden.

EIGHTEEN

It wasn't groceries. It was a saw and as many bottles of drain cleaner as Abe could fit into his bags.

It would draw too much attention to go to one shop and clear their shelves of the product, he may as well walk into a hardware store and purchase a knife, some rope, masking tape and bin liners.

Abe was a reader. He had read a non-fiction book about a particular tiny village in Germany that had somehow produced many of the top business people at the big automotive companies like BMW, Volkswagen and Mercedes. It was also home to a woman who had started a pretzel company in her garage. And he remembered that she coated her pretzels in lye. Obviously an incredibly corrosive material, however, once heated above fifty degrees, becomes completely safe and gives the pretzels that shiny brown colour that people are so used to.

Abe considered using this as a reason to buy an industrial-sized container. If asked, which was likely, he could claim the pretzel defence.

Then he remembered a fictional thriller he had ingested in one sitting where the killer liked to bathe his victims in bleach but, so as not to raise any questions, he would purchase the six bottles required from different places.

That was the route that Abe chose over the stupid pretzel idea.

He couldn't see Mrs May and Blair talking outside The Beresford because he wasn't looking towards the house. The bags weighed too much and every time he looked at his destination it seemed to step back a few hundred metres. Abe decided he would focus on what was directly ahead of him. One step at a time. One sawn leg. One burnt arm. One dissolved hand. If he stayed on course, this would all be over before he would know it.

By the time he reached the front door, everybody had gone back inside. He quickly paced to his apartment and threw the bags on the floor inside. He shut his door and rested his back against it, breathing heavily. Relief. Another step forward.

Once calm, Abe took two bottles of Draino out of one of the bags and replenished the supply cupboard in the communal area.

'Jesus!' Abe was startled to see his landlady standing behind the cupboard door as he closed it.

'I'm afraid not, Mr Schwartz, it's just little old me.'

Neither of them spoke for an uncomfortable moment.

'Is everything okay? I noticed that some of the drain fluid had been used. Something I need to take a look at?'

Panic. Sweat. Wide eyes.

'No no no no no no no no, it's fine. Honestly.' Abe spoke so quickly, the words seemed to morph into one long garble. 'The water was going down slowly in the bathroom sink but it's sorted now. Just a little blockage. I'm not sure what it was, but it's gone now.' His lips quivered into a shape that was worse than the painful smile he was attempting.

'Little? You used both bottles of drain cleaner.'

'Oh ... well ... I'm an idiot. I knocked the first one over, so had to come back and grab the other one.' Mrs May looked at Abe as though trying to remember the right letters to complete her daily crossword. 'I'm sorry for being so wasteful but I went out early this morning so that I could replenish the store. That's what I was just doing.'

Another awkward silence.

'That's very good of you, Abe. And you're sure I don't need to get a plumber in or anything? It's all cleared?'

'Honestly, it was nothing. It looks like a bigger deal than it was because I spilled that first bottle. It's fine.' And he repeated for good measure, 'It's fine.'

Mrs May nodded an acceptance, turned and started to walk back towards her apartment. For such an old lady, her movement did not match her age. She wasn't hunched over. She didn't drag her feet. She almost floated. Silently. Softly. The stealthy assassin.

Before Abe could take a breath, Mrs May had swivelled on her heels.

'Sorry, Abe, I meant to ask, have you seen Sythe recently?'

He thought he felt his cheeks instantly flush, but Abe had, in fact, turned completely white. Mrs May didn't seem to notice.

'He's in and out. I may have seen him around but not even long enough to say hello. You need him for something? Want me to tell him you're looking for him if I see him?'

There. That seemed genuine.

'No. It's nothing in particular. I just feel like he hasn't been around. You know how he is. Always disappearing for weeks on end. I'm sure he's just caught up with his work.'

He watched her scuttle back to her corner of the house. He looked up at Blair's front door, then down and left to where Sythe once lived. Then went back to his own place, bolted the door shut and, once again, rested his back against it until his heart rate dropped.

Take two.

Abe took all his clothes off and put them on the floor at the foot of his bed – there was going to be a lot of blood. He walked over to his shopping bag and took out the saw. The blade was covered by a cardboard sheath, which he ripped off to reveal the sharp teeth of his new tool. An image of Mrs May swept through his mind. She was dancing.

She didn't matter.

She suspected nothing.

He could forget about her.

One step at a time, Abe.

This was phase two: limb removal.

NINETEEN

Mr Conroy had woken up with a terrible headache, just as his wife had warned him he would.

She was always right.

To look at them, it would seem as though neither had moved an inch throughout the night, both of them hugging the covers around their knees, lying in a ball, facing away from each other. In truth, they had both tossed and turned in their sleep. Mr Conroy had dreamt of the Devil, offering anything the man desired in return for his soul. It was a first and it scared him.

Mrs Conroy's mind was not so creative, it went straight to Blair and remained there. Blair's first day at school. Blair graduating. Blair singing at church. Blair coming home late. Blair getting a boyfriend. Blair moving out. Blair doing drugs. Blair getting into trouble with the police. Blair getting raped. Blair getting killed. Blair killing herself.

Things spiralled. She woke up several times in different positions, sweating, while her husband snored off the extra glass of whisky she knew was too much for his constitution. Yet, by morning, the Conroys had regressed to the comfort of routine. Waking up back to back.

Mr Conroy was always first up. He would stroke his wife's arm affectionately and head straight downstairs to make them both a cup of tea.

'I dreamt ferociously last night.' Mr Conroy needed to share.

'Well, I dare say it'll have something to do with all that cheese you polished off.'

'I'm serious. He was in my dreams. He was in my head.'

'And who is He?'

Mr Conroy looks at his wife for a moment and doesn't say anything. He's either embarrassed or frightened or disappointed in himself.

'Him,' he nods. '"Who..."' there is a pause as Mr Conroy tries to recall something from the book of Peter '"...walketh about, seeking whom he may devour"'. The quote is whispered with shame.

'Oh. Darling, it was not the Devil in you. I don't believe that for a second. It was the mixture of red wine and dairy.'

'He offered me my heart's desires in exchange for my soul.'

'And did you accept?'

'Well, no. I don't believe so. I guess I must have woken up at that point.'

'There you go. You are of God.' She stands at the table. '"Greater is He that is in you"' – she points at her husband's chest – '"than He that is out in the world"'.

It is this kind of tender but blind conversation that Blair was so anxious to escape.

'Now, would you like some toast?' And she is already walking over to the bread before her husband has the opportunity to answer.

'Thank you. Yes, please. I know I'm being a bit crazy. Probably something to do with Blair moving out, too.' It hangs in the air for a moment. 'I feel better for getting it out there and being honest.'

His wife returns a few minutes later with two slices of toast and strawberry jam.

'Enough about me, how did you sleep, dear?'

School. Graduation. Singing. Church. Boyfriend. Moving. Drugs. Rape. Death.

Drugs.

Rape.

Death.

'Like a log, as always.' She smiled, like she'd had no dreams. As though her conscience was clear.

And they overcame him by the blood of the lamb, and by the word of their testimony.

TWENTY

Blair's parents believed in God. They believed that Satan had been defeated but that he would never stop. And, while they waited patiently for Jesus to come around again, the Devil was already here and working hard to ruin things.

Blair's own belief was that her parents were deluded, that they may as well believe in mermaids and unicorns because when they spoke of the second coming, when they uttered the words 'glorious rapture', they sounded like idiots. She didn't want to think of them in that way.

But now she lived at The Beresford, if she wanted she didn't even have to think about them at all.

Her phone vibrated.

She was in the bedroom with a towel wrapped around her and wet hair that she just wanted to dry and straighten after having it tied up for her run.

Her mother:

Hello darling. Hope your first night was peaceful and you're settled in to your new place. Your father and I went out for dinner and drinks last night. Was quite odd to come home to an empty house but I'm sure we'll get used to it.

Blair rolled her eyes and threw the phone onto the bed. It was the same passive-aggressive bullshit her mother always pulled; there had to be some sour subtext to everything she said. Was Blair supposed to feel guilty that her parents would have to 'get used to it'?

It buzzed again.

Blair left it. Probably her mother signing off. 'God's grace' or some other pointless nod towards her Lord. Always cautious that He might be watching, listening in on her calls, tapping her phone, reading her texts. She loved Him and she feared Him.

The Beresford's newest tenant blow-dried her hair then straightened it, all the time wondering what to do with her first full day of freedom. She would definitely take full advantage of the quiet and solitude to read for a while. She would unpack her clothes and make a list of items that could add a splash of colour and personality to the place. And she thought about the man downstairs. Abe. She felt it would be a kind gesture to take him for a coffee or drop off a four-pack of beer. Perhaps she could split it with him in the communal area downstairs, get to know him.

She didn't necessarily have to 'love thy neighbour' as her mother would say, but she could certainly like him.

Then the music.

Mrs May's God-awful melodies. Depending on the time of day, residents were treated to either instrumental flute pieces or whale song or what sounded like Buddhist chanting. It faded into the background for the other tenants or was washed out by traffic noise, but Blair's apartment was directly above the old lady's. She had a front-row seat. Even so, she couldn't quite make out the racket coming from below.

It was either a vinyl record being played at the wrong speed or somehow being played in reverse. Either way, Blair didn't want to hear it. She'd slept well, she'd exercised, she was clean. She had purpose.

Blair grabbed her keys off the drawers and picked her phone up from the bed. She couldn't resist looking.

It wasn't her mother.

Morning, sweetheart. Hope you're settling in nicely. I put a little money in your account so you can spruce the new place up a little. Let me know if you need anything specific, though. Love you. Dad.

She smiled.
The better parent.
The better Christian.
It lifted her spirits so much that Blair could no longer register the din coming from Mrs May's place. She almost skipped down the hallway and out of the front door, down the stairs and over to Abe's.

Five spirited raps on his front door and Blair waited for him to answer.

This was it. Her new life. Her new freedom. She was independent. She could take care of herself. She could go out for a coffee with a new friend on Saturday and not worry about when to get home. She didn't even have to worry about coming home at all. She could turn those coffees into wine and shots. She could dance until midnight and lie in bed until noon. Because there was no more church on Sunday.

Blair had spent twenty-five years existing.

Now she was ready to live.

TWENTY-ONE

That fucking busybody, Abe thought, when he heard the knock at his door.

'Just a second,' he called out from the bathroom.

In Abe's left hand was Sythe's right arm. Abe had held it over the side of the bath tub so that he could cut it off. At first, he'd stupidly tried to go through the shoulder but there was muscle and cartilage and sternum to work through, so he decided to take a line through the top of the humerus. It meant that there was only one bone to saw through and it was much easier than he had imagined. Such a pro.

Abe ditched the severed limb and the hacksaw into the tub with the rest of Sythe's dead body. He wiped the sweat and blood from his face with the bottom of his shirt and went to answer the door, mumbling to himself about how he was just trying to get something done and blah blah...

He unbolted the door and took the chain off in a way that sounded like he was annoyed at whoever was disturbing his morning of amputation. Then he tried to make his eyes look tired as he opened a five-inch gap in the door.

'Oh, it's...' Abe widened his eyes to seem more alert and straightened the collar of his shirt.

'Blair.'

'No, I know it's you, I just thought it was going to be somebody else. So ... er ... how are you? All settled in?'

'Yes. Thank you. And thank you for your help last night with the boxes.'

'Not a problem.' Abe smiled the smile of a man who was genuinely pleased to have been able to help, who would do the same for anyone and wouldn't expect anyone to repay the favour. Good, old, dependable Abe Schwartz. Polite Abe Schwartz.

Abe sometimes-cuts-up-his-neighbours Schwartz.

'So, I thought maybe you might fancy a coffee?' Blair pushed her hair behind her right ear as she said this. Abe didn't notice. He was too busy interrupting.

'Not in here.'

It was too quick. But Blair took it as awkwardness rather than guilt.

'No. Not in there. I thought you might know somewhere nearby. I could see a little of the area. You know?'

'Yes. Yes. Of course. Sorry. It's just a mess in here at the moment. Work and books and stuff.' He waited for a response but nothing came his way. 'You mean now?'

'No time like the present, as they say. But if you're working I could find my way around, I'm sure.' Blair took a step away as if contemplating the idea.

'No, no, no, that's fine. Great even. I could do with some caffeine. Are you okay to wait over in the communal area for a few minutes while I just freshen up quickly?'

'Of course. I'll see you shortly.'

'There's books and chairs over there, if you wanted. I won't be long.'

'Take your time.' That country-girl conviviality was second nature to Blair and she wondered whether she would have to lose some of that if she planned to make it in the city.

Abe shut the door and instinctively locked it, replacing the chain, too. Then he leant his back against it and didn't even try to stop his face lighting up. It wasn't a date. He knew that. But it was something. More than he'd had in months.

He felt light.

Abe's mobile phone was on the bed and he danced his way over, unlocking the screen with his thumbprint. He wasn't scrolling through ideas on decapitation or possible uses for a person's skull – though liquorice bowl would have been his favourite – he was swiping to his music collection and hitting play on Curtis Mayfield's 'Move On Up'.

He carried the phone into the bathroom and laid it down on the sink. He was whistling along to the parts that were too high to sing.

'Right. Where were we? Ah, yes. The other arm.'

Steady, honest, blend-into-the-background Abe Schwartz took Sythe's remaining hand and pulled his still-attached arm over the side of the bathtub. He reached for the hacksaw and pressed its teeth into the artist's biceps.

'Try to stay still, okay? This won't hurt.' He was looking directly at the dead neighbour.

And started sawing.

And singing.

'*Hush now, child,*' sawing through muscle, '*and don't you cry,*' he hits the bone.

The plan had been to take off all the appendages and soak them in a bath of lye, meanwhile, Abe would burn the fingers and toes in the back garden to see what happened.

It was day two as a killer, and Abe had already lost focus because a pretty woman had asked him to walk her around town and pick up a coffee somewhere.

One of the real problems about getting away with murder is that it can make you feel invincible.

TWENTY-TWO

The music stops, and Mrs May is out of breath. She's old but she's not dead and she can still move, she can still dance, and she can still sing along when she wants to. The only thing she is too old for now is caring what the younger residents of her building think of the way she lives her life.

She can't really dance, she just moves around in a circle and, as it's almost past eleven, she is free to drink a glass of red wine as she does so.

And God help anybody who judges her.

This is what keeps her alive. This is what she enjoys about living.

She doesn't hear Blair in the communal area but she knows that's where the young girl is hanging around. The Beresford was Mrs May's building and nothing happened there that she didn't know about. That's what she told herself and that's what she believed.

Blair is flicking through one of the books on the shelf when Mrs May appears behind her, two mouthfuls of Merlot still in the bottom of her glass. Blair smells the alcohol and turns around; it reminds her of church.

Blood of Christ.

'You can borrow any of those, dear.'

'Well, I was very surprised to find this among your library, Mrs May.' Blair holds up a tattered copy of *The Anarchist Cookbook.*

Mrs May laughs, her top lip stained purple.

'Oh, the things that have been left by the tenants here over the years will astonish you, I'm sure. I remember finding that underneath a mattress. And let me tell you, it's probably the least-offensive piece of literature I've uncovered in that hiding place.'

That is Abe's cue to arrive.

He looks like he's made an effort with his appearance. But not too much effort. Something Blair knows can take even more effort. She notices.

'Building a mail bomb?' he asks, jokingly.

'Sorry?'

'The book. Has somebody upset you? Or are you just tired of the way we are all controlled by technology?'

The Unabomber reference triggers in Blair's mind.

'Oh, yes. I'm thinking of going off the grid entirely.'

It's an odd subject to flirt with, but it's natural and playful and Mrs May can feel the ease with which her young tenants appear to act around each other.

'Have I stumbled upon a book club or something?' The old lady takes in one of the mouthfuls of wine.

'We were just heading out for a coffee, Mrs May. Abe here is going to show me around a little.'

'There's a good boy, Abe.' She isn't trying to sound patronising but that is how it comes across. 'I'm going to do a little pruning before my lunchtime nap, so I guess we're all living life on the edge, eh?' She turns away for a second as if to leave then brings herself back. 'The strange thing is, I remember leaving my pruning shears in the back garden and somehow they ended up in a flower pot at the front of the house.'

Mrs May keeps her focus on Abe as she speaks. In her periphery, Blair motions tipping a glass of wine into her mouth while rolling her eyes. Abe bites his lip.

Then says, 'I'm always doing things like that. Took me ten minutes to find my keys this morning and they were in the key bowl the entire time. I mean, why would I ever look in there?'

Cue polite laughter.

'Well, enjoy yourselves.' She finishes her wine. 'Time for my siesta.'

The youngsters watch as she dodders merrily back to her corner of The Beresford.

'Well, doesn't she have the life?' Blair offers, her face aglow with youth and naïveté. 'Does she ever leave the place?'

'I think she came with the building. It's like the ravens at the Tower of London, if she ever leaves, the whole place will fall to the ground. Shall we?' Abe puts his hand out for Blair to go through the door first.

Chivalrous Abe. Abe the protector.
Abe the amputator.
It was good for him to get out of the house.

TWENTY-THREE

She couldn't get Abe out of her mind. Something seemed different about him. Not bad, necessarily, but unsettling for the old lady.

On returning to her apartment, Mrs May poured herself another glass of wine, smaller this time. She closed all the curtains in every room, and lit two candles in the lounge. She sat, staring at the flames for a minute, conjuring as vivid an image of her favourite tenant as she could.

Then she took a large gulp of her midday wine, set it down and adjusted the charm bracelet on her right wrist. One of the charms, a small, silver bell – a gift from a lover long gone – tinkled quietly, asking the air to be purified.

Mrs May spoke to the fire. She asked for compassion towards Abe. That perhaps he may find the courage to pursue things with this new girl. She envisaged his face in detail, hoping that any God listening would know exactly who she was thinking and speaking about.

With Abe so vivid in her mind, she found herself feeling tearful. She didn't feel sorry for the skinny, Jewish wallflower. It wasn't pity. She liked Abe. She always had. She watched him struggle. With himself more than anything. She just wanted him to have something for himself. Something that would pick him up a little, maybe. Something to make him feel positive about the world.

People pray for things every day. A school shooting, people pray for the families. A terrorist attack, they pray for peace. Yet, there are still guns that are easily available and there will be more school shootings. Another splinter from another religion will drive a truck into a crowd of innocent tourists or a bomb into the bottom floor of a high-rise building.

The prayers didn't seem to work.

But these people probably did not pray like Mrs May.

She wept. And she meant every saline droplet. She cried and she did not hold back that emotion. She envisaged that forgettable face and she passionately called out for some kind of sympathy towards his efforts. That he might understand the sensation of success.

Her plea flowed without constraint.

Then she whispered something to herself and blew out the candle. 'So it is done.'

The curtains were opened – apart from in the bedroom – and she looked out of the window, but the young coffee drinkers were long gone. Mrs May would have to wait and see whether she'd had any effect.

There was still a little wine left in the glass, but she could have that later. The old lady was true to her word and her daily schedule. She lay down on her bed, in the darkness, and was asleep within minutes.

TWENTY–FOUR

Your daughter leaves home and moves in to a big house with a bunch of strangers that is run by an old woman who drinks all day and listens to strange music and cries when she prays, the person you want showing her around town is Abe Schwarz.

The old lady seems harmless, but unsettles you with her idiosyncrasies. There's the tortured artist in the building that seems perfect fodder for a one-night encounter, or he'll lead her on and break her heart. You don't know that there's no need to worry about him because he has been cut into twenty-three pieces – so far – and part of him has already melted away and been flushed down a plughole or toilet.

So, by default, your daughter ends up with Abe Schwartz.

But even if Mrs May was a straight-talking businesswoman and Sythe was in one piece, and he didn't have a pretentious name and he was benevolent and grateful for his success, you'd want that little girl of yours to be across the table from Abe Schwartz, spooning the cocoa powder from the top of her cappuccino with a wooden stirrer.

The man she is looking at across that table is the man you want him to be. He's nervous around her because he respects her, he doesn't want to say the wrong thing. He wants her to enjoy his company. He's not thinking about fucking her. Not yet. And he hasn't rushed ahead to what might happen later that day, that week, that month.

Abe Schwartz lives in the moment.

And he appreciates it.

In this moment, he is a friendly tour guide. He's a knowledgeable neighbour. He can talk about coffee and books and local plays. He can make her laugh.

The only problem with Abe is that moment he lives in. It's so rare for people to stop and take notice of the world that is rushing by. To really have gratitude for what they have rather than worrying about what they don't have. This is Abe's gift. But also his flaw. Because, when he is there with your daughter, he is nowhere else. She feels like she has his attention, like she is being listened to – maybe for the first time. The Conroys would want that for Blair.

Then there's that other moment. The time an artist lost his temper and tried to take out his frustrations on the little guy. The moment of retaliation. The killer moment. When Abe Schwartz felt angry and bullied for the last time. He felt strong. Abe was lost. Punching Sythe's arrogant face repeatedly until he was too weak to fight back against Abe's tightening choke around his neck.

There was nothing else.

Sythe got all the attention.

Maybe for the first time.

Certainly for the last.

Abe Schwartz had never hurt another person in his entire life before then.

It was a moment.

It wasn't a lapse in concentration, you can't blame it on that, it was complete concentration. Utter focus. He meant it. And maybe that's why it seems as though he is okay with it. Maybe it's just because he's out of the house. He's away from it.

'So, this is the posh stuff. One cup of coffee costs as much as a new paperback but it's just amazing, right.'

Blair nods, licking foam from the stirrer.

'And you can choose any of the pastries and they will light up your world. Honestly. Also, you can throw that cup in any direction when you're finished and find a novel/screenplay/poem written on a MacBook or a well-manscaped beard, if that's the kind of thing you're into.'

Abe paused as though waiting for a confirmation that she preferred the slender Jewish type. But Blair just laughed along with his seemingly effortless quips.

He let her talk and she was pleased to have someone who would listen. She told him that her parents were very religious but that she had fallen out of love with that side of life quite early on. Not because anything traumatic had happened to her, it was that it was everything to her parents, and that was tiring.

She apologised to Abe in case he was offended by her atheism, but Abe brushed it off, saying that he had come from something similar, though his memory of it was hazy. He was veering towards agnostic rather than atheist, more out of hope than anything else.

Blair had never been comfortable enough around anyone in her hometown to ever discuss such a thing, yet there she was, divulging diary-entry information to an almost-stranger.

'You come here a lot, then?' she inquired.

'I rarely sit in here, it's not really my scene. Tries to be cool, which isn't really cool. I prefer something simpler. But the coffee and pastries are delicious. I generally grab and go.'

'So why did you bring me here?'

'I don't know what your scene is.' He sipped at his black coffee and shut his eyes for a moment to savour it. 'I wanted to show you this before I take you to my place.'

Blair was trying to get the measure of Abe. Was he, actually, cool because he didn't care, because he didn't try? Whatever he was, she felt at ease with her new friend.

There was a period of silence. In no way uncomfortable. The way old friends can just be together.

Abe broke the silence.

'You want to see it?'

Blair nodded, emphatically.

'Okay. Let's get out of here.'

'This place is dead, anyway.'

TWENTY-FIVE

The doorbell to The Beresford rang and Mrs May woke up from her early siesta in the dark of her room.

She waited to see whether the person would go away and she could return to her slumber.

The bell rang again. This time more aggressively. Six or seven times in a row.

Again, she waited.

Again, aggression. This time there were ten rings.

'Oh, for crying out loud.'

The old lady sprung out of bed like a person half her age. She wrapped a dressing gown around her and stomped to the front door. When she got there, the woman was making her way down the steps. She turned at the sound of the door opening.

'Can I help you?' Mrs May spat out the word 'help'.

'Oh, you're in.' The woman was in her forties. Straight blonde hair. Dark eyes. She looked ill.

'I am in. And I am awake after my doorbell sounded fifty times.'

Mrs May was not the kind of person who was this short with anyone. She was a woman of few words, and those words always meant something. She was old and did not have time to waste on verbosity or frivolity.

'I'm sorry, I just...' The tired-looking woman began to move closer to the house. Mrs May could see her face more clearly. It was not a look of tiredness. It was desperation.

'I'm looking for my daughter.' The words were breathed out of her as though they could almost be her last.

Mrs May had never had children. She had come close several times, some more devastating in their loss than others, but she recognised that look. The sunken eyes. The black bags. The day-overdue hair wash. She had been it and she had seen it.

Her first thought was that the new girl, Blair, had run away from home. She looked wholesome and sweet and clean, but you never could tell. The rent was low at The Beresford and it attracted all types. And Mrs May was not one to discriminate.

Some were running away from something, and others were heading towards it.

None of that mattered. Pay your rent and stay, stop paying and leave.

The rooms would always be filled.

She remained cold. 'And who is your daughter?'

The woman explained and Mrs May listened. She did not invite her into The Beresford, and the door remained open just enough to frame its owner's face. Her daughter had left home and she thinks she may have got involved with the wrong crowd while in the city. Her messages became abrupt. She didn't sound like herself. She cut off some of her friends and family 'back home'. Blah blah. She had definitely lived at this address at some point, and it was a long shot but perhaps her daughter had left a forwarding address for the mail because nobody had heard from the girl for a couple of months now and yawn, cry, roll the eyes.

Two months?

Mrs May remembered the girl. Her mother was right. She *had* started spending time with the wrong people. She *had* changed. She was dirtier and lazier, and she had male visitors. And, more importantly, she disappeared and stopped paying her rent, and her room was filled by a young, unknown artist, who went by the name Sythe.

'I see a lot of people come and go in this place. Some leave without saying a word, others are more polite. But none leave a forwarding address, I'm afraid. I'm old. I don't have time to wrangle everyone's postal affairs.'

The desperate mother said nothing.

'I'm sorry I can't be of more help. I hope you have better luck elsewhere.'

And the door was closed.

Mrs May watched the bedraggled searcher slink off the veranda, looking like Nicole Kidman's corpse, and two things entered her mind. A sigh of resignation that this missing girl was undoubtedly dead. As dead as her mother looked. And relief that it wasn't Blair that she was looking for.

It was time for her afternoon drink.

TWENTY—SIX

The floor wasn't clean, the windows were smeared, the coffee smelled burnt and bitter, and it tasted cheap. It was perfect.

Blair could see that Abe was more relaxed in the second coffee shop. The clothes were more casual as you looked around the place, and the beards were scragglier. Nobody there was trying to be anything that they were not. What you saw was what you got. You knew the coffee wasn't great, and that was okay because it wasn't boasting the finest Arabica roast or a foamed milk that was enhanced with the flavour of tonka beans or the essence of Peru.

It was simple and honest and real.

Like Abe.

'This is more like it, eh?' Abe laughed as he handed Blair a coffee that looked as though it had come out of a vending machine.

'It's very different to the last place.' It dawned on Blair that this may be some sort of test from Abe. That he was examining her reactions to see which coffee shop she preferred. If she chose the first one, it meant that she was like those people, but if she picked this one, she was like Abe. 'I prefer it.' She smiled back at him. It was true. She meant it.

They talked about anything. It was either the beginning of a close friendship or the start of something more romantic. At that point, neither of them knew which it was. And neither of them cared. They spoke about food and religion and political leanings. They discussed their childhoods and education, and even dipped into sports. Even the odd silences were comfortable.

'That Mrs May is quite eccentric, isn't she?' Blair offered.

'She certainly is one of a kind. But she is a lovely old lady; she means well. She has been around forever, and if you get the chance to hear some of her stories, you're in for a real treat. I have no doubt that she will offer to have you over for dinner or drinks at some point. She does it with almost everyone.'

'Did you say "almost" in case she doesn't ask me?'

'Ha! No. It's just that some people have only been there a couple of weeks before they disappear.'

'Unlike you.' Abe nods. 'And the artist guy.'

Abe keeps his cool. 'Oh, Sythe. Yeah, he's been there a good few months, and I don't think he's going anytime soon.'

For the first time since leaving the house with Blair, Abe finds himself wondering how long it would take for the flesh to dissolve from Sythe's arms and legs.

TWENTY—SEVEN

They could be heard laughing from thirty yards away. Mrs May was drinking another glass of red wine when she spotted Abe and the new girl from her window.

She knew young love when she saw it.

Moments later she was opening the front door and giving them a knowing raised eyebrow.

'Having fun?'

Blair answered. 'Abe has taken me to some of the area's best coffee spots.'

'Well, isn't that kind.'

Abe blushed at this but Blair came to his rescue.

'He's a very kind, young man. With awful taste in coffee.' The new friends laughed again.

The very kind man bid his housemates a fond adieu before very kindly returning to his own apartment, kindly removing his clothes before kindly sawing through both of Sythe's thighs, dumping his limbless torso into the tiled corner of the bathroom and submersing the arms and legs in a bath of lye, kindly.

He lay down on his bed, his hands behind his head, and he disassociated himself from the situation in the room next to him in order to think about Blair.

What was going on? He'd been with women before, he wasn't the asexual idiot the kids in his school had teased. He'd fucked around at university, but there was no emotion there. Not like the connection he felt with Blair. But, then, he'd never been friends with a woman, either. Maybe that's what it was.

Abe was starting to tie himself up about it. If he tried to advance things and Blair thought they were just friends then he would blow that and end up with nothing. And he was so sick of having nothing.

If it was more than a friendship, if Blair liked him in the way that he thought he liked her, he could have everything. He could have love. He wouldn't be alone. His books were company, of course, and there was someone in his apartment with him, but the conversation was rather one-sided.

Abe decided that he would let his own emotions flourish and develop into whatever they wanted, and he would wait until there was a clear sign from Blair. If it was friendship that she wanted, he would take it. If it was love, he would grab it with both hands.

So rational.

In a bag, Abe threw an old hooded jumper he no longer wore, a copy of a courtroom crime thriller he had no intention of ever reading, a wicker basket he had bought on a whim to spruce up the lounge, though he had never decided on what he could place inside the thing, and the bones from Sythe's fingers and toes.

He took them out into the garden – knowing that Mrs May still had half a glass of wine to finish because she'd brought it with her when she came to the door, so was not going to be out there pruning her flowers just yet – and he lit a fire using the pile of old local newspapers and kindling from the storage cupboard.

Once the flames were roaring inside the metal burn bin, Abe dropped the contents of his bag on top. First the book because it would burn easily. Then the bones. Followed by the wicker basket, which went up almost instantly. He decided to hang on to the hoody a little longer, then dumped the plastic bag in the fire with some more of the kindling.

He was well on his way to getting away with murder.

And the timing was between two meals, so he knew the smoke wasn't going to be pissing off his irate neighbour over the back fence. But if he wanted to come back, shooting his mouth off again, then Abe could always just kill him.

TWENTY-EIGHT

Blair's hometown was not particularly adventurous. Like The Beresford, there was a routine to everything – harvest festival, Halloween, Christmas, farmers' market, bake sales – the cute idiosyncrasies of the small, rural, Christian community. Though Blair was trying to make her world a little bigger, to gain more experiences, it was this provincial life that had made her the way she was today.

There was something about the grocery store in her village that offered possibility. The owner, a dangerously overweight woman in her late thirties, was, seemingly, the happiest person in town. She had found her calling. Food.

Her business would have done no worse had she kept things traditional with the fruit and vegetables she selected to sell in her store but, having never really left the place where she was born, decided that her tastebuds would do the travelling for her. A culinary Columbus.

People of the town went with her. They started putting papayas in their shopping baskets and avocados and Romanesco broccoli. And she would give them ideas of what to cook. When she introduced cacao nibs, there was scepticism, at first, but her passion for superfoods was infectious. And the chia seeds had been a hit, so she was trusted.

Blair liked to run in the mornings. That hadn't changed. But what she also loved was getting home after a run and eating peanut butter. Often on toast but sometimes straight off the spoon or a dipped finger. It was tasty and fatty and unctuous, perfect after an hour of physical exertion.

Then, one day, out of nowhere, something was different. Blair went to the grocery store to pick up another jar of her favourite post-run fuel, and that barrel of a shop owner had jars of almond butter for sale.

'What is this?' Blair held up a small jar. Smaller than the peanut version but more expensive.

'Life-changing. That's what it is.' That contagious grin of hers, followed by unrivalled enthusiasm, and, within a minute, Blair was standing at the till, parting with her money for a small jar of spread made with a different kind of nut and a bag of free Granny Smith apples to take with her.

'When you get home, I want you to slice one of the apples into wedges and dip them straight into the jar. You can thank me next time.'

Blair did as she was told, that's how she'd been brought up. She took the variation of her favourite snack home, found a sharp knife, cut the apple and took off the jar lid. A layer of oil lay across the top, which didn't look appetising. A sign on the packaging said that oil separation was natural and it would just need a stir.

She used a piece of the apple to do so and then took a bite.

The woman at the shop was right.

A perfect combination.

Abe was up early. He knew that Blair would be out running before she got ready for work and was waiting at the window to watch her leave for her morning exercise. He crept out of his apartment, across the lobby area and started making his way up the grand stairs to Blair's place.

Mrs May came out at just the right time to catch him.

'Morning, Abe. Are you heading up to Blair, I think you may have just missed her.'

'Good morning, Mrs May. Yes, I know. She's out on her run. I just ... well ... I got her a little something. A surprise for when she gets back.'

Mrs May smiled and said nothing. She didn't want to embarrass Abe any further. It was sweet. Whether they were admitting it to themselves or not, she could see something budding that was more than a platonic friendship.

'I'm just going to leave it outside her door.'

'Well, don't let me keep you, Abe.'

He turned and continued up the stairs, and Mrs May went out into the garden.

Blair came home twenty minutes later and completed her morning workout with a rousing bound up the stairs to her apartment. She stopped at the sight of something on the floor in front of her door.

It wasn't flowers or chocolates or champagne, Abe would never be so unoriginal or obvious. Blair crouched down and picked up the gift that had made Abe smile to himself the day before while out shopping.

A large jar of almond butter with a Granny Smith apple on top. A yellow Post-it note was attached to the piece of fruit:

Saw this and thought of you. Life-changing. A perfect combination.

TWENTY-NINE

Nobody had seen Sythe for two weeks. It wasn't unusual for him to disappear for this length of time. He was artistic and passionate, and that often affords such people an amount of leeway that others, who aren't tortured by their own brilliance, are not.

He was gone.

The smaller bones turned to dust and were disposed of with the rest of the ash from Mrs May's garden debris. But the larger bones took a little work. It would get hot in that bin, but not hot enough to disintegrate Sythe's femurs. They did dry out considerably and become brittle, and that was enough for Abe to crush them into smaller fragments himself with a hammer and gradually deposit in the rubbish or while walking through town or in the woods with Blair, who was showing signs that she wanted more from their relationship than the closeness of friendship can bring.

Abe had done it. He had escaped. He had killed another human being – a deplorable narcissist, but a living thing nonetheless – and there was no evidence left that could possibly tie him to the crime. His conscience was clean, as was the bathtub that he was now able to use again.

He didn't suddenly have a taste for it. He wasn't trying to recreate the thrill of murdering somebody. He didn't want to outdo himself. Nor had he unlocked some deep desire to become the next Dahmer.

Abe Schwartz had acted in retaliation. He was the one that was attacked. He defended himself. The whole situation was blown out of proportion. Abe was concerned for Sythe's welfare. He'd heard the argument on the doorstep and was checking in on his neighbour.

Abe was kind.

Abe was thoughtful.

Abe was not in the wrong.

And this is what he told himself. Of course, in retrospect he could have attempted to resuscitate the artist. He could have called an ambulance or the police and explained the accident. But he panicked. And the doorbell rang about a minute after the event to herald the arrival of the woman he thought he might in fact love.

That's no excuse for cutting up a person, dissolving their flesh and burning their bones. Abe knows that. He's not stupid. But to Abe, it was done. In the past. Scrubbed out. He never had to think about Sythe again.

A knock at his door.

It was Mrs May. She was holding up some keys in her hand and she looked nervous.

'I'm worried about Sythe. I know he goes walkabout from time to time, but I have a bad feeling. I know I'm probably being a little crazy, but I'm going to take a look in his flat.' She jangled the keys.

Abe's first thought was, *Does she just go into our apartments whenever she likes? What has she seen?*

'I'm a bit nervous. I don't really want to go in there. And I definitely don't want to go in there alone.'

'You want me to go with you?' All thoughts gave way to curiosity.

'Would you mind?'

She seemed trepidatious. As though she expected to find a body in there. Abe was less so, expecting to see piles of acrylic paint tubes and canvasses on easels and sketchbooks.

They were both wrong.

WHAT DO YOU WANT?

Talent is a tricky subject. There's a school of thought that suggests it does not exist. Yes, physiologically, culturally and historically, you may find that Jamaica produces more powerful world-class sprinters while Kenya appears to have a predominance of long-distance runners. And neither is particularly dominant in the swimming pool. But with a mere ten thousand hours of practice at anything, one can become proficient or even an expert in a given field.

Of course, this doesn't explain Mozart, who composed his first symphony at age five. Of course, if he played piano for six hours every day from the age of one, he would have clocked up the requisite amount of time to do such a thing.

Some people choose to believe that we all have a gift for something, a predisposition to achieve in one area. Having a gift isn't enough, the hard work has to follow. The hours of practice are still needed if you are born with perfect pitch or outlandish speed or strength or intellect.

And in a world where everything can be so instant, wouldn't it be great to dispense with all the hours of graft? To suddenly be able to play blues guitar like nobody ever has, or run around a stadium faster than any person in history.

But maybe you live in a remote part of Ireland. Your family is wholesome and industrious. The farm has been in their name for generations and you have been helping since you were a kid. But you don't want that life. You don't want the early mornings. You don't want the smell of manure. You don't even want to be outside in the air.

You're an artist. You want to be alone. You want to be around other artists. You think you've got something. Friends say you have a talent. But they are your friends, it's not constructive. Your parents don't understand. How is that going to make you any money?

You don't like your name.

What are you going to do, Aidan Gallagher?

Change it.

What do you want?

I want a space to paint. I want opportunity. Fame. Notoriety. I want to know whether I'm good enough. And, if I'm not, I want to be good enough. I want the skill. I want the talent.

What people rarely say is that they want it in that order. You can be famous or notorious without having any skill. Pick any serial killer in 1970s America. None of them had a skill for not getting caught. They didn't exhibit the precision of a surgeon when removing a victim's head. They could pull a trigger or thrust a knife.

Asking for talent is pointless because it can go unnoticed, unrewarded. You can die poor. You will most certainly go unappreciated but rarely uncriticised.

So be honest.

What do you really want?

To have the financial success and renown of somebody who has talent and has worked hard. Without having talent or having to work hard.

You want to make an impact and you don't care what it's for.

THIRTY

The rent was so cheap at The Beresford, Blair could have worked at Old Bean (the less-pretentious coffee shop that had become a regular haunt for her and Abe) and still have been able to afford her weekly food bill and a night out for drinks.

Blair had higher hopes than that. She hadn't just left the Bible belt on a whim; she was prepared. She had been trying to escape the country since returning from university. Her hometown did not offer much in the way of a career. She didn't want to be a farmer, and as interesting as her part-time job in the local bookstore had been, she didn't want to be the manager and she would never own it.

And the very last thing she wanted was to find herself a good, local Christian man to take care of her financially while she tended to the house and baked cakes and got fat before spreading her legs in an attempt to bring another small mind into their community. Sex to procreate. Never for fun. Nothing for pleasure.

Sinner.

Praise the Lord.

Please only the Lord.

Fear the Lord.

Minutes after graduation, Blair was scouring the internet for jobs in the city. She would delete her browser history after every search, like her dreams of escape were pornography. She was sure her parents didn't even know what a browser history was but there could be no trail. No evidence.

She didn't have any experience so everything she applied for was entry-level. It didn't matter. It was a golden ticket.

Then there were the interviews. More lies. Fake lunches with friends from university became frequent. She would disguise her interview outfit beneath a jacket or long coat, or hide shoes in her handbag. Several failed attempts were heartbreaking. Blair cried in her room at night, wondering if there was any other way out of town, out of that life.

Out of becoming the one thing she never wanted to be: her mother.

Then she started widening the net. Applying for jobs in fields that did not interest her. Sure, she could work as a recruitment consultant. Her technical knowledge was limited but she could learn how to sell a laptop or computer monitor. She could work in distribution – whatever that meant. Just not there.

It came. An offer of a position as a PR assistant for a media marketing company. Blair had a degree in English, she had a brain, she could pick things up, she was creative. But she also had that country-girl disposition, whether she wanted it or not. And she came across perfectly at the interview. A team of young, professional women. Twenty-somethings taking over the world.

It wasn't what she had envisaged herself doing but it was exactly where she had imagined herself being. Away.

Goodbye, paper town.

So long, off the map.

Time to grow up, get a job, have her own place, maybe meet somebody she liked, finally have sex.

Some of the girls from back home had chosen to rebel against their parents' strict beliefs by fucking anything that moved as soon as they could. But Blair, although wanting a way out, didn't want to rebel. She didn't want to disappoint her family or shame them in some way. She just wanted independence. A chance. A choice.

And that day, sitting on the sofa of her very own apartment, reading the latest bestseller, she thought about Abe and how she would like to take things forward, how she would like to make things more intimate.

THIRTY-ONE

'Grab your keys.'

'What?'

'Just grab your keys and come with me.' Abe held his hand out to Blair as though he was going to lead her. Neither of them knew whether or not they should be holding hands with one another, though they both wanted to. Abe lowered it and made a motion for her to follow him.

'Do I need a jacket?'

'No, no. We'll only be outside for a second.'

They exited The Beresford but, instead of walking down the driveway and in towards town, Abe turned right and walked along the outside wall of his home.

'Where are you taking me, Abe?' Blair was excited and nervous. Abe had been showing that he cared about her more and more. He was thoughtful and polite and interested.

She was also interested.

'To the dark side,' he quipped. She screwed up her face in mock irritation.

Thirty seconds later, they arrived.

'Here we are.'

'Abe. What is this?'

'It's The Beresford.'

He explained that this was the entrance to the rest of the building, the part that they never see because they are kept separate.

'We can't just go in there.' Blair was intrigued but it felt edgy.

'Actually, you just can. It's not like our part, where you need a key. Come on, I'll show you. We can walk in and go up in the lift, see how the other half live.'

It felt colder to Blair in the other half of The Beresford. It was less like a home and more like a hotel or conference building.

'Wait. I am not going up in that.' Blair pointed at the old-fashioned lift. Abe laughed. 'Does that even work? It looks like a death trap.'

'It's fine. Honestly.' Abe pulled the iron door to the side to open the lift. 'They don't make 'em like this anymore.'

'With good reason, I'm sure.' Blair was concerned but she was saying this as she stepped inside.

'We'll skip level three because there's nothing there, but we can stop on a couple of the other floors.' He shut the door himself with a loud clang and lowered a metal lever to lock it.

'I feel super safe now. Thanks.'

Abe pressed the button for levels four and six. There was a key slot above the top floor. Abe stroked at it with his finger.

'What's that for?' Blair wondered.

'Penthouse living, I guess. No idea who lives up there or what it's like.'

The old lift disappeared behind dark bricks for a couple of floors before passing the open area of up-for-hire conference space. It was dimly lit, and Blair gave it nothing more than a glance.

Then things got loud.

They stopped at the fourth floor.

'Oh my God. Are we in the same building?'

Abe had done this journey once before. He was curious about the rest of The Beresford and why the building had been separated. Most people had heard about the couple who allegedly fell from an upper-floor window, but the split also made sense commercially for Mrs May and afforded her a more comfortable lifestyle in her elderly years.

There was a long corridor that branched off to either side at the end, where a window showed the same view that Blair had from her bathroom.

She counted. 'There's five doors on each side.'

'A couple more around each corner, too.'

'I wonder what they're like inside.'

'Small, I guess. I'm not sure. But we have thick walls and I can still hear Mrs May's music, so I'm sure they can all hear this racket.'

Some kind of rock music, death metal, screaming, guttural noise.

Blair guessed it was a young kid whose parents weren't at home. It was crazy that neighbours weren't banging on the door and telling the owners to have some damned respect.

The sound was an assault. Blair and Abe had to speak up to hear one another, and somehow it added an edge to what they saw before them. It was dark. Perhaps she imagined the dampness. Suddenly it smelled different. Cinnamon, perhaps. Some kind of spicing, at least.

'Can we go, Abe? This doesn't feel comfortable here.' It felt like something was going to happen. Something she didn't want to witness.

Abe shut the door and Blair shut her eyes.

The lift moved upwards.

'Not up, Abe. Let's just go.'

'This thing is old. Let's just get away from this floor, see what's up there and we can come straight back down if you like.'

The noise faded as they moved through the fifth floor, which looked the same as level four. Blair was convinced that there would be no difference to the floor above that, and they could press the button for the ground and walk back to their well-lit, spacious, separate dwelling.

The sixth floor was silent.

Blair didn't want to say it but the corridor looked narrower and longer, though there was still the same number of doors on each side. The paint was peeling. She felt cold.

Abe took off his jumper and gave it to her.

'Put this on. I feel fine.'

'Are you sure?'

'Of course.' He rubbed her shoulders affectionately, like he was showing her that he would protect her. He would keep her warm and safe.

Abe asked if she wanted to get out, but Blair declined.

'This is where it happened, you know?'

'Where what happened?' Blair didn't know if Abe was teasing.

'Some time in the eighties. Mrs May was running the place even back then. A couple were in that apartment,' he pointed to the fourth door along on the left, 'nobody knows what happened, but they both ended up on the street six floors down.'

'What? Why are you telling me that?'

'Because it's the truth. It's part of the history of the building. Apparently they seemed like a happy couple – though you can't tell what's going on behind these doors, right? The window wasn't smashed. There were no signs of a struggle. They found an ashtray on the windowsill outside. So the thought is that they were smoking out there and fell.'

'Or they jumped.'

'Wow, Blair. That's dark.'

She could see he was trying to lighten the mood.

'Says the guy who takes me on a date to a haunted house.'

Before either can laugh it off or question the validity of the date, two people can be heard arguing and somebody exits the door, which is fourth down on the left.

Tall and angular, he spouts some profanity, slams the door shut and makes his way towards the lift.

'We need to go,' Blair whispers. 'We need to go now, Abe.'

'Hold the lift,' the figure calls out, picking up his pace.

Blair pulls Abe into her and wraps her right arm around him as if in a romantic embrace. With her left hand, she feels behind her and hits the bottom button. The lift judders and squeaks.

'Hey, hold on.' He's running towards the door now, but Blair keeps her focus. She speaks into Abe's ear. 'Don't look up.' Then to the lift, 'Come on, come on, come on.'

She doesn't want to but she thinks of God.

The lift starts to descend.

The man above them thrashes at the cage door that he can't open and calls one of them a motherfucker.

Blair prays that nobody tries to get in on level four as the sound of the music picks up again. She sees somebody walking around in the dark on the conference level. And when they get back to earth, they run. They run back out the door they entered. They get to the corner and turn left and they do not stop until they get back to their own entrance.

Abe doesn't have the same fitness level as Blair and arrives shortly after her on the porch and is surprised to see her giggling hysterically.

'That was fucking crazy. Please, can we just go to the cinema next time.'

Abe tries to catch his breath.

Blair continues. 'When we first saw there was a penthouse, I wondered why Mrs May wouldn't want to live there. I mean, she owns the entire building, right?'

Abe nods, his hands resting on his knees.

'But it's obvious now we've been up there.'

'Yeah. She's not very good with stairs.'

They laugh again and Blair unlocks the door.

Home, sweet home.

The good side.

THIRTY—TWO

Sythe had destroyed his apartment. Abe could tell that Mrs May had never been inside because her reaction was exactly the same as his.

There were tubes of acrylic paint, that part had been correct, but most of the canvasses were on the floor. Some with giant holes through them made with a stomping foot or fist, or the sharp end of a paintbrush.

There were buckets. Filled with water and mixed with paint. And there were mops. Coloured mops, strewn across the wooden floor of what should have been a lounge but was obviously a studio.

The mops had evidently doubled up as giant paintbrushes, and the walls of that room in The Beresford had been used as the blank canvas. It was expressive and angry and, Abe thought, utterly enchanting and beautiful. The guy had talent.

Mrs May could not force herself towards the beauty through the shock.

'What has he done?' She sounded weak. Abe had never seen her like that. He didn't know what to say. He couldn't tell her that it was striking. He stayed silent. Looking around, he manoeuvred himself back out into the hallway towards the bedroom. (Or what would be the bedroom. It was the mirror image of Abe's place.) He found himself wandering away from the old lady, mesmerised.

Each of the apartments on the lower two levels of The Beresford had one bedroom. Walking through the front door, it was the first room. Spacious. Plenty of natural light. Opposite was a smaller room that most residents used as a study, home office or for storage. Many treadmills had gone unused in those rooms. For Sythe, it was an oversized supplies closet.

What should have been a bedroom was the same as the room that should have been Sythe's lounge. Eight feet of splashes and dots and angry mop strokes. There was a broom in there that he had used to create a scratched effect on the paint in one corner.

There's a thin line between passion and madness, and it was difficult to tell on which side Sythe had found himself while doing this. But the fact that he had attacked Abe with no provocation led him to believe that the man had boiled over into a very dark place.

A place that produced breathtaking art that nobody would ever see. And a place that got him killed.

Mrs May was muttering outside. Something about not having any furniture and how could someone live like this. And how he'd got his big break. She trailed off. Somewhere between anger and resignation.

She appeared at the door.

'Oh, here, too. Of course. Every room. Every goddamned room is covered in his scribbles. There's mops everywhere. Paint on every surface. I was only ever nice to him. I helped him. Why would he do this to me?'

Abe wasn't sure if she was asking for his opinion or it was confused catharsis. But he kept his mouth shut.

'I'll have to get someone in to clean this all up and repaint the walls...' She walked off, still mumbling.

Abe followed.

In the kitchen, there were three canvasses resting against the wall. Each one was around four feet by three feet in size. Abe pulled them apart, realising that they formed a triptych – the picture on the right was the only one signed in the bottom corner.

Mad swirls of brown with splashes of yellow ochre and pale-blue rectangles. He had no idea what it was or what it meant but Abe loved it. Mrs May caught him mid-admiration.

'You like this stuff?' she asked.

'I know it's not the time but I do feel drawn to it, yes.'

'Take it.' She waved a hand in good riddance.

'Sorry?'

'Take it. There's no chance of him coming back here, is there? You'll be doing me a favour. It's one less thing to be removed.'

'But it's his property.' This was Abe's natural reaction before remembering that Sythe definitely would not return to collect it.

'This house is my property. He has gone against his contract. So now he is gone, and it belongs to me. It can cover the rent I'm sure I'll never see. Let's just say that. Take it. Please.'

'If you're sure.' Abe knew she was sure. And he had an unseen piece of art from the late Sythe. Could be worth some money in the future.

'Yes. Take it, and let's get out of here. I need a drink.'

THIRTY-THREE

They went to the cinema after experiencing the other side of The Beresford. Abe can't remember a thing about the film. He and Blair shared an arm of the chair. Their bodies were so close he felt paralysed, terrified to move in case he touched her and gave off the wrong impression.

They had touched before but it had ended in laughter. Blair seemed to giggle when she was nervous.

Although she had pulled him, quite forcibly, into her in that lift, her form pressed against his. Was it so that the man on the sixth floor would think that she hadn't heard him calling for the lift, or was it a ruse to get closer to Abe?

That had also ended in laughter.

Tonight they were having a night in. That meant popcorn, wine and a movie at Blair's apartment.

It never happens at Abe's.

He doesn't want Blair at his place. That's where he did what he did to Sythe. What he had to do. He didn't want to. It was an accident. He's not a killer. A stupid mistake. But Abe just wants to get past that.

As Blair is providing the accommodation, Abe is left in charge with snacks and drinks. Two bags of popcorn: one sweet, one salted. A packet of chocolate-covered sweets. And two bottles of red wine. The first to be savoured, the second to help bolster his courage.

'Good evening, sir. Won't you come in?' The ever-playful Blair. Masking her feelings with awkward humour.

Abe felt like Blair's flat was lighter than his. Even though the rooms were almost identical in layout and size, it seemed bright and homely. The way flat two had felt when he had first moved in. Blair was only one level up from him, it wasn't that much closer to the sun. Abe's place used to be like that. Beaming with a sense of possibility and promise. Now it looked more and more like the corridor up on the sixth floor.

The walls decaying at the same rate as hope.

Blair had chosen the film. *10 Rillington Place*. She said she wanted to see if it still creeped her out after what happened upstairs or whether she was much braver now.

Courage was a problem between them. Both of them wanted to take a risk with the other. She didn't act through a lack of experience, while he liked her too much to throw it all away by making a false move. Neither was chasing the thing that they wanted.

A quarter of the way into the film, Blair is startled and fidgets on the sofa, her arm nudging into Abe's and somehow falling onto the sofa between them with Abe's hand on hers. She looks at it and laughs softly.

'Oh, God. I'm sorry, I didn't mean to...' He pulls his hand away and thinks about getting up to leave. He's blown it.

'No, no, no. Don't be silly. I just wasn't expecting it. Come back. It's okay.' She looks him in the eyes. 'I like it. It's nice.'

Grandmas are 'nice', Abe thinks to himself but he follows her lead.

They watch the rest of the film, hand in hand. Nothing more. Neither of them attempts anything braver than that. A step closer.

More than friendship.

Blair wants more.

Abe has decided that this is the woman for him, the one he is supposed to love.

THIRTY—FOUR

Very reasonably priced, 1 BED flat in large apartment building –
The Beresford. City location. One mile from nearest train station.
Available immediately. No long-term agreement required. Separ-
ate kitchen, lounge and spacious Victorian bathroom.
Unfurnished. Communal library and large garden.

Mrs May was particularly proud of her garden and felt like it should be mentioned. The 'library' was an overstatement but also something she was pleased to offer.

As every wall – and two of the ceilings – in Sythe's apartment would have to be repainted, she decided to add 'freshly decorated throughout' to her description.

She wasn't worried about filling the room, they always got filled. And, now that the dust had settled on her discovery of the unknown art project, she was no longer worried about Sythe. He could be covered in petrol and on fire in a ditch somewhere after what he did.

The old lady felt no remorse for feeling this way. She was tolerant but Mrs May was no hypocrite. She did not believe in turning the other cheek to her enemies. She had no faith that they would be judged by God, and, if they were, that would not be enough for her.

Mrs May was kind. She had experience. And she knew what it was to love. But she would not love blindly. She would not love indiscriminately, because it lacks nuance. It takes away a person's ability to be selective. It is unnatural. As is penting up your hatred towards people.

She believed that it caused ailments in the body and worse still, the mind. She would express her hate freely so that she had the room to love with everything. There was no confusion.

Those who deserved love, received love.

And those who brought out hate would also get what they deserved.

She was raging. And much like her exhausting plea for the

protection of and compassion towards young Abe Schwartz, she put everything into her prayer for wrath and violence towards the young, ungrateful artist who had so disrespected her.

Every day for her was a ritual. Cold coffee in the morning. Siesta in the middle of the day. Garden care in the afternoon. Glasses of wine spliced throughout. And her prayers were also followed habit.

Darkness. A candle. Fondling the bell charm on her bracelet. And if she was praying for somebody or about somebody, she would either picture them vividly or have some kind of item that she could focus on that belonged to or reminded her of the person in question.

Mrs May had let Abe take one of Sythe's abandoned pictures, but she had gone back and kept several for herself.

The entire apartment was black but the candle flame. A gulp of that full-bodied red wine. A solemn gaze at the picture ahead of her; she hung it on a spare nail in the wall. The prayer could begin.

She spoke with a spite and venom and malicious forethought.

She spat thunder and wrath and weeping.

She spewed scorpions and sulphur and poison.

It sounded as though she were recalling every putrid word or malevolent image in her mind before puking it out in a stream-of-conscious hate babble.

She roared thunder and earthquakes and agony.

Mrs May looked at Sythe's painting and she imagined him being struck down by the world. Her next swig of wine was aggressive.

She'd had a lot of alcohol throughout the day and had woken from her afternoon nap still with a spirited buzz that she would swiftly top up.

Whether angry, drunk or passionate, her hatred spilled over.

She shouted. She shook. And with the same ferocity that her eyes wept with hope for Abe, her mouth foamed and tensed for Sythe.

Mrs May sat until her heart rate dropped to a normal level then finished her wine.

She would post her new advert for the room once the painters had finished.

PART TWO

ONE

It was the same routine. He'd go out for a 'few drinks', say he'd be home by ten and she would wait up for him until a couple of hours after the bars had shut. He'd fumble with his keys for a minute until finally letting himself through the front door, demanding a sandwich and insisting that he wasn't drunk.

No apology.

She would tell him to go to bed.

He would tell her to 'fuck off'.

He'd call her a bitch.

She'd make him the sandwich and watch in disgust as he ate it.

Then he'd start in on her again. About how she sits at home and does nothing. How he provides for her so should be allowed to have a drink when he wants and with whomever he wants. And he expects to come back and not have to argue about a sandwich.

He'd bring up her looks, her mother, the way she is with other men. How *she* treats *him* badly. Eventually, he'd have her pinned by the throat to a wall. And he'd scream in her face so loudly that it made her ears ring. A couple of times he'd spat in her face. Once, he used the other hand to rub it into her eyes and mouth. Then he'd laughed as it made her gag.

If she didn't back down, which she never did, he would hit her. The last time, she was on the floor and he raised his foot as though he was going to stamp on her head.

Never again.

She had tried going to bed whenever he went out drinking, but it wouldn't be the sandwich he wanted when he got in. After letting him do that for so long, she decided that it was better to take a beating than be fucked by that animal.

He had come home from work and not even showered before going out again. Just a spray of deodorant and a clean shirt was enough. He kissed her goodbye at the door, told her that he loved her and said he'd be home around ten.

She had to stop herself from wondering why he couldn't just be like that all the time. It was the reason she always came back, and she had to break the cycle. Seeing his foot raised above her face, ready to smash down on her skull was the push she needed.

If she didn't get out, he was going to end up killing her.

She gave it half an hour in case he came back because he'd forgotten his wallet or phone or something. To keep herself busy, she washed up the plates and cutlery, and threw his dirty clothes on a fast wash-and-dry cycle. She even cleaned the shower. He'd never do that. Wouldn't know where to start.

Everything she owned managed to fit in the suitcase they'd used on their holiday to Spain three years before. When she thought they were happy. It went into the boot, and she drove off without looking back. Her heart punching the inside of her chest.

Once clear by a couple of miles, she pulled over and cried.

She was free.

Her plan was in motion.

There were no texts on her phone. Good. She tapped in the address that the landlady had sent, placed her phone into the holder on the dashboard and pulled back out onto the road.

It was seventy-eight miles to The Beresford.

She had informed Mrs May that she would be arriving at night, though she didn't say why. The old lady had guessed something was wrong, but a lot of the people who passed through her building were running from something. It wasn't her business what that something might be. As long as they paid their rent.

Gail Castle had fallen for a strong and sensitive man. A disciplined man. A military man. She loved that about him. But he was a different man when he came back from that war. A tortured man. An anxious man. A spiteful and violent man. She had held on to the memory of the first man, but sightings of him were becoming rarer. And that size-eleven boot above her head was the full-stop that said he was never coming back to her.

She started searching for a place the next day. She'd been saving for almost a year. Her getaway fund. The rent at The Beresford was so cheap that she wouldn't have to get a job for months if she didn't want to. But, as with all good plans, there had to be a bump in the way. And that bump was only going to get bigger.

Gail was two weeks late, and her periods ran like clockwork. She was too scared to take a pregnancy test because it might make her change her mind about leaving. So she had put it off. She could confirm either way once she got to her new place.

The roads were fairly clear, and she made it to her new home in less than two hours. She knew the place was unfurnished apart from a bed, but that was all she'd need. So she parked up, pulled her suitcase out of the boot and walked up the steps to the front door of The Beresford, just about the grandest building she had ever seen. Maybe eight floors high but in Gail's mind it seemed like twenty. The central window on the top floor was surrounded by a triangular battlement. An art deco feature that stood out from the style of the upper-floor balconies.

Gail wondered what floor her apartment would be located on.

Within ten seconds, a slender, dark-haired man arrived at the door. He wasn't intimidating. He didn't look strong. In fact, he seemed a little out of breath. But his face was kind. He smiled a greeting and asked how he could help her.

'Hi. I mean, good evening. I'm Gail Castle. I'm due to move in.' She glanced to her left at the suitcase.

'Now? In the middle of the night?' He was joking. It was just after eight. Another smile. 'Come on in.'

Abe Schwartz introduced himself to another new housemate. He was polite. He did the right thing and asked her whether she had come far and how her journey had been. He offered to knock on Mrs May's door, though he knew her well enough to know that she would emerge at exactly the right moment.

The old lady did exactly that, again offering Abe's services should Gail require any assistance with boxes or furniture. When his presence was deemed worthless, Abe bid both women a fond farewell and returned to his own apartment where, only moments before the doorbell rang, he was dragging Blair Conroy's lifeless body into his bathroom, so that he could start disassembling it, and wondering why he had done this again.

TWO

The thing is, not once in the history of that small town had there been a community fundraising event, like the cake sales that Blair had learned to hate so much, that had turned into a food fight, a riot or anything sinister. One year, Mr Hammond had accidentally switched the paper signs on two of the cakes so that the 'gluten-free' muffins were actually packed with wheat.

The worst that happened was a little bit of bloating and a complaint about constipation, which was nothing to do with a gluten intolerance, anyway.

One time, at church on Sunday, Mr and Mrs Beecham sat on separate pews. Nobody knows why. They had been married forever and the next week they had returned to their usual spot – three rows from the front, on the left. It was the talk of the town for the next few days. People wondered but were too polite to ask, and too afraid that it was something serious, which would require considered discussion somewhere down the line.

That's as bad as it ever got.

The time the school band played on the village green for the harvest festival and got all their timings wrong, the ovation was stronger than any other year because they supported each other. They cared. Nobody beat the flautist around his head with his own instrument. The conductor wasn't sacked. The tubas were not filled with custard. And the drums weren't punctured.

Nothing bad happened.

Nothing ever happened.

That's why Blair wanted out.

She wanted to get away from the nothingness.

She had put through an order in the bookshop for *Mein Kampf*. It was requested by one of the school history teachers. He'd never read it and had been teaching about the Second World War for years.

It was obvious that it was sensitive for him. He wasn't a Jew-hater. He wasn't a Holocaust denier. He was a scholar who had been delivering information to students for years, without taking in the information that was at his disposal. He was fair and balanced, and he knew that the book wasn't going to change anything for him, but he wanted to know what it was about.

He was curious.

So he asked the local girl at the bookshop to order in a copy for him. He didn't go online, because he wanted to support the town's businesses. And that screwed him in the end.

Blair wasn't like the others, she understood the reason he had come to her. She put the order through the system to arrive for her next shift and got the teacher to pay up front so that she could slip him the book a couple of days later.

The owner saw the order and cancelled it.

And phoned the teacher.

And told the town.

The teacher had to explain himself and have an in-depth discussion with the priest. It was a mess. Over a book. And a quest for knowledge.

He left. And nobody thought about him again, apart from Blair. It became something of an urban legend. Business at the bookshop wasn't affected, but Blair was forever changed. It was unfair to her. The world was bigger than their little town. Life didn't stop at its borders. In fact, Blair was almost sure that that was where life began.

She ditched a bookshop that told people what they should and should not read. She threw away the horror of the mislabelled muffin.

So that she didn't have to go to church.

So that she could have her own space, her own place.

So that she could get lucky and meet the guy of her dreams, only for him to stab her to death in his apartment.

And, as that life drained from her body, she didn't think about her parents, or how she was too young or that she had got Abe so incredibly wrong, she was just glad that she hadn't died in the town where she had been born.

THREE

Another moment.

Abe doesn't cry or scream. He should do that. He should freak out. He should be kicking himself for letting this happen. Again. And it's not like Sythe. He had no real emotional attachment to his first victim. That was easier to compartmentalise.

He'd never met anybody like Blair. There was an instant connection. Something you rarely find. Something you can't fake. He had fallen fast. Quicker than she had. He meant it. So he should have been thinking about his mistake and his rash behaviour, how this time he had really fucked up. Her left eye was bloodshot where he had hit her with the back of his hand, and the blood had spilled everywhere from her neck and her stomach.

All Abe was thinking was that he had to cut up another body. He had to dissolve more flesh and pulverise some bones.

The only thing that was puzzling young Abe Schwartz was the arrival of Gail Castle. One minute after Blair's heart stopped beating. It was the same when Blair arrived. Sythe wasn't even cold. He'd only recently been dragged into Abe's room when the doorbell rang with a new tenant. It seemed like too much of a coincidence.

But it had to be, of course. It wasn't something supernatural. It wasn't God or the Devil, because Abe knew those things did not exist. He wasn't cursed. It was chance. That's all. Maybe he could kill the new girl and see if somebody new turned up. A little extreme. Even for Abe.

This time, he didn't wait. He dragged Blair's body into the bathroom. He cut off her hands and feet. He sawed the legs below the knee then through the top of the femur. He cut the arms below the elbow then through the humerus.

It took less effort than he expected to get through the neck, because he'd rammed the scissors into her throat so many times. To make sure that she wasn't coming back.

Abe threw the pieces into the bath tub and leant the torso upright.

He stared into the oesophagus and swore he saw it move. As though it was trying to push something out. Air, perhaps. Blair's soul, maybe. He looked into it. The blood so red it almost looked black. And he thought about how his dick would probably fit in that hole.

He didn't want to do it. And he wasn't sure why the notion even entered his mind; he wasn't that kind of killer. He didn't get off on it. There was no gratification. As there was no real sense of wrongdoing. He wasn't in shock. He wasn't numbed by his actions.

Abe was nothing.

He cut up the woman he thought he was in love with and felt no sorrow at her passing or remorse for the way it had occurred.

What was wrong with him?

When did things change?

In his mind, this was not a case of what Abe had done, but the question of why this was happening to him.

He washed the blood off his arms and face, and changed his clothes. He put the bloodied garments on a cool wash, even though that hadn't worked last time and he'd had to burn them. Abe just wanted to get himself into more presentable shape because he remembered the last time, with Sythe, he was interrupted by Mrs May requesting that he help Blair unload her car.

He didn't want to get caught out again.

He had to be prepared.

Abe pictured Mrs May's face for a moment, and it was then that she knocked at his front door.

FOUR

He called out Gail's name as he tripped up the front step. He'd been fumbling around with his keys like he always did, knowing that eventually, the sound of metal scraping against the lock would send her so insane that she would open the door for him.

And he would smile at her, drunkenly, to give her that glimpse of the man she remembered. The one she loved. Before he stepped inside to tower over her and remind her of the man he had become.

'Gail,' he shouted again, giving her name two drawn-out syllables.

He shut the door and his eyes lit up with promise. Perhaps she was upstairs in bed. He could wake her. A bit. Not totally. He liked it when she was lying on her stomach and he could crawl into bed and put his weight on her.

He'd whisper drunken nothings into her ear while she stirred. Then he'd take down her underwear while still pressing down on her back and he'd force his way in. She'd lie there until he was finished. It didn't take long but any time was too much. He thought she was enjoying it because she made noises, but it was just the air being squeezed out of her as he crushed her ribs.

Former Staff Sergeant Castle made his way up the stairs, walking with his hands and feet like the dog he was. Expecting to get the bone.

The lights were off. It was dark. He didn't want to wake his wife because she might turn over onto her back, so he only flipped on the switch in the hallway. Leaning against the doorframe of their bedroom, he tried to look seductive.

He could see she wasn't there.

It made him feel stupid.

Which made him get angry.

'Gail.' He was shouting again as he moved swiftly down the stairs, holding the bannister for support. He made his wife's name last the entire journey.

He peered into the living room briefly then headed straight for the kitchen. She wasn't there. He went back to the living room.

'Where the fuck are you?' he mumbled under his breath.

He sat on the sofa and typed that same sentence in a text, which he sent to his wife. Eight seconds passed with no reply. No notification that it had even been read.

He could have been worried about her but he wasn't. He was annoyed. This wasn't how things were supposed to be. He was supposed to get home and have his wife in the house. So that he had somebody to talk to when he got back. Somebody to tease and antagonise and frighten and demand things from and shout at and hit and fuck while she was half asleep if that was what he wanted.

Castle was confused. He thought that maybe she had gone out herself. At no point did it cross his mind that she would ever leave him. Though, when he wasn't drunk, it was often something he thought that she should do.

He calmed himself down and switched on the television. He could wait up for her, this time.

He got a beer from the fridge.

And he made himself a sandwich.

FIVE

It couldn't be. It was too much like before.

Abe opened the door. First the chain, then the lock beneath. He looked to his right, at the bathroom doorway down the hall, inhaled deeply, then turned the latch.

'Mrs May. What can I do for you at this hour?' He didn't really know what he meant by that. He was either being playful, cheeky, tired or annoyed. For the first time in a while, Abe was flustered.

'For an old lady like me, it's the middle of the night, but a strapping young man like you...' She did this a lot. Commenting on her age like she was 150. Nobody had a clue how old she really was. Abe assumed that she would live forever and was probably pickled on the inside from all the alcohol. He laughed off her comment.

'Is it the new tenant? Would you like me to help take her things upstairs? I'm more than happy to, I just need to throw on a jumper and shoes.'

'Oh, no. No, no. She's not moving in upstairs. She'll be opposite you, in Sythe's old place.' She whispers behind her hand, 'You'd never know he'd been there.' Abe pictures the original Sythe tryptic in his apartment. 'Besides, she only brought one suitcase. Seems she needs a fresh start.'

The sentence hung in the air for a moment. Abe wasn't sure why but he was becoming increasingly paranoid that Mrs May knew more about him than he would like.

'How can I help you, then?'

Mrs May had come to ask whether Abe would be interested in going over for dinner and drinks at the weekend. She said that she wanted to make Gail feel welcome, that she had a feeling about her and that she may need some support. Abe did not falter in his immediate response.

Of course. He would be delighted.

The old lady said that she was pleased and was on her way up to speak with Blair to see whether she was also available.

'I'm sure that she will be there with bells on, Mrs May. I can always ask her for you, if you like. Save you the trouble of going up there. We are supposed to be going for a coffee after her morning run tomorrow, anyway.'

Just like that, Abe fell back into the comfort of his lack of empathy. He could lie at will with no tells that would give away the truth of who he was now.

A murderer. Though he did not see himself that way. That was not how he thought he should be defined.

'That's fine, dear. I can manage.'

'Well, thank you for asking me. I shall see you tomorrow, no doubt.'

He shut the door and replaced the locks then watched through the peephole to see what the old lady would do. She was heading toward the stairs but seemed to change her mind at the last minute. Maybe it was too late for her, she couldn't face the stairs. Perhaps she had come to the realisation that Abe would ask Blair the next day so it made Mrs May redundant. All she had to do was cook the meal on the weekend and keep the wine flowing.

She glided back to the biggest apartment in The Beresford, and Abe kept his eye on her until she was safely hidden away.

He brushed his teeth for two minutes, the pieces of Blair Conroy's body stuffed into the bathtub behind him. Abe was annoyed with himself. When he'd pictured her naked, this was not how he'd seen her.

SIX

It looked so bright in there. Gail thought of the place she had just left, her marital home, so dark and oppressive. No matter how much she cleaned or tidied, it had deteriorated. A slightly longer look at a skirting board or the paint around the light switch and you could see that the finish wasn't to a high standard.

Cracks everywhere. A symbol of their marriage. You hear that owners often end up looking like their dogs – or the other way around – but a person's house takes on the characteristics of its owner, too. They have a specific scent. For every grey hair there's a fallen roof tile. A wrinkle is a crack in the wall. And Gail's new place looked as though it had recently had some work done, a major facelift. What that said about Mrs May was anyone's guess but, to Gail Castle, it seemed that every surface in that place, every wall and ceiling, had been painted. There was not a mark on anything.

Not sterile. Just ... covered up.

Gail dragged her case behind her even though she could have left it in the hallway and explored. But it had everything in there. Her life in a suitcase. She felt like such a cliché. A battered ex-military wife, fleeing in the night from her tormentor.

Her phone buzzed as she admired the kitchen area.

It was him. One of his more polite messages:

Where the absolute fucking hell are you?

That was it.

She told herself that he probably didn't know how to make his own goddamned sandwich, and it almost made her laugh. She was too distracted.

Gail should not have read the message. Every text or social-media post was a way of worming his way back into her heart and brain. She should have purchased a new phone and dropped that one out of the window as she weaved around the back roads before she hit the city.

Now she was thinking about him.

What if he wasn't okay?

What if he was so drunk that he fell over and hit his head and ended up in a wheelchair, dribbling over himself and screaming in his mind?

She was spiralling.

What if he made himself something to eat and did a Mama Cass? Maybe it was too abrupt.

She should have talked to him and revealed her decision.

Another text.

Bitch.

Gail shook her head and laughed at herself for being so absurd. Why did she still care? What hold did he have over her?

She rubbed her stomach. She knew. She had to do the test to confirm but she knew. She could feel it. A poison inside her but, at the same time, the most joyous accident of all time.

Gail wheeled her suitcase into the bedroom. She had emailed Mrs May and told her that she wouldn't be bringing any furniture with her, and the old lady had agreed to leave Sythe's bed so there was somewhere to sleep, at least. There were also four pillows and a quilt. Gail had packed one set of covers and cases.

Once the bed was made, the case was placed on top and everything was taken out. There were two flat, fold-out boxes inside. She filled one with her underwear and the other with the few electrical items she had packed — a hair dryer, straighteners, three phone chargers and her laptop.

She was looking for the pregnancy test. She'd had it in the kitchen when she was filling a plastic bag with food she wanted to take. It wasn't in there. It wasn't underneath.

Gail pulled her clothes out and dumped them, one by one, onto the boxes she had neatly filled; it may have got caught between two pairs of trousers.

It hadn't. The case was empty. And as much as she knew, without the test, that she was definitely pregnant, she was equally sure that she had left her pregnancy test on the kitchen counter for her drunk husband to find.

SEVEN

He felt nothing. A whole lot of nothing. Not sadness. And certainly no joy that he could remember. He'd snuffed out any possibility of love when he plunged the scissors deep into Blair's throat. Abe stared at her and exhaled a sigh. The same kind of sigh another person might give if they dropped a plate and it smashed on the floor. A sigh that says, 'That's a waste', but in a way that is more irritated than contemplating the sheer gravity of a lost human life.

Abe didn't smoke weed to numb himself in some way, he did it to open himself up; to experience more of the world than he could with his regular five senses and their dull limitations.

There was a corner of the garden that was safe from prying eyes, though there was no doubt the neighbours must have noted the distinct aroma. Still, it was more pleasant than the usual burning of oil paintings and human skeletons.

This was how Abe had first met Sythe and had a real conversation with him. They'd passed one another while entering or exiting their apartments or taking out the rubbish and recycling on a Sunday night, but it was outside in Mrs May's perfectly handcrafted garden where they became more than passing acquaintances.

Abe was in his favourite corner, lighting up. He took a long drag and hid it behind his back when he heard footsteps coming toward him. At first, Sythe did not see his neighbour, lurking behind some foliage. He was carrying a large canvas and swearing at himself, 'It's a piece of shit. You're a piece of shit.' He was heading toward the burn can, breaking the wooden frame of his canvas as he walked.

There was a movement near the bushes, and Sythe spotted Abe. He was startled. 'Jesus. What the fuck are you doing in there?' A little of his Irish accent seeped out. Abe noticed.

'Sorry. It's just me. Abe. I come out here sometimes when the world gets on top of me, you know?' He takes his hands from behind his back as though surrendering the evidence. 'It just chills me out. Calms me down. Please don't tell Mrs May.'

Sythe laughed. 'We're not in school, Abe. You can eat, drink, smoke and fuck what you want, it's none of my business. I'm sure the old lady probably knows, anyway. She sees everything that happens in this building.'

Abe stepped out of the bushes, pulled a tin out of his pocket, opened it and offered it towards Sythe.

'Well, don't mind if I do. You could probably tell that I am in need of some chill and calm.' He reached into the tin, took out one of the pre-rolled joints and put it to his lips. Abe produced a lighter and lit it for his co-conspirator.

'What are you doing out here?' Abe asked.

'As you may know, I'm an artist.' Abe nodded and took another drag. 'Well, this thing in my hand. It is not art. And I don't want it anywhere near me. So I am smashing it up and setting fire to it.'

'Sounds cathartic.'

They both giggled.

'Oh, it is.' Sythe pulled the still-wet-with-paint canvas away from the frame and ripped it down the middle. He threw it into the bin, followed by the frame. Mrs May kept a pile of old newspapers and kindling in a cupboard outside. He scrunched the paper into balls, threw them in the bin and tossed in a match. Abe helped by dropping the kindling on top, and they both stared into the glowing can while smoking.

'You're the literary type then, huh?'

'I'm sorry?'

'Every time I see you, your face is inside a book. And it's a different one, every time.'

'Ah, yes. I read a lot. Kinda my thing.'

There was a moment of silence when Sythe wasn't sure where to take the conversation; he couldn't remember the last book he had read.

'I need to stop lending books out, though. I gave one to the guy who lived above you for a while and he just upped and left one day without giving it back. I hate that.'

Sythe went white. And it was nothing to do with drawing too much into his lungs. He wasn't sick. He wasn't cold. He was thinking about Abe's unreturned book. He was remembering the housemate who had disappeared, the one who had 'upped and left' and never looked back. He was thinking about what that guy would look like now. Because it had been so long since Sythe had killed him. The week after it had happened, Sythe's career had blown up. He was a success. And he'd forgotten all about that night until Abe brought it up.

'Yeah. You're right. I hate that, too. People do tend to leave this place quite suddenly, eh? It happens.'

Abe nodded in agreement.

Sythe continued. 'I'll tell you what, if I ever decide to skip town and move on to somewhere new, feel free to take the books I leave. I'll leave you a painting, too.'

EIGHT

It was the size of a nut. Probably. Or a grape. Or the seed of a grape. She didn't know. But she knew it was in there. It wasn't a boy or a girl, or even anything that resembled a person yet. An amoeba. A zygote. Whatever.

Gail was pregnant.

Two to four weeks according to that little screen on the test.

She thought back. It had been about that long. She had managed to keep it staved off for weeks. Maybe five. A record for her. She could concoct an argument before bed that would dampen the mood enough that she would be able to turn her back to him and he wouldn't try anything on. He could be drunk and she'd screw up the sandwich or bring something up that he didn't want to discuss or say that he was like his mother. That would always work.

But it could only last so long. She couldn't keep him off forever without getting into a conversation about how she didn't want to be with him.

That very thought made her feel young and stupid.

Gail had let him in. He had climbed into bed and got onto her back. His favourite. She'd shut her eyes and hoped it would end quickly, but near the end he pulled her hips up and knelt behind her. She let it happen. She didn't know what to do, how to get out of it.

Was this her forever?

It couldn't be. It was the last time. It had to be.

Of course she was pregnant.

Stupid Gail.

Young Gail.

It wasn't even really a person. No feelings. No hair or nipples or lungs. If she got rid of whatever was inside her, it wasn't really a person. She wasn't killing a human being. She was causing more damage by stepping on an ant or swatting at a fly.

To ease her mind a little, Gail looked up 'baby sizes through pregnancy' online. At forty-one weeks your baby can be the size of a watermelon. At forty-two weeks, the size of a jackfruit. She didn't even know what a jackfruit was. But there it was, at the bottom, four weeks. The size of a poppy seed.

A goddamned poppy seed.

It would be another couple of months before it was even a lime. And at that stage, they can't have a personality. They don't know what books they're into or if the sound of jazz makes them want to cry. They don't have a political stance or favourite cartoon.

They're not real.

He doesn't like his steak medium/well done. It's not because he can't have solid food yet or that he doesn't have teeth, it's because he isn't even a he. He isn't a she, either. So Gail could terminate things quite easily. A strong night on the gin might do it. There was probably a pill for something like that. She wouldn't even know it had gone because it was a poppyseed.

Nothing more than a poppyseed.

She could pull the plug on a poppyseed. One made out of fear and hatred. One that had not been produced through calculation of her cycle and ensuring both parties were eating healthily and exercising to give that seed the best opportunity for growth and thriving.

That stupid, dumb seed was made out of bad maths and worse decisions. The father was drunk and fucking her from behind so neither of them had to look into the other's eyes. That poor, unknowing seed had come from something cold and senseless and scary.

And Gail would love it more than anything in the world, and protect it with her life.

NINE

In that freshly painted room, all magnolias and off-whites and eggshells, where there was once a swirling mural of chaos, where a lonely woman rubs her stomach that contains a life no bigger than a poppyseed, where once there lived another domestically abused woman, and a carpenter and two accountants and a sportsman who had broken his leg, there lived a struggling artist, who had moved away from Ireland and changed his name in the hope of finding success.

A new life.

And in that room where a lonely woman had found out she was going to have a baby, where a carpenter had constructed a bespoke entertainment unit, where one accountant had calculated many a tax return while the other sadly took their own life, where a sportsman ferociously attempted to maintain fitness by performing push-ups while wearing a cast up to his hip, an artist choked his neighbour to death and had no idea how it had come to that point so quickly.

Something of a blur, as so many first kills attest to being, but Sythe had managed to hook his right arm around his friend's throat, grasping onto the biceps of his left arm. He squeezed. Tightening his muscles enough to close the airways of his victim. It wasn't an aggressive strangling, where Sythe pushed his thumbs deep into the sides of his neighbour's windpipe. It was quiet. Almost loving. Coaxing towards death rather than hurtling.

His victim tried to break free by throwing a fist behind his head. A couple of good shots caught Sythe on the cheekbone, but muscles require oxygen in the blood and breathing was being slowly cut off.

When the body went limp, Sythe held on for ten more seconds before releasing his grip and seconds later, his emotions.

He cried for the man he had become in the hunt for success and recognition. And he cried for the man whose life he took so effortlessly. And he cried because he couldn't remember how it started. Maybe his critique of Sythe's work was too harsh. But it wasn't enough to kill the guy.

Sythe had no time for reflection. A minute after he had massaged the life out of his critic, the front doorbell rang. He waited, hoping that Mrs May would be past her daytime siesta, but the doorbell rang again and he listened.

Nothing from across the hall. The bell rang again.

Sythe pushed the dead body onto its side, marvelling at how heavy it felt for such a slender client. He flicked some water onto his face and towelled it off before heading out into the hallway, hoping to determine the identity of the caller.

He didn't recognise the man on the doorstep.

'Hello. Can I help you?'

The man tried to look as though he wasn't staring at Sythe's face, spattered with water, eyes red from crying, ashen in disbelief at his cruel act.

'Er, yes, sorry, I'm here to see Mrs May.'

He was a smartly dressed black man in his late fifties, well spoken. There was something in his eyes, too. A magic. A calmness. Sythe wondered whether there was some romantic connection with the old lady.

'Of course. Come in. She's usually first to the door, so I'm guessing she must be asleep. Or perhaps she's in the garden and didn't hear.'

'That's okay. Thanks for letting me in. I just need to get my key.'

'You're moving in?'

'Yes. For a short time.'

He wasn't lying. Jonesy stayed for seven weeks. He was pleasant. He played jazz music at an appropriate level. He was considerate and polite and quiet, keeping himself to himself, mostly. He would occasionally dine with Mrs May, and nobody really knows whether there was something going on there. And nobody asked why he stayed for such a short time, though he had mentioned family in the area and the fact that he wasn't feeling quite as young and healthy as he had, so there was some speculation that he may have even been dying.

But he did not die at The Beresford. He did not see out his lease, but he did pay for everything up front, and he had very few belongings to take with him when he left.

He left.

Walked out that front door as modestly as he had entered.

He wasn't killed.

He didn't murder somebody else.

It doesn't have to be like that.

That's not how it works.

TEN

Another early-morning trip to the city saw Abe picking up drain cleaner from several different stores. This time he wasn't going to start with the hands then move on to legs and finally torso; he knew what he was doing.

He was going to get rid of the flesh in one go.

The bones he could do in batches, just like before. It would be safer that way. But the quicker he could get rid of the body and the smell, the better chance he stood of getting away with it again.

Mrs May had seen him leaving early and asked if he'd spoken to Blair.

'Er, no. Not today. Not yet. But I'm guessing she's not that far behind me for her morning run.' Abe didn't wait for a response from the old lady, he didn't want a conversation. So he pulled his large headphones up over his ears and started walking.

The old lady was not offended. Abe was her favourite tenant. He always paid on time. He was always courteous and helpful. He had seemingly found love. But something was slightly off. She was worried about him. She wanted the best for the boy.

As he wandered towards the smog of the city, Mrs May went back inside the house and straight up to Blair's apartment. She knocked. And waited. And knocked again. And waited more. Perhaps she had gone for an even earlier run and both she and Abe had missed her.

Coming down the stairs, Mrs May focussed on Abe's front door. She gripped her keys and wondered. What was going on with him? What was happening in his life? Of course, she couldn't just let herself into people's apartments on a whim, but if she was worried about them...

First, she needed to check on her new addition to The Beresford.

'Morning, dear. I just wanted to make sure you're all settled.'

Gail looked as though she had been crying. Because she had been crying. And she was distracted by the buzzing of her mobile phone as she received another abusive text from the husband she had left the evening before. She had been reading them as they appeared on her home screen but then so many came through at once, she stupidly opened up her texts to see what she had missed and it had alerted him to the fact that she had read it.

Stupid Gail.

Young Gail.

The messages were getting worse. Spite disguised as worry for her whereabouts. And it was the morning, so he couldn't hide behind the twelve beers he'd drank the night before. She wouldn't answer him. She wouldn't go back. She couldn't.

This was who he was now. He was mean. He would hit her.

Saying those words in her head made Gail feel at once juvenile and free.

'It did not take me long to unpack.' She faked a laugh.

'And you have everything you need?'

'I'll need to stock up on food, and I slipped out last night to pick up a few essentials.'

Essentials like bread, milk, tea bags and a pregnancy test.

Her phone buzzed again. Both women looked at it.

'You need to get that, dear? Something important?'

Her ex-husband telling her that she was a piece of useless shit. It could wait.

Gail shook her head.

'You have the essentials you say? So you have a bag of Blue Mountain coffee beans that you can grind yourself for the freshest, most delicious coffee in the world?'

'I can't say that I do, no.' Gail looked puzzled but heartened.

'Well, I always have them. And once you've tasted it, you'll find that it is as essential as de-ionised water for your iron.'

Mrs May's eccentricities made her immediately endearing and intriguing.

'I have some at my place now and it goes perfectly with the chocolate and walnut cake I also have. If you'd like to talk...'

'I think I need to understand what all this Blue Mountain fuss is about. That would be lovely. Thank you Mrs May.'

Gail picked up the keys from the shelf by the front door and left her phone, face down, on that shelf, inside the apartment. It buzzed again and she shut the door behind her.

*

Mrs May was right. The coffee was incredible. As was the cake. Somehow, each one made the other taste better. It was ludicrous to Gail. She felt spoilt.

They talked for a while. The old lady asking most of the questions and doing the majority of listening. Gail spoke of her childhood and her parents and school and work, and it all led to meeting the best man in the world, who turned out to be a monster.

Without too much graphic detail, but enough to get the message across, Gail belted out her story and was pleased to have a receptive audience. She had tried to speak about it with her mother once, and the woman who had given birth to her ended up defending the abuser.

Pressure.

War.

He's a man.

Gail needed to talk about it. She needed the release. She needed somebody to tell her that she had done the right thing. But she left out the part about the poppyseed inside of her. It was too early, anyway.

Mrs May had lost track of time so was unaware that Abe had returned. There was no opportunity to let herself into his flat, even if that was something she had wanted to do. He was back.

When she opened her door to let Gail out, Abe was standing in the foyer with a cardboard cup holder and two take-out cups of coffee.

'Hello, Abe. Back already.'

'Just a quick trip. Grabbed myself and Blair a nice cup of coffee. I assume she's back from her run?'

'I can't say I've seen her.'

'Well, I'll go up and give her a knock.' He gave a polite nod to Mrs May. 'Nice to see you again, Gail.' And another nod to his new neighbour.

He knocked and waited. Knocked again and waited. Then returned downstairs, where the two women were still talking outside Mrs May's door.

'Seems she's still out. Would either of you care for a coffee?' Abe took one of the cups from the holder.

'Not unless it's Blue Mountain,' Gail smiled, conspiratorially.

'Oh, looks like I'm no longer the favourite.'

They all laughed lightly before Mrs May broke the moment.

'Why don't you come in, Abe? It's almost time for wine, but I can squeeze in a coffee.'

Blair was dissolving in the bath, there was nothing he could do to speed that up, so Abe agreed. Gail went back to her abusive messages, and Abe went in for his interrogation.

ELEVEN

Jonesy only had one dinner at Mrs May's. That was enough. From that day, he would still visit her for coffee and even a glass or two of red wine. But no meals. Nothing so long that he couldn't escape.

The old lady could cook. She was a little old-fashioned in her choices and presentation but she knew her way around a stove, that was for sure. She did not buy into the vegan or vegetarian movements one bit and believed that humans were flesh and they desired flesh – both sexually and nutritionally. Perhaps even spiritually.

Though, strangely, she would not touch milk. The idea of drinking juice from another species did not sit well with Mrs May. Stranger still, she loved cheese.

On that solitary occasion where those two elders of The Beresford did meet for food, Mrs May finished with a very generous cheese board. This was accompanied by a bottle of Barbaresco Riserva San Cristoforo from Piedmont. Jonesy had no idea how much the wine would have cost but he understood that it was delicious. As was the prawn starter, beef main and chocolate pudding.

The conversation was never dry – they had enough years between them on Earth to find something worth saying. Mrs May seemed incredibly interested in her new lodger and had many questions for him. Jonesy managed to sidestep the probing a few times where the subject was, in his eyes, irrelevant. But he did open up.

'You're not from round here, obviously, so what brings you this way?'

Standard dinner-party fodder but it was of a personal nature to her guest.

'I've come to visit family. Family that I haven't seen in a long time, for one reason or another.'

Mrs May nodded and forked some food into her mouth so that Jonesy would have to continue.

'My son and his wife. And my two grandkids. I haven't seen them since they started school. They're teenagers now.' He looked off to the side, picturing the kids when they were little. His face soon dropped into an expression that Mrs May knew well: disappointment and regret.

'I'm sorry, Mr Jones, you certainly do not have to talk about it, if you don't want to.' Then she shoved more food in her mouth so that he would have to.

He explained, in that soft, soothing voice of his, that he was unwell. Stage-four cancer. The doctors are surprised he's still on his feet but think he has a couple of months left. Maximum.

'That's why I signed such a short lease and paid you up front. You won't lose any money, and I don't want you to worry, you won't find me dead in there. I won't die. I won't let myself until I've sorted things out.'

Mrs May put down her cutlery and slid her hand across to hold her guest's arm. She was saddened and wanted to support him. They looked at each other for a tender moment, then she slid her hand back to take a drink of her wine.

'So, you've travelled here to reconnect with your boy. Does he even know you've been unwell.'

'We haven't spoken in so long. I tried to get through it myself, but it was caught too late. I stopped the treatment and packed my bag. The next time I go home, it will be to die.'

The room went cold.

There was a short silence as they digested the gravity of Jonesy's situation.

Then Mrs May spoken again. She could have tried to change the subject. She could have tried to stay on a supportive course. Instead, she asked, 'What if there was something you could do?'

'I'm sorry.'

'What if there was something you could do to get rid of that blasted illness within you?'

'I tried. Chemo. Radiation. The usual things.'

'I mean something else. There are people out there who would kill another person if it gave them their fifteen minutes of fame, but this is more than that, Jonesy. This is your life. A chance to reconnect and have a family again. If there was something, would you try it?'

Jonesy looked decidedly uncomfortable for a moment, and this section of their conversation was the reason the two had only shared one dinner.

'Are you asking if I would kill a person in order to save myself from cancer? Maybe buy myself some healthier organs on the black market?' He placed his knife and fork on the table, and Mrs May was afraid that he was going to get up and leave.

She changed tack slightly. She'd offended him and that was never what she had intended. She wanted to show that she cared, she understood.

'I'm sorry, I don't think that came across right at all. I wasn't suggesting anything like that. I just ... I just wondered whether there was an experimental treatment or something. You hear about those things...'

He picked up his cutlery again.

'I understand your sentiment, Mrs May, I do have some friends who have reacted in the same way. I'm old. I have lived a long and varied life. I have travelled. I have loved. I have lost. I have loved somebody else. I have read great novels and played my own music. I have drunk great wine and bad whisky. I've tried drugs and lived through war. It is my time to go. There is nothing left for me to do but tell my son that I was wrong and I never stopped loving him, and that he should always be the bigger man with his own kids because I only have one regret in my life and it lasted for ten years. That's more than this cancer ever took from me.'

He took a deep breath that was somewhere between a sigh and complete resignation.

'So, I guess to answer your question, there is no experimental drug out there that is going to save me in time, there's no voodoo or magic, and I wouldn't kill somebody to get an extra fifteen minutes on this planet.'

They never spoke of it again.

Mrs May knew that there was no need to push the subject.

Jonesy was going to die soon, but there was no need for it to happen at The Beresford.

TWELVE

The coffee was already going cold but that didn't bother Mrs May. She'd had her cold cup in the morning and this lukewarm crap was eating into her wine time. She just wanted some face-to-face with Abe. So that she could gauge what was happening in his life. Something was making her uneasy. It wasn't maternal instinct, but she wanted to look out for the boy.

She asked how things were going with Blair and he lied. He told her that they were close, that he felt some connection with her and that he believed that she felt it with him. He was worried that their backgrounds were too similar, and that might make them hold back. But he was willing to take it slowly because they were having a great time together.

She probed a little further, because Blair had been absent since the night before and it was unlike her to not be seen around, running or in the library. It wasn't like with Sythe, where he would disappear for weeks on end then suddenly reappear.

'Remember Jonesy?' she asked.

'Of course. Wasn't here long but left his mark. Left a couple of poetry books in your library, too, if I recall.'

'Have you read them?'

'Nobody really reads poetry anymore, Mrs May.'

'Ah, so you have read them.' She swigged the final dregs of her coffee. 'Oh, thank the Lord below that's finished. I need a glass of wine.'

Abe stayed in his seat while she unscrewed something cheap and poured it quickly into a glass.

She continued.

'Jonesy was the real deal. You know? A proper gent. He wasn't here long but he didn't just leave without a word. He paid up. He said his goodbyes. He went on his way. I wish more people would do that. I'm getting tired of the deserters. If you ever want to leave, Abe, that's the way I want you to go.'

'Of course. I wouldn't just—'

'I mean it. Do it the right way.' She interrupted. A warning, masquerading as concern.

'Okay.' He felt like a child being scalded by a parent for misbehaving during class. 'I don't have any inclination to move on just yet. I like it here. Blair is here...'

The switch in Abe Schwartz was mystifying. The way he lied so effortlessly. Either he was in denial and was convinced that he would return to his apartment and find Blair there, still alive and sorry, or all empathy had evaporated from his being. He couldn't feel bad about what he had done because he did not believe that he was in the wrong.

He had bought Blair a cup of coffee from town, knowing that she was chopped up in his bathroom. He was talking about staying at The Beresford because he felt a connection with her and wanted to see how it developed, yet her fingerprints were already starting to melt away, and any other soft tissue that could help identify her was eroding.

The old dependable, affable, awkward Abe was in there somewhere but buried deep beneath the pretence.

As were his memories and his morals.

'I understand that, Abe, and you are a great tenant, but there is a world out there, and when you find that it's time for you to see it, I want to make sure that you do things in the correct way. Leave the same way that you came. Okay?'

'Okay, Mrs May.' To Abe, it felt like her worry or consideration had given way and, in the end, what she was doing was asking him to leave The Beresford. To get out and explore the world. To leave this all behind. Start anew.

He swallowed the last of his coffee.

'She's right, you know?'

'I'm sorry?'

'Gail. This stuff was no Blue Mountain.' He smiled and Mrs May caught a glimpse of the kid she knew. The scrawny Abe, who had arrived with no idea how to take care of himself. The Abe who hadn't killed anyone. Who hadn't lost something with every second his thumbs had squeezed Sythe's airways shut.

The Abe who would have picked up on Mrs May's not-so-subtle hints.

'I should be getting back.' The chair screeched as he pushed himself away from the table.

'Of course. Oh, I meant to ask. How is the sink?'

'The sink?'

'Yes, you had some drainage trouble a while back. Nothing since then?'

'Oh, that. No. It's all good. That was just a one-off, I think.'

'I do hope so.' And she looked at him like she knew something.

Abe's paranoia kicked in. All he could think about was getting out of the old lady's place and back to his own, back to Blair. He had to melt her and burn her and crush her to nothing. He was starting to panic, and panicking almost always leads to mistakes.

Abe's biggest mistake was that he hadn't really been listening to Mrs May, he thought the conversation had taken an odd turn. His anxiety would make him forget what they spoke about, that his initial inclination was correct. She was telling him to get out of The Beresford.

WHAT DO YOU WANT?

It's Valentine's Day. The loneliest day of the year if you are single. And, for many, if you are in a relationship.

Men can be seen scrambling through buckets of supermarket detritus or petrol-station wastelands for the last bunch of dying flowers because, for some reason, if they don't give their wife/girlfriend/fiancée a box of chocolates or an expensive candle or make them something meaningful, it means that their love is not real.

And it's made worse when love becomes public. When somebody posts a picture of the breakfast they were made that morning and accompany it with a long spiel about how great their partner is and how long they have been in love. In fact, throw in some extra images of you as a couple over the years, that way everyone will be envious of your everlasting commitment and ongoing sexual ardour for one another.

Disguise the fact that you are showing off or papering over the cracks by cutting and pasting a set of questions about your relationship onto your social-media platform of choice.

How long have you been together? Who asked whom out first? Which of you does the driving? There's nothing emotional in there that you have to commit to. It's supposed to look cute. You're just joining in.

You laugh off the question about what you do on 'date night', because you don't do that kind of thing anymore and you're already dreading the fact that one of you has to spread your legs tonight for a day made up by card companies. And the people who are like you feel awful because they know they have to do the same thing this evening. And the people who are in love feel bad for you because they can see the lie. And the singletons hate you because they'd be happy for some contact with another person, even if it's not that good. And, in the end, every voyeur feels like crap as a result of your public declaration, even you.

Love, whether real or troubled, makes others feel hopeless.

Private love is the dream. The kind that makes you want to scream from the rooftops but gives you the security to know that it isn't necessary.

What do you want, Abe?

I want to be loved. Needed. I want other people to look at what I have and feel short-changed that they don't have anything that comes close.

Love is so easily confused. For the most part, it is interchangeable with madness, but nobody would ask to be mad.

You ask for it because it seems unattainable. It's a myth. Something you can't get by yourself.

You ask for it because you were born into this world alone and you will die alone and love ensures that for some point in the middle of your existence, you have somebody else.

Is it really love that you want?

THIRTEEN

He can tell his therapist that his dad was also a mean drunk, that he used to take a large wooden spoon out of the cutlery drawer and smack his son across the knuckles or the back of the legs.

It doesn't matter.

You don't hit your wife, Castle.

The things that happened in that war, that he saw, that everybody saw, or heard. The screams. The fear. The heads on the side of the road. All the things they never shared with anyone when they got back. Those events that fucked them all up so epically. How the military just left them. They fought for their country in the blind faith that what they were doing was right. And then they were abandoned by the very people they were fighting for, to protect, as soon as they got home.

Yeah, sad story, Castle. But you don't hit your wife. Ever.

Gail didn't even know her husband had been in therapy. It was the one thing the army had thrown his way to help him deal with whatever made-up syndrome was fashionable for veterans that month.

He didn't want to hit her. He couldn't control his rage. He was scared of himself so he knew how scared she must have been. And he hated himself for that.

The therapy proved to be a useful outlet for him. There was somebody to talk to who had to keep things confidential – as long as no laws were being broken. It doesn't stop the rage, though. No amount of deep breaths or tapping yourself on the forehead fifteen times was going to outweigh the devastation he had witnessed and the hatred he felt for himself as a result.

And his therapist knew all of this. His therapist knew more about what was going on in former Staff Sergeant Castle's mind than his own wife ever would. His therapist had seen this with other ex-military types who had served. His therapist understood the psychology and the history. When Castle wept on that couch and said that he was drinking again and came home to an empty house, and that he thought Gail had probably left him for good this time, his therapist said all the right things – get to an AA meeting because the booze isn't helping – but, inside, that therapist was thinking, *Of course, you idiot, because you don't hit your fucking wife.*

He truly was an idiot. The kind of idiot that seemed to make a breakthrough in therapy, agreed to attend his first Alcoholics Anonymous meeting before going to a bar to drink away his sorrows, then going home and smashing up his own kitchen and throwing away the pregnancy test because he thought it was a box of his wife's tampons.

And, because he was the type of idiot who would make a breakthrough with his mental health and throw it all away the next minute, he was also the type of guy that would slide his back down the kitchen cupboard, sitting next to the now-broken microwave he threw against the tiled floor, swig another beer, then text more abuse to the wife he claimed he didn't want to hurt.

FOURTEEN

You ruined my life, Gail. You fucking ruined it all. I wish I'd never met you. I hope you fucking die.

Gail did not need this. She had done nothing wrong. What she needed was to change her number or get a new phone. One of those pay-as-you-go things. She'd seen them in cop shows. The criminals used them then threw them away. Burners. That's what they called them.

She needed a burner.

Sure, she could have blocked him, deleted all the messages, but that wasn't final enough. There was no cleansing. The Beresford was her fresh start. She needed to be rid of her old life.

It would have been easy to look up the nearest phone shop, but she decided to ask Mrs May. She was pleased to be away from her situation but she didn't really want to be alone; she craved human interaction. Something real and unthreatening.

'Oh, dear. I'm sorry. I can use my computer for listing the rooms, but that's the extent of my technological skills.' Mrs May seemed genuinely dismayed. 'I'm sure there is somewhere in town. There are probably lots of places. I don't venture out of the house much.' She laughed uncomfortably. 'You could maybe ask Blair. Introduce yourself while you're up there. Or Abe if that's no good.'

Gail was worried about meeting Blair but didn't know why. Mrs May was nothing but complimentary and apparently Abe was smitten. She traipsed up the stairs and knocked meekly on Blair's front door.

Nothing. Of course.

Gail tried a more authoritative knock. Four, in fact, and a rasp to end with.

She'd not been there a day and already she knew that tenants would often leave without a word. She'd heard about the famous artist who had lived in her flat. And it already seemed to her that this Blair woman had run off but nobody wanted to admit it yet.

Poor Abe.

That's what Gail thought. Abe wasn't like her husband. Nobody, not even his so-called friends would be saying, 'Poor Castle.' He was a monster. But Abe didn't seem that way. Still, the Blair girl must have left for a reason.

Gail hit Abe's front door with a little more confidence.

He spoke through a very small gap between the door and its frame, but he was friendly looking and courteous.

'There are a few places not that far from here, actually. If you can give me a few minutes, I'll just freshen up and I can show you.'

'Okay. That would be great. Thank you. I can wait over there by the books.' She pointed.

'Mrs May likes to call it the library. But, yes, I won't be long. And if you drink coffee, I know a couple of really good places near the phone store, if you fancy it?'

Gail was immediately concerned about her baby. She knew that there were certain things she wasn't supposed to consume while pregnant. Alcohol, obviously. She had heard something about cheese, but then the French would eat cheese and drink wine while pregnant and they weren't a nation of three-legged hunchbacks or anything.

'Of course.' Coffee was okay but not too much. She was going to order decaf. Just to be safe.

Safe. Just like good old Abe Schwartz.

He shut the door.

Gail waited by the books.

All that was needed now was for Mrs May to come out of her apartment at the right time to catch them both before they left and things were repeating themselves almost exactly.

FIFTEEN

Take a lamb shank. A little oil in a hot saucepan. Sear the outside of the meat on all sides. Brown it off. This gives it great colour but it also seals in all the juices. Now you make your stock. Onions or shallots with garlic. Carrots and celery. Mirepoix, they call it. Get some herbs in there and season. Some tomato paste, too. Add water until the meat is covered in liquid and the top of the bone is poking out of the broth.

Leave it on a low heat for a couple of hours.

It will probably be ready before then but the extra fifteen minutes is what you need to get the effect you are looking for. You want it to sit upright on your plate, perhaps on a bed of mash with some vegetables. But it is all about that meat.

You want to be able to touch it with a fork and have it separate from the bone entirely. You want to be able to do this with ease because you know how tender the flesh is after being cooked for a long period of time on a low heat. You want it to fall away and leave the bone clean.

That's how you want to eat your lamb shanks.

And that is how Abe wants Blair's flesh to come away.

If she sits in the lye solution for long enough, Abe should be able to take a gloved hand, grab the end of a humerus and watch as a bicep slides off cleanly into the water. Or he could grip her ankle and admire the way her calf slips away.

He was sad that her breasts were gone but pleased that he had more bones to burn.

Then the new girl knocked on his door and interrupted him.

He agreed to help her. Straight away. And it was as natural to him as strangling Sythe or melting his neighbours.

Abe was a nice guy.

The nicest murderer you could ever meet.

He met Gail over by the books. She was reading the back of some tattered classic.

'You know, I really should read more. I've always wanted to.'

Abe tilted his head to the side to read the title of the book. 'Well, don't start with that one, otherwise you'll never get going.'

'Oh, really? That bad?'

'It's okay, it's just one of those books you can only love once you love reading. I think there are better gateways.'

Abe could talk about books all day, but Mrs May appeared, like a meerkat popping up from a hole in the ground. Abe looked around to see whether he could spot anywhere that might be concealing a camera. How did she always know?

'So you enlisted Abe, did you?' The old lady asked Gail through the side of her mouth.

'Yes. I tried upstairs but there was no answer.'

'Oh, so I'm your last resort, am I? Your back-up.' Abe said it jokingly but he found himself hurt by this.

'Of course not. I just wanted to introduce myself to her.'

'No answer? I'm starting to get worried about her.' Mrs May looked straight at Abe. 'I didn't have her down as a defector.'

'I think you're probably jumping the gun a bit there.' Abe tried to sound comforting. 'I'm going into town to help Gail sort her phone, and I'm sure Blair will show her lovely face soon enough.' He was keeping it light, knowing that her cheeks and lips had already separated from her skull.

'I'm sure you're right. Good luck getting the phone sorted.' She walked back to her apartment slowly, without the usual kick to her step.

'Shall we?' Abe opened the front door, presenting his hand for Gail to lead the way out.

Things went almost exactly as they had with Blair. Abe showed her the swanky coffee place and the grubby one. And somewhere in between they got her a new phone at a good deal. She opted to change her number completely so that she wouldn't have to receive abuse or death threats or messages of life regrets. She was worried that he might try to kill himself and she didn't want that on her conscience. Better to bury her head in the sand. She could contact the few friends she had left and give them her new details – the ones whose husbands weren't Castle's drinking buddies.

Abe and Gail had covered a lot of ground. She had ordered decaf coffee to protect her poppyseed, and he had recommended some books that she might enjoy. He'd said that his family was rather traditional in their views, and she had explained that her husband had not been the same person since returning from the war.

Good old Abe had found himself angered by the information, that a man could attack a woman, unprovoked. Gail wasn't like Blair. She wouldn't belittle him. He could see that. He liked her. He didn't like her husband. That guy sounded like a monster.

Like before, Mrs May was pruning when the pair returned. Abe told himself that he was being paranoid, that history often had a way of repeating itself. The old woman was always tending to her flowers. So, the fact that she was doing it now, just as she had done it when he had come back to The Beresford that first time with Blair, it was coincidence; it had a high probability. If he went out at the same time tomorrow and came back on his own, Mrs May would be outside with those secateurs he had used to cut off Sythe's fingers and toes. Which reminded him, there were bones ready to burn.

'Look, I'm sure you've got a lot to do, and you need to transfer your information from one phone to the other, but when you're done, come out into the garden, I'm lighting a fire – just something I like to do – and you could throw your old phone onto it. Might be cathartic, you know? Get rid of all those horrible messages that you don't want to read. I don't know. Just an idea.'

Abe looked shy. It was endearing to Gail. A couple of days ago, she had watched a man contemplate stamping his boot down on her skull, and today, she had a different man, a kind man, a thoughtful man, offering a way to erase the abuse that had been thrown her way after the incident.

'That sounds like a perfect bloody idea, Abe. Thank you.'

A genuine smile that made Abe want to get rid of Blair as quickly as possible so that he could move on.

He was done with grieving.

'Well, I have been known to have them. You come out whenever you're ready. I have a few things to finish up and then I'll head out. It probably won't be hot for another half-hour or so.'

They parted ways. Gail went to sort out her burner phone. Abe went to put some of Blair's bones in a pillowcase. And Mrs May marched back into her apartment, stripped off her clothes, shut the curtains, poured a wine and said another prayer for poor old Abe Schwartz.

She wanted him to leave.

She wanted him to make that decision for himself.

SIXTEEN

The women of The Beresford, the ones who were still alive, both had requests, desires, things that they desperately wanted. And they were asking for them. Begging. Praying.

In different directions.

Gail had moved the few numbers she thought that she might use in the future to her new phone. She was on her knees at the side of the only piece of furniture she owned at the time – her bed. (Formerly Sythe's.)

She didn't want her husband to kill himself because she had left. He'd sent seventeen more messages to her since she last looked. She could tell he was drunk – they were putrid. Straight from the mouth of Satan, it seemed.

One moment he loved her, he was sorry.

Next she was a whore, a sorry sack of shit.

Gail looked up to the ceiling and asked a god, any god, for forgiveness. Like anyone with self-esteem so low from years of being beaten down and held back, from all the lack of encouragement, from being told she was nothing for so long that she built her own daily mantra that told her she was worthless, she was apologising.

She was weak for leaving. Maybe she didn't try hard enough. She should have pushed harder for him to talk about that war. She should have gone softer on him when he didn't want to speak about it. She could have been a better wife.

After all the apologising for being a sorry sack of shit whore, she eventually got around to what she was there for, to implore the Lord to intervene somehow into her husband's thoughts and stop him from going to the darkest of places. She wanted him to suffer and struggle and own his mistakes. She just didn't want him to kill himself.

Perhaps she thought more of herself than she realised. Maybe she wouldn't be able to take that gesture. She asked God for Castle to weep and howl and realise, maybe even change. But she was never going back.

Amen.

She picked up her old phone. Three more messages. Something spiteful about her mother and sister. She skimmed over them and hit reply:

> *The first time you hit me was too much. I should have left then. Get some help, ~~you sorry excuse for a man.~~ I'm not coming back. I hope you find some peace ~~when you fucking die~~. Don't message me again.*

She hit send and turned off her phone forever.

Mrs May was in the dark, on her feet. She was not looking towards the heavens. She knew that Gail's God had stopped listening a long time ago. You can't explain away the injustice and famine and greed and rape and war and sickness with a Lord working in 'mysterious ways'. It's a cop-out. Blind faith.

That was not for Mrs May. She put out what she wanted to get back. And when she put it out there, she meant it. She was passionate. She screamed out her vitriol if that is what she was feeling towards somebody, and she tensed her body rigid and wept when she felt compassion.

That day, with Gail on her knees in the flat above, Mrs May lit her candle, rang her bell, drank her wine and paced in circles as she begged.

She begged for Abe to find his way. She could see how lost he was.

She begged for him to leave The Beresford. It was time for him to move on. Abe had been there long enough. Longer than anybody else. He had grown. He had changed. Now he needed to get out. But he had to come up with that idea by himself.

Or maybe with a little help from Mrs May.

The old lady knew that she had to have conviction in these rituals. She had to believe wholeheartedly in her plight. She tried. She gave it everything. She was sweating and tense and emotional by the end. She gave out everything that she could. But she knew without a doubt that Blair was gone and was never coming back. There would be more broken parents knocking on the front door of The Beresford in weeks.

And she could see that Abe, for all his talk of connection and love, had moved on to the new girl, Gail. If he didn't get out now, she was going to be next on his list.

SEVENTEEN

There was an undeniable connection, that part was true. Abe and Blair had been seeing so much of one another that any onlooker would be forgiven for thinking they were a couple. They looked content and comfortable, they were interested in what the other person had to say.

The coffee mornings had progressed to lunches and Abe had even attempted to join her for a run that one time. But it was the last. He could drag a dead body into a bathtub but running around the block was too much. That's why he didn't want to get bogged down with burying his victims, he'd never get through it.

Lunches had turned into cinema trips. Blockbusters with buckets of popcorn and French art-house productions at the independent houses where you could sit on a sofa and drink wine while you read the subtitles. Eventually he had been brave enough to rest his arm alongside Blair's so that they were touching throughout the film. She hadn't pulled away. She wanted the contact, too.

Then came drinks. Nights out at a bar with alcohol. Abe had no friends, and Blair knew nobody in the area, so they were always out as a two. Their attention was devoted entirely to the other person. No distractions.

They could joke about and laugh and be silly because the gin alleviated many inhibitions. They would hold hands and dance about. They were getting closer.

Then there were dinners and walks – because running was now out of the question – and movies in Blair's apartment. They would sit in the communal library and read in silence. They had hugged, playfully, and been caught in the odd embrace where a kiss should have happened to evaporate that last bit of sexual tension.

Blair was inexperienced. She came from a Christian community where the citizens mated for life, whether they were happy or not. There hadn't been a serious boyfriend, even at university. She was no prude. She knew how to get herself off, but she was less sure about how to get somebody else off. Abe needed to take the lead on this one. His sexual experience was limited, three girls in college. None of them were a one-night stand, he'd had to chip away at them gradually, afraid to take a chance because the thought of rejection was crippling.

So, with Blair in front of him, that amazing woman, that beautiful, intelligent, kind and interested woman, he could have seized the opportunity – on more than one occasion. And he had not seized once.

He masturbated over thoughts of them together once a day, sometimes twice. There was a picture of her on his phone that he'd taken as she was heading out for a run, and he would zoom in on her form from behind before beating himself off vigorously.

But he couldn't lean in for the kiss.

What if she pulled away?

It would all be over. The coffees and lunches and drinks and bottles of Malbec while watching her VHS copy of *L'Appartement* for the fifth time.

Someone had to do it.

Someone had to take the plunge.

Abe and Blair very rarely spent their time in Abe's apartment. It wasn't as light as Blair's place. It wasn't decorated. It wasn't pretty. There were very few candles or cushions or pictures, apart from the giant triptych that Sythe had painted before he died.

He invited her down, said he had something for her and that she doesn't need to bring anything as it was all taken care of.

Blair arrived at his door to find an envelope hanging from the knocker with her name printed on the front. Inside, she found a ticket that said 'Admit One Person'. She held it in her hand and knocked on the door with the other.

Abe answered.

'Ah, Madame, you must be here for tonight's screening. May I see your ticket, please?'

'Abe, what are you—?' He took the ticket out of her hand, ripped it and gave it back.

'This way, please. You are in row A, seat one.' He gestured down the hallway. It was dark, but she could see the flicker of light coming from his lounge.

For somebody who was scared of taking that leap from friendship to something more intimate, this was something of a grand gesture from anxious Abe.

He had converted his living room into a cinema. His simple two-seater sofa was the only seat, it faced the largest wall space. On the coffee table in front of the seating there were two boxed pizzas – still warm – and a bucket of salted popcorn that he had also melted butter onto.

'Abe, this is very cool.' She was beaming.

'If you take your seat we shall begin the presentation.'

They took their seats. On the table was a small projector, no bigger than a can of Coke, that shone a bright, white hundred-inch rectangle onto the wall. It was plugged into a new DVD player that was tied in a large red bow. Next to that lay a cellophane-wrapped copy of *L'Appartement* and a pair of scissors.

'If you would like to do the honour.'

Blair laughed that genuine laugh of hers that wrinkled her nose in the way that Abe loved. She opened the case and took out the disc, picked up the scissors and ceremonially cut the ribbon on the player. Abe clapped with comic earnestness. He poured some wine and they sat back and watched the film.

The mood was right. The lighting was perfect. The wine was going down, and Abe's courage was creeping up. He felt full after the pizza so decided to make his move after.

The credits rolled. Gail Castle was checking her phone for the final direction to her new home at The Beresford. She was eight minutes away. Blair turned to Abe to thank him for such a wonderful surprise. She put her hand on the side of his face and told him that it was 'incredibly sweet'.

That was the moment.

But Abe did not take it.

Blair did.

Her left hand on Abe's face, she leant in. She kissed him gently on the lips and said thank you. He kissed her back and said that she was very welcome. They kissed again, delicately but with want.

Abe had his green light, he was no longer afraid of the rejection. He wasn't going to fuck anything up between him and Blair. He could seize the moment.

Abe seized.

And fucked everything up.

He reciprocated Blair's movement and held her face in his hand as they kissed. Eventually, he moved this down her shoulder, onto her arm, before grazing the side of her breast.

She laughed. Like she always did when she was nervous.

'Why are you laughing at me?' He was embarrassed.

'Oh, no, I'm not laughing at you. Not at all. I just, I don't know, I wasn't expecting that. But also, I was. Just nerves. It's okay. Come here.'

They moved back into position. This time, she didn't laugh. But she did flinch a little. He felt his way around. But her lips were tightening and she let out another laugh.

'Don't laugh at me.' Embarrassed but angry.

'I'm not. I'm not. I'm an idiot. Sorry. Look, I just think I'm ticklish. Put your hand here.' She grabbed his hand forcefully and placed it on her leg, and they tried again.

Blair put her hand on Abe's leg, too. He could feel himself getting excited but was paralysed by the thought that she might laugh at him again. He wanted her. There, on the sofa, the smell of pizza and popcorn in the air, wine-stained teeth and lips. He wanted her.

Her hand moved up and found how excited he was. She didn't laugh, and that relaxed Abe again. He started to stroke her leg while she felt her way around a penis for the first time. His hand moved between her legs – a little too soon, that didn't bode well.

She had to fight hard to keep the laughter in but she managed it, rubbing her hand against him more and more. He did the same to her and she made noises that suggested she liked the way it felt, even though she wasn't sure that she actually did. (It wasn't the way she did it.)

And it wasn't that she had great technique or that there was something wrong with Abe, but he got to the end quicker than he would want. He stopped kissing Blair to open his mouth and make the noise he always made when he came.

'Wow, I had no idea I had such talent.' Blair wasn't bothered. She didn't care, he could clean up and they could try again in the bedroom. But she shouldn't have been so bright in her understanding. She should not have kept it light and smiled. But it probably didn't matter how she reacted, Abe still would have sat forward on the sofa, not looking at her, saying, 'Don't laugh at me. Don't you fucking laugh at me.'

He still would have reached forward onto the coffee table and picked up the ceremonial ribbon-cutting scissors and jabbed them repeatedly into Blair's virgin neck. Abe would have still continued to stab at her throat while telling her not to laugh, however that sweet country girl had reacted when the idiot shot his second load of the day straight into his pants.

It wasn't him. It wasn't Abe.

It was somebody else at the start of a series of killings. Everybody coming to The Beresford was now a potential next victim.

The moment Blair got into any kind of relationship with Abe Schwartz, one of them was going to die.

EIGHTEEN

It wasn't a carbon copy, history wasn't repeating itself in exactly the same way, Abe wasn't living one day over and over, but there was too much similarity for it to be classed as coincidence. At least in Abe's mind, which had a gift for compartmentalising information, it would seem.

He was in the back garden and the burn can was raging. He stood there watching the flames dance around a batch of Blair's bones while he smoked weed and gazed over the fence at the back of his irate neighbour's house. It was the same way he had initially bonded with Sythe, although that night it was the artist in charge of the fire.

'Abe?' Gail asked timidly as she approached her new friend from behind. She knew not to startle him, that kind of thing always annoyed her husband. He could have explained that sudden movements or sounds reminded him of explosions or gunfire during the war, she would have understood. Instead, he had pushed her aggressively into the corner of the doorframe. The force caused her to crack her head against the wood. She bled and slid down to the floor. Her husband walked off and left her there.

What could she learn from that? It didn't explain anything about his apparent post-traumatic stress, it told her what she already knew: he was an abusive piece of shit, and she could never get it right. So, she somehow convinced herself that it was maybe her fault that he hit her.

When Abe turned around, he was not threatening or overbearing. He looked happy. He was smoking. She could smell what it was. He offered some, but Gail declined. She didn't want to stunt the growth of her poppyseed; it would be an apple pip before she knew it.

Gail already thought of herself as a mother, and she would do anything to protect the child she didn't yet know.

'What are you burning?' Gail asked, looking towards the flames.

'Just some wood and paper and things. I don't know, there's just something quite empowering about starting a fire and maintaining it.'

'It's very manly.'

They both smiled.

'It's comforting to do it at night. Like a hobo, keeping warm. With this wonderfully grand house as a backdrop. It relaxes me.'

Gail nodded, there wasn't much that she could add to what he was saying. He seemed to be in his own world. Maybe it was the drugs. Maybe he did feel comforted and manly and all the other words he'd used.

'Anyway, have you got it? Are you ready to cathart the hell out this?'

'Cathart?'

'Yes. Like catharsis. It'll be cathartic. You are about to cathart. I know it's not a word, I was trying it out.' He takes another drag.

'Oh, well it works. Big time. Let's cathart this.' Gail produced her mobile phone from her pocket.

'Is there anything you want to say before you toss it in?'

Gail took a step towards the hot can, her phone held to her chest in mock ceremony. Her words were inaudible to Abe. Her lips were moving but the sound coming out was nothing but a hum.

'Damn you, Castle.'

And she threw her phone into the fire.

She wouldn't have to read or hear his poisonous words again. He couldn't find her now. He couldn't hurt her again. He would never see his child.

So it is done.

'What now?' Gail had only felt a tremble of catharsis. She was hoping for more.

'Up to you. You can stay and watch it all melt away, if you like. Or you can walk away and leave it behind.'

'And what are you going to do?'

'I'm going to stay out here for a while. I can look at the sky and think. I can make sure that phone is nothing but a puddle of plastic by the time I go back inside.'

Gail decided that she'd head back to her place. She tried to use

Abe's made-up word in a sentence, but it made her feel stupid. Then she got awkward. And she left Abe outside alone.

'Goodnight, Abe.'

'Night, Gail. Excellent work today.'

He watched for a while as the sides of the phone began to sag and melt. The screen came away from the body, the insides were eventually exposed. The phone lay on a bed of fingers and toes, which would be brittle enough to crush into a fine powder by the time the night was through. Blair's arms would only be broken into small fragments, but enough that they would be easily disposed of.

Gail had burned her phone and was ready to move on.

Abe had to get rid of Blair completely before he could fully cathart.

NINETEEN

Abe froze. It was him. It was definitely him. He'd only caught a glimpse at the time, but his body was reacting to the stranger's presence in the same way it had when he was running towards the lift in the other half of The Beresford.

Abe was frightened. All the adrenaline his body could produce had moved into his legs.

Why was he in this part of the building?
Was he looking for the couple in that lift?
Was he looking for Abe and Blair?

They exchanged a look. Abe tried to be brave, give a friendly smile as though bidding a passer-by good evening. The stranger did not reciprocate. He screwed up his eyes, trying hard to focus on the man across the foyer.

Then Mrs May appeared.

She walked straight up to the stranger, put a comforting hand on his back and said something quietly to him, which Abe was both thankful for, because it took the man's gaze away from him, but was also intrigued by, because he wanted to know what relationship his kind, old landlady had with a man like that.

She ushered him out through the front door. Abe's door. Gail's door. The good door. Abe's legs still couldn't move. Mrs May turned around to see Abe, but his legs were still stuck in place. The man from the sixth floor gave one final glance through the window, and Abe knew that he'd taken in the image of the guy who hadn't held the lift for him.

Was he dangerous?

He was from the upper levels. Abe had killed two people, but it wasn't him, it wasn't the real Abe. He wasn't a thug or a gangster. He wouldn't be able to handle himself against somebody like that. He'd only got the better of Sythe through the element of surprise.

'Abe? Is everything okay?'

Her words seemed to release him from the spot where he was rooted.

'Yes. Of course. Good evening, Mrs May. I've just been outside, lighting a fire, watching the stars.'

'Getting to know the new tenant.'

Abe didn't quite know what she was suggesting.

'Gail seems very nice. I see you had a visitor...'

They kept their distance. Neither of them moving. Abe was avoiding the window, Mrs May was avoiding walking further than she had to.

'Ah, yes. Nothing important.'

'A friend of yours?'

The old lady raised a friendly eyebrow at this line of questioning.

'No, Abe. Not a friend. He lives in one of the apartments on the upper levels.'

'Ah. Okay. Just ... I've never seen anyone come down before, that's all.'

'It does happen occasionally. Only when they really want something.'

'And he ... really wanted something?'

She exhaled and nodded her head a few times, slowly.

'Yes, dear boy. He wants to leave.'

'I'm sorry to hear that.'

He wasn't. Part of him hoped he might leave through that sixth-floor window.

'It's absolutely fine. I prefer it when people leave the way they arrived. It's so much better than when they just disappear. Better for them. Better for everybody.'

She walked back towards her apartment, slowly. Sometimes the old lady appeared to have a spring in her step, and others it was like her slippers were filled with gravel. Her movement was inconsistent.

It was one of the gravel nights.

The old lady turned back as she reached the door and bid Abe a good night. He was left alone in the open space between the apartments, and he wondered whether the better thing for everybody was to never leave The Beresford.

WHAT DO YOU WANT?

But that's not how we do things.

You can hide behind tradition, but that's not what it is. It's fear. You watch a film that you have already seen a hundred times, it's not because you love it – though you clearly do love it – it's because you know the outcome. It's safe. There are no surprises. There's no twist that you didn't see coming. Nobody you loved will die. It's predictable.

Get a fucking life.

Try something new.

Maybe you live in one of those towns where everybody knows your name. Still has a bakery on the high street and a pub that everybody goes to. Maybe even an independent bookshop that refuses to go out of business. A place untouched by the ravages of time. The same as it has always been.

So that's how you are.

You are part of a community. You work better as a whole than as an individual. You come together and support one another and you believe in God. The people around you treat you with kindness, and you do the same to them.

And it's all very nice. But it's all very nothing. And you have made your world so incredibly small and insular. You are cut off.

Yes, some of you are old and some are young. There are athletes and there are bookworms. There are sheep and those with some entrepreneurial drive. Black, white, male, female and everything in between. But you are, essentially, the same person.

Your identity is that of your group.

The kicker is, if you buy into it, your life is full. You do not feel as though you are missing out on tall buildings and jazz music and one-night stands and pollution and coffee shops that stay open all day and night. But as soon as you realise that you do not want the small-town life, your world becomes even smaller – but your options are greater. Because there are so many places that you can go, that is not where you are now.

You can go anywhere, do anything, be anyone. As soon as you stop dwelling on what you don't want and focus on what it is that you do want.

What do you want, Blair?

I want to get away. I want my own identity. I want independence. I don't care if it's hard, I want to feel hardship. I want to struggle. I want to find me.

You have a clear idea.

I want life.

You need appreciation.

TWENTY

'**W**as there ever a Mr May?'

The dinner had progressed swimmingly. Blair had not been around all week, so it was only Abe and Gail who joined Mrs May. Gail had said 'no' to alcohol, citing her drunken ex as the reason she wanted to cut down. The hostess didn't even pause for judgement before offering her guest an alternative.

Then, somewhere along the festivities, she asked Mrs May whether she had ever been married herself.

Abe had almost completely disposed of Blair's crushed and broken remains. Just some ribs and spine left. The ribs broke down easily, but the spine was as tough as the hips; it was dense, it was a problem. But nothing that he couldn't handle.

His bathroom was almost back to normal. Another nightmare over. But he was quieter than usual at the dinner, so Gail was doing most of the talking with Mrs May, which is probably why she ended up prying too far and asking her gracious host whether she had ever loved and lost.

For as long as Abe had been at The Beresford, he had never known anybody to ask the question. Many who had dwelled there had ventured guesses: she came with the building; she was born inside The Beresford; she had killed her husband and taken his money, that's why the rent is so cheap; she was a wrinkly, old virgin – that was one of Sythe's least flattering notions – and Blair had once suggested that Mrs May seemed very regimental, and perhaps that had something to do with grief. 'Like Queen Victoria wearing black every day as a widow,' she had suggested. 'She seems very together. But that is often the face of someone who is just holding it together. Besides, she's about eight hundred, so she probably outlived anyone she loved.'

It turned out that Blair was the closest, if you believe what Mrs May said.

'Ah, my dear, I am not often asked that question.'

'I'm sorry. I didn't mean to—'

'No, no. Don't you worry. It's absolutely fine. There was a Mr May. He was a wonderful, patient, funny and talkative man. And I miss him dearly.'

'I wasn't sure, because you don't wear a ring.' Gail couldn't help herself. 'My grandmother kept her wedding ring on her finger for sixteen years after my grandfather passed, so I wasn't sure. Everyone is different, of course.'

Mrs May reached into her blouse and pulled out a gold chain looped through a simple gold band.

'I keep it next to my heart, dear. Never take it off.'

Abe was speechless. He'd never seen Mrs May like this. So sad and sincere.

'I'm so sorry.'

'Oh, don't be, dear. I had a lot longer with him than I was supposed to.'

Mr May was diagnosed with stage-four bowel cancer and given weeks to live. His wife was distraught. It wasn't long enough to do all of the things they'd promised one another. It couldn't be weeks, surely.

The doctor explained that the couple may get a month together but they should also be prepared that it could happen much sooner than expected. He spoke of palliative care and other things the Mays did not want to entertain, and the doctor's voice whistled by their ears and into nothingness.

The Mays had been servants of the Lord for their entire lives. This felt unjust. It felt wrong. It felt like a punishment, not a test of faith. They had prayed every day, for each other, for their community, for distant relatives. They were good people. They helped more than they hurt and they listened more than they preached.

Mr May was feeling weak. He wasn't quite ready to give up, but he was done with prayer.

It didn't work.

He wondered how often he had sent out his 'thoughts and prayers' and it had meant nothing, made no difference. You think the families of that school shooting felt any different? You think the victims of rioting or suicide bombings would be comforted to know that Mr May was sending out his thoughts and prayers in the direction of the families left behind?

Mr May lost his faith.

Mrs May's grew stronger.

This was no time for a kneeling-beside-the-bed-at-the-end-of-the-day prayer. That wasn't going to cut it. This had to be more. It had to be passionate. It had to be a selling-your-soul type of prayer. She had to mean it. She had to make the Lord sit up and listen.

She got one more year with her husband. One glorious year together when all the experts had told her she would get two more weeks. And since that day, since that sweaty, tear-filled purging, that is how Mrs May has prayed. With vigour. With meaning. With truth.

She made that deal.

'A year? That's a miracle. I can't believe it.' Mrs May hadn't told Gail and Abe the entire story but they were shocked all the same. Gail looked as though she was about to cry.

The old lady nodded, but she didn't believe in miracles.

She believed in passion.

And she believed that she had made it happen.

'You lived here together at The Beresford?' Abe finally joined in, forking some restaurant-grade Dauphinoise potatoes into his mouth.

'No. I came here straight after and I've been here ever since. Never left. Never will.'

'How long has that been?' Gail was trying to gauge how long Mrs May had been alone, but Abe was more interested in her age.

'Fifty years. A hundred years. Who knows? Time doesn't really matter. Would anyone like a top-up?'

Abe happily obliged while Gail held on to her water. She thought about divulging her own secret about the baby after Mrs May had opened herself up so honestly, but it made her feel too vulnerable.

And she was worried. She needed a roof over her head now more than ever, and she didn't want to lose the apartment because she violated some clause in the contract that she hadn't read through before signing.

Dessert conversation was lighter. Abe noticed how often Mrs May put her hand to her chest. It was something he had never seen before. If he had, he would have assumed it was something to do with her heart or digestion, but now he knew that she was checking for her wedding ring, maybe even pushing it into her chest.

Abe made himself a part of the conversation, as though Mrs May being so exposed was somehow comforting to him. He was back to himself, forgetting about Blair and the bones left in his bathroom for long enough to get to the end of the evening.

He gave both ladies a kiss on the cheek and thanked them for their company. He praised his host's food, asked whether Gail would like to be walked back and, when she politely declined, he stumbled back to his apartment alone.

Gail stayed behind for a moment. Clearly inspired by Mrs May's openness, too, she reciprocated.

'I'm pregnant.'

Mrs May opened her mouth to say something but nothing came out.

'That's why I didn't have the wine tonight. It's the reason I drank the horrible decaf the other day when Abe helped with my phone. I'm so sorry for not saying but I didn't know until the day after I got here. I mean, I thought I knew, but I hadn't done a test, so I did one and then I knew, knew. You know?'

Mrs May put her hand on the rambling woman's arm to stop her.

'It's fine, dear. I take it that the father is...' She let it hang in the air.

'Yes. It's him. I can't tell him.'

'So, you're definitely...' Again with the trail-off.

'I am keeping it. Of course.'

'Of course.'

Gail explained her worries about breaching contract by introducing what would essentially be a housemate. But again, Mrs May reassured her.

'It won't be the first baby to be born at The Beresford.'

'Thank you for being so understanding. And thank you again for a wonderful evening. Please could we keep this information between us?'

'Mum's the word.' She tapped the side of her nose and winked. Then she disappeared back into her apartment. She cleared the table and placed everything into the dishwasher. Then cleaned down the surfaces in the kitchen. Before dimming the lamps and lighting some candles. She took a wild gulp of red wine from the bottle before refilling her glass, and she prayed for Gail's baby.

TWENTY-ONE

Apple seed, pea, blueberry, raspberry, green olive, Kumquat and lime. Gail had ticked them all off, week by week. Her baby was now the size of a plum. And she was convinced that she was showing.

She wasn't, of course. She didn't even look as though she had eaten a plum. It was still early in the process. She hadn't even gained any weight. She hadn't experienced any sickness, either, so a part of her felt as though she was either not getting it right or that she was somehow cheating.

Gail wanted to feel pregnant. She wanted to feel like a mother. And that wasn't happening while she was keeping things secret and not experiencing morning sickness or not showing a plum-sized bump at the front.

So, she decided to tell Abe.

That would make it more real.

She was nervous for some reason. It wasn't like telling Mrs May, she was a woman, she would understand. (It was at that point Gail realised that she had asked her landlady about being married but had never asked whether she had any children of her own.) Abe was different. He was a man. She didn't want her pregnancy to change their relationship in some way.

There was nothing romantic between Gail and Abe, but they had been spending time together. She was not giving off any signals – she had been very careful about that – because she was not interested in being with anyone after her previous relationship. (At that moment, Gail began to wonder about the sex of her child. It would be wonderful to have a girl, a little version of her. But better. It could just be the two of them and that would be enough. But a boy would be wonderful. She could raise him to be the man who would treat a woman how they should be treated. He would respect his mother and all women. He would never raise his voice or his hand. He would never know his father, he would never need him.)

There was music playing from Abe's apartment. The guitar sound was heavy and not to Gail's liking, but it was a welcome break from the noise that leaked through the walls from Mrs May's place.

'Hi, Gail. Is everything okay?' He looked paler than usual, or perhaps his eyes were darker.

'Yes, thanks, I just wondered whether you might fancy a walk to grab some coffee. I've got a hankering for a cinnamon swirl.'

'Not today. I'm not feeling great, to be honest. Maybe tomorrow?'

'Ah, yeah. Okay. That's fine. You rest if you're not feeling well.'

She looked disheartened.

'Are you sure everything is alright?'

'Well … yeah … I … look, I'll just come out and say it: I'm pregnant. A few months.' She rubbed her stomach and immediately felt stupid.

'You're happy about that?' It was an odd thing to say but Gail was behaving strangely.

'Of course.'

'Then congratulations.' He faked a smile. 'I'm sure I'll feel better by tomorrow. We can talk properly then, okay?' He was already shutting the door before she could answer.

His well wishes had not seemed particularly genuine to Gail and, instead of suddenly blossoming with maternal fervour, everything fell flat around her. But she realised that she hadn't been lying about that cinnamon hankering. Perhaps she was experiencing cravings, she wasn't sure when they were supposed to kick in.

It helped.

She walked to the coffee shop alone.

Abe had woken up the day after the meal at Mrs May's and felt like death. At first, he had assumed a hangover – not talking had left a hell of a lot of time for drinking, and he'd been putting away that Bordeaux like it was grape juice.

But the afternoon came around and he felt worse. Stomach cramps. Retching. This was no hangover, it was like nothing he had ever encountered.

And it had been happening on and off, every other week since. This was the sixth time.

He felt cursed.

And there was an overwhelming sensation that he should leave, get out of The Beresford. Where had that come from?

Then Mrs May came over with some leftovers from the party and a soup she had made that morning, which seemed to make him feel even sicker. Every time he is ill, she brings over her magic broth.

He'd woken up sweating but shivering. The room spun. He could see Sythe and Blair standing at the foot of his bed, both with their arms folded in disappointment, shaking their heads.

Abe knew he was hallucinating, he'd rid the world of every molecule of his victims, and assumed that it must be food poisoning because he'd eaten some bad chicken once while he still lived with his parents and the same thing had happened. But it couldn't have been Mrs May's food because she seemed as sprightly as ever when she dropped off her care package, and Gail was positively glowing in the way that only expectant mothers can. And neither had been sick since.

It couldn't be the food.

He thought about his mother but couldn't recollect her face.

That was a long night of searching for Abe. Crippling cramps and never quite throwing up, which was so much worse than actually throwing up because there was no respite.

The walls were breathing. The ceiling appeared to be lowering to a few inches above his face then raising back up. Lowering. Then raising. The same thing had happened the first time he tried magic truffles on a trip to Amsterdam while still at university.

Abe shouted at the apparitions to leave him alone, to get out. 'I know you're not real. I fucking killed you.'

They unfolded their arms and looked at one another, then back at Abe, then each other, and they started laughing. A silent laugh. A tormenting laugh.

Abe sensed the rage he had felt at Blair when she had laughed at him for ejaculating prematurely. But he was too weak this time to attack her with a pair of scissors; he couldn't even sit up.

She wasn't really there.

Sythe wasn't there.

It wasn't food poisoning.

It was the house. Playing tricks on him.

It was The Beresford.

It wanted him out.

When we hit our darkest moments, when we are so low and it seems like there is no way out, that is when, in our desperation, we lean towards the fantastical. We turn to aliens or magic or ghosts or, worse, God. Abe didn't believe in any of that crap. He put it all down to the house. That The Beresford was a living, breathing entity. That it had seen what he had done and was now punishing him.

Or the man in that bed masquerading as Abe.

He loved that apartment. He loved living there for almost no money. He even loved old Mrs May in his own peculiar way. He didn't want to go. He wanted to smoke weed in the garden and read in the limited library and be cooked for by his geriatric landlady. He liked knocking one out in the bathroom where he cut up two of his neighbours while thinking about the woman who was never his girlfriend.

But he hated the pain and the sweats and the ghosts in his bedroom.

And he thought, *Maybe it is time for something new, to move on.*

The cramps ceased.

The spectres evaporated.

And Abe slept.

TWENTY-TWO

Gail's baby was the size of an avocado when she called Blair a bitch. Then another man was trying to hit her.

Mrs May had emptied Blair's apartment after ten days of not seeing that kind country girl. She could have searched through all the woman's belongings to find her parents' details. She could have let them know that she had moved on from The Beresford and forfeited her small deposit. But that wasn't how Mrs May did things.

She would wait. A week, maybe three, and Blair's God-fearing mother and father would be on that doorstep, demanding to know what had happened to their daughter. They'd look ten years older than they felt, and all three people in the doorway of The Beresford would have the feeling that Blair Conroy would never be seen again.

Her parents would comfort themselves by saying that she was with God now. And Mrs May would know that she was not.

Abe still hadn't moved out but was useful in taking Blair's things to the local charity shop. Her clothes. Her books. They couldn't get into her laptop so that was thrown away. It didn't make sense, of course. Why would she leave without any of her personal possessions?

Mrs May never asked the questions. She just had to get the room ready for the next tenant.

Abe and Gail were talking in the library area. She had asked him more about Blair.

'Mrs May said that you two had got close.'

He admitted that, and then riffed on the truth. Saying how she had led him on. She was showing him affection and then pulling back. Blair was a bit of a user. He would buy her things, and had lent her money.

'I won't see that again. I think that's probably what she used to get out of here.'

Gail, matter-of-factly, just-for-something-to-say, wittered the words, 'Sounds like a real bitch to me.'

It was nothing. A throwaway comment to show that she was on Abe's side.

'What did you call her?'

'A bitch. The Blair Witch. The Blair bitch.' She laughed at her own joke.

'Are you laughing?'

'What?'

'You didn't know her. You don't call her a bitch, you hear me?'

Abe should have left. He should never have had another opportunity like this. Getting sick had been his missed cue to leave.

He got up from his chair and stood over the pregnant woman, snarling. She'd seen that look before a hundred times, when Castle wanted his sandwich or to turn her onto her front and fuck her dry.

Abe was mad.

He slapped Gail hard around the face.

He drew his fist back next, and Gail reacted to all the beatings she had taken over the years. She wasn't going to lie down and wait for a man to stamp on her head. Not again. She had escaped that.

Another fight at The Beresford.

It was happening again.

A minute after it was finished, the doorbell would ring.

PART THREE

ONE

Abe was dead.

And Gail had sixty seconds before the newest tenant of The Beresford knocked on the front door.

She didn't try to hide it, at first, which was something that very few people who murdered somebody at The Beresford did.

Gail knocked on Mrs May's door.

She was crying.

'What's the matter, dear? Is it the baby?'

'I didn't mean to do it.'

'What? What do you mean? What have you done?'

Gail stepped aside. Mrs May could see along to her beloved library. Abe was lying on the floor.

'Oh, no, no, no , no, no. Abe. No.' The old lady pushed past Gail, forgetting for a moment that she was pregnant. It was anger and panic, then utter devastation.

She moved like a much younger version of herself – there wasn't much time – and was kneeling over Abe within a few seconds. There was a wound on the side of his head, and the smashed vase was on the floor next to where he lay. A large shard of that broken vase was protruding from his left eye. Mrs May could see the marks in his face where it had cut him before being rammed into the left socket.

She checked quickly for a pulse.

Nothing.

Breathing.

Nothing.

Although Mrs May knew that would be the case because Gail was still alive and it had to be one of them that perished.

She was talking to herself (or Abe) as she shook her head.

'I prayed for you, boy. I tried to get you out. Couldn't you see that? You kept getting sick here. You needed to leave. You had to decide. You could have just walked out. Now look at you. Dammit.' Every word was hissed at him through her teeth.

Gail appeared. There was not much time left.

'It was self-defence. I swear. He hit me.'

Mrs May had to act fast.

'That's not how the law will see it. There's a piece of porcelain poking out of his eyeball.'

And she convinced Gail to drag Abe's body into his flat and wait there. She couldn't call the police because she would end up in prison, and then she would have to give birth there.

'And then they'll take the baby away from you and put it into care. Or worse, back with his father.'

It all happened in a moment, and the young mother-to-be was confused and she couldn't believe what she had done, and she also couldn't remember it because it spiralled so quickly as her rage grew out of control.

Before she knew it, Gail's hands were around Abe's ankles and Mrs May was saying, 'Quickly, dear, we don't have a lot of time.'

TWO

Not everyone who ever lived at The Beresford was running away from something or somewhere. Or somebody.

And not everyone had to kill or be killed.

Aubrey Downes was sensible. Methodical. A little boring, perhaps. She came from a family of well-intended tedium. Her father worked in the insurance industry. In fact, he ran his own company. A company that made him proud. A company he devoted a lot of time to. Yet he always made time for his family.

When he died, from obesity-related heart failure, his funeral was attended by his wife, his two children and the people who had worked for him. Almost one hundred people, who realised upon his death that they never really knew anything about John Downes and, worse still, found they didn't actually care about that fact.

The company continued to thrive. They all kept their jobs. And the remaining Downes family members reaped the benefits. John Downes knew a thing or two about insurance, so not only did he leave his family with a profitable business, there was a lump-sum payout that would ensure they never had to struggle.

Aubrey was not running away. She missed her father, of course, but life was simple. Her brother would take over the business once he had graduated, and was old enough and qualified enough to do so. Aubrey already fit the bill but wanted to go for something on her own.

With the money she had in her bank, she could have stayed in the centre of any major city in a high-end hotel room for a year. But Aubrey was cautious. And that would not teach her anything about living alone, would it? It would be frivolous and superficial. Two words that nobody would use about Aubrey Downes when they eulogised her life.

She had scoured the internet and stumbled upon a place that was ludicrously reasonable yet also befitting her current lifestyle. It seemed too good to be true, but she had done her due diligence and everything seemed above board.

Aubrey Downes was leaving the family home to pursue her own interests. To make something of herself. If it didn't work out, there was always the option to fall into a position in the business her father had built from nothing. But she was confident that she could follow in his footsteps rather than ride on his coattails. It was important for her to do so. Her brother did not share the same entrepreneurial spirit.

He stood next to his mother as they waved Aubrey off into her bright, new future. A brave new world. She watched them in her rearview mirror as they walked back into the light of the house, shoulder to shoulder, her brother with his arm around their mother, comforting her.

They were not extraordinary people. They were not cut-throat or malicious. They were safe and secure, and planned within an inch of their lives so as to avoid any opportunity for spontaneity.

Aubrey was flying against that. But safely.

She left her family but she wasn't racing away.

Not everyone who ever lived at The Beresford was running from something or somewhere. Or somebody.

Aubrey Downes was not everyone.

And not everyone had to kill or be killed.

Aubrey Downes did.

THREE

'I told him he had to leave.'

Mrs May was talking to herself. She sounded disturbed.

'He could have got out.' She was shaking her head.

There was no time to lament. No time for reproof. Somebody was at the door, and Mrs May was the only one who could answer it. She had to greet her new tenant.

Aubrey Downes was wearing a tan coat that stretched down to her slender ankles. Her rectangular glasses sat flawlessly on the triangles of her cheekbones and, just below the left rim, she had a perfectly placed mole that her father had always referred to as a 'beauty spot'. Slung over her right shoulder was a laptop bag and in her left hand was her mobile phone. She looked as though she was arriving for a job interview.

'Hello. I'm looking for a Mrs May.' There was no hint of an accent that could place her.

'As far as I know there is only one Mrs May and I am her. You must be Aubrey.'

The new tenant seemed perfectly polite.

So had Abe Schwartz when he first arrived.

Mrs May looked Aubrey up and down as subtly as she could muster, though her mind kept wandering to Abe; what he could have been and the image of him with part of her vase protruding from his retina.

Audrey was somehow plain but striking. It was probably the red hair. She was pretty but not beautiful. There was a confidence in the way she carried herself but an awkwardness that almost betrayed it. She was mysterious but not in the way that made you want to get to know her.

Mrs May could not make her out. She seemed out of place. But not lost.

Gail was so clearly damaged, arriving in the middle of the night. And Sythe smacked of desperation from the offset.

'Well, come in, dear, you'll catch a cold out there.' The old lady turned on the charm.

'Thank you. I do have some things in the car, but I can collect after getting in to the apartment?'

'Yes. Yes. Of course. We used to have a lovely lad here who would have helped you with your boxes, but he's gone now. Currently just myself and another lady at the moment. And she's ... pregnant.' She mouthed the last word like it was dirty, rather than sensitive information.

'It's no trouble at all. I can manage.'

'You do seem like the independent type.' The old lady smiled, and Aubrey took it as a compliment – that she was projecting the correct image.

They walked upstairs together, and Mrs May gave Aubrey the keys to Blair's old apartment. She explained that there were two keys for the flat, one for the front door, another for the store room out at the front of the house, and a couple of other keys – for what, she couldn't remember. Then she left her new tenant to look around and plug in her laptop. But not before pointing in the direction of the garden and her beloved library, which was now a crime scene.

The old lady ran down the stairs like a woman half her age. She looked over her shoulder once at Aubrey's place before scooting across the foyer to Abe's.

Gail was a mess.

'What the hell are we going to do?' She gazed at Mrs May, lost.

'I'd say you're going to have to get rid of the body.'

'What? What are you talking about? Get rid of the body? And how am I supposed to do that?'

Mrs May wanted to say, *Well, Abe used to chop them up and soak them in a concentrated lye solution.*

But then she would have to explain how she knew that, how she knows everything that goes on in The Beresford.

She couldn't do that.

She wasn't allowed.

It wasn't in her contract.

FOUR

The Mays had no mortgage and, by the time Mr May finally passed, their savings had dwindled by half as they crossed off places and buildings and experiences from his list. The doctors had suggested there were a matter of weeks left, but Mrs May managed to get another year out of the old boy.

He had always wanted to see the *Mona Lisa* in real life. They did it. He said it was a lot smaller than he'd imagined. He'd never set foot in Africa. So they did that, too. A full safari trip was too much, with everything they needed to tick off the list, but they managed a walk with lions. Mrs May still remembers her husband's face when the park ranger told him to lean into the wild animal as it walked past him to show that he was not afraid. He tried to be so brave, even through his frailty.

They ate alligator and kangaroo. They drank at a club Oscar Wilde had attended and slept in a hotel that Princess Diana frequented. They lived more in that final year than most do in sixty.

And when he finally passed, she was prepared. Emotionally and financially. It wasn't a relief to see him move on but there was a peace that came with it, a peace that would never have materialised had he been taken as abruptly as she had thought he might in the beginning.

Mr May had died in his favourite chair after finishing a book he had always wanted to read but hadn't particularly enjoyed. His body was taken away, and Mrs May was left alone in the quiet of their home, not knowing what would happen next.

She poured herself a glass of red wine and sat on the sofa, staring at her husband's empty chair. He would never sit on that again. On the coffee table was his cup that he would never drink from again. Next to that was the local newspaper, folded in half at the property section. She couldn't understand why, as Mr May always skipped that part.

She gulped down half the wine and picked up the paper.

There it was.

She put in an offer and bought The Beresford without knowing why. It was the right paper on the right page at the right moment.

She would live in one part and rent the rest out. And she would not have to spend the remainder of her days looking at chairs her husband would never sit in again, or sleep in the room they had shared for decades, or pick up the shoes he would never leave on the front step rather than putting in the shoe rack right next to the door.

That would be everyday hell.

It didn't take the old lady too long to realise that life at The Beresford was not normal. It was different, and that is what she wanted, of course, but she began to notice things that were happening. That life had a strange way of repeating itself. As did death.

It dawned on Mrs May that having that final year with her husband meant that anything after was going to be everyday hell. A living hell.

Mrs May had chosen Hell.

And there was nothing she could do to change that.

FIVE

Every time it seemed that Gail wavered, Mrs May pulled on the right string to reel her back in. Just a dollop of fear at losing her child and the old lady was sure that she could make Gail do anything. But her patience was wearing thin.

'How would I even know where to start with getting rid of ... this.' She pointed at Abe's sad corpse.

'Oh, Google it, Gail.'

'What? Look up how to get rid of a dead body? Are you insane?'

'Or try common sense. Cut it up. Crush it up. Burn it. Ditch it. I don't care. Just get it out of my building.'

Then there was an argument that wasn't really an argument, it was both women venting their frustrations towards one another. Gail wanted to know why she had to do it on her own, and Mrs May told her that it was nothing to do with her because she had not killed anybody – accidentally or otherwise. Besides, the old lady was going to keep quiet about the whole situation, and that was more help than she needed to give.

She did help Gail pull Abe's dead body into the bathroom.

'Whatever you're going to do, do it in here. It's going to be easier for us to clean it up afterwards. I'm happy to help you with that. I'm an accessory now, anyway, aren't I?'

Gail was so confused. Why was the old lady helping her? Why wouldn't she let Gail call the police? But why would Gail risk going to jail? Would it even matter that it was an accident? She had lashed out at her husband a few times in self-defence, and there were occasions when this would make him back off and go to sleep on the sofa. There were also times when it made him plough into her harder. They could use that in court. Say she was aggressive. Suggest she had a temper.

Everything came down to the baby. The unborn, unformed foetus inside of her. She could tell herself that what she was doing was selfless; she was protecting her child. If she ended up in jail and the baby was taken away from her to be with its father, it was ultimately going to be worse off. If he got drunk and hit his wife, what was going to stop him from getting drunk and hitting his child? Gail could be locked up until the kid was eighteen. It would grow up hating her, resenting her.

She couldn't have that.

So Gail did what Mrs May wanted and she used her common sense. She looked around Abe's flat – mostly books and films and wine – she found the tin he kept his weed in that she'd seen him use in the garden. After twenty minutes of acquainting herself with Abe's possessions, she found the things she thought she would need.

The scissors were useless, and she threw them across the room in agitation. But she soon found her groove. Talking to her baby as she went. 'I'm doing this for you. I'm saving you from him,' she chanted as the teeth of the saw cut through Abe's flesh and bone.

She tried to pull the piece of vase from his eye, but it wouldn't budge, so she cut out his eye with a sharp knife instead. Telling her little embryo that everything was going to be okay.

It took her hours, and not once did Mrs May check up on her to see how things were going. Gail placed all the pieces she had hacked off into separate bin liners. She rolled them up and taped around them with masking tape, hoping it would contain any blood but also prevent the smell from seeping out.

All the bags were different shapes and sizes. She wasn't a carpenter or an experienced murderer. She did the best with what she had. All the while telling that doomed zygote inside her womb, 'This isn't me. This is not who I am.'

It wasn't Abe either. Reliable Abe.

And it wasn't Sythe. Poor, tormented artist.

When you scroll through the terms and conditions or you sign a contract without reading and comprehending every word, there's a good chance that you don't really understand the deal that you have made or with whom you have made that deal.

WHAT DO YOU WANT?

Parenting is tough. Your friends who had kids before you tried to explain this. On those Sundays where you slept in until midday after drinking and eating anything you wanted the night before. After you went another month without using your gym membership. After you wasted all the wonderful time and expendable income you frittered away on things you never wore or used.

They told you what it was like once you had to care for a small human and keep it alive.

And you thought they were exaggerating. Or being dramatic.

Then you had a child of your own and realised they were right and you wasted all that time you had before. All the opportunity to chase the things you wanted.

But you didn't know what you wanted then.

You thought you wanted children.

You know how awful the world is. You know it's unsafe. War and disease are met with a shrug of the shoulders or a roll of the eyes when they should be devastating. Real-life bullying is now accompanied by cyberbullying. Everyone feels awful and anxious and they don't know why.

You brought a child into it anyway.

And your friends tell you about the terrible twos. You don't believe it.

The gut-wrenching fear and dislocation of their first day at school. You don't believe it.

How much the child you are doing your best for will make you feel like you are the worst person in the world. How they will become unmanageable in their teen years. You don't know how a parent could call their own offspring a 'little shit'. You will feel like a failure. Yet you won't give up.

Eventually, they will leave. And that thing that has terrorised you for two decades will suddenly leave a great hole in your life.

What do you do now?

What do you want?

Mr Conroy, what do you want?

I want my daughter to thrive. To be the person she wants. To be respectful. To keep the Lord in her heart. To not forget her mother.

And Mrs Conroy?

You do the best you can for somebody else, every day. Their existence proves to you that there must be a God. You hope that you are doing the right thing. You've made hard decisions and you have disciplined where needed, even when it has hurt you. A lot has hurt you.

Then they leave. And it hurts you.

You put everything into them, and now you must find out who you are again.

I want something that is mine, something for myself.

Something bigger than being a mother.

I want a message from God.

SIX

The people who lived at The Beresford did not belong. They had that in common. The kind of people who wanted to sit in the centre of the circle but existed on the side of a square. They were outside. They floated on the periphery.

They weren't outcasts. They hadn't been banished. They weren't weird. They just didn't quite fit.

Something wasn't tessellating with them and the world. They weren't living up to their parents' expectations or their own view of what life should be. Gail knew that a marriage should not come with a physically abusive husband. Abe wanted to use his technology on the Sabbath, and, while he was there, he didn't feel the need for a Sabbath. That segregated him from his family. Blair was a secular girl in a devout world, and Sythe was a boring narcissist.

Each of them, and those before, were trying to run from their own personal hell. The Beresford was their escape.

Their halfway house.

Their waiting room.

Their Purgatory.

Aubrey was different. She was solid. She came from good stock. Hard-working and devoted parents. Her father hadn't adhered to the healthiest of lifestyles and he worked more hours than was ideal, but that did not detract from his loyalty to his family or the time he spent with them.

There was no abuse. She was disciplined, but it was appropriate. She was not neglected in favour of her younger brother. There was always encouragement. Aubrey became the woman she wanted to be. Strong, striking and independent. She was eased towards a position in the family business, but there were no hard feelings when she decided to go at things alone.

Aubrey had the same reaction to her apartment that Blair once had. It was clean and bright and huge. So huge. She was paying hardly anything and the lifestyle she had been used to while growing up was not the greatest leap from what was being offered at The Beresford.

That apartment meant freedom. Freedom to the lonely girl who did not fit in to her Christian-with-a-vengeance country community, and freedom to the woman who wanted to try something different from wealthy, protected suburbia.

But that did not mean they were the same.

Blair was like Abe and Sythe, and the carpenter from years before, and the prostitute before that. She did not belong.

Aubrey did belong.

She just didn't belong at The Beresford.

And that was going to make it even harder for her to get out alive.

SEVEN

Gail was waiting. Mrs May hadn't come back to Abe's flat, and hours had passed. She looked into the corner of Abe's bathroom where she had stacked the parts of his body, which she had sawn up and wrapped in plastic, into some kind of abstract pyramid. The old lady didn't seem like she was coming back anytime soon, even though she had mentioned lending a hand with the clean-up process.

The act of sawing and rolling in a black bin liner and taping down the edges had proved to be a kind of repetitive therapy for Gail. It occupied her mind. But now that she was finished the young mother-to-be was on edge.

She wondered whether the baby could feel what she was feeling. The guilt. The anger. The shame. Somehow, no regret.

What if her baby's first experience was feeling those sorts of emotions? How would that play out? What did it say about Gail as a mother?

Gail needed more monotony; the nothingness caused her mind to wander and whir. In Abe's kitchen she found the mop. Dirty with Beresford blood. But she filled a bucket with disinfectant and warm water, and made her way back to the bathroom. The old landlady obviously wasn't going to help at all.

It wasn't her fault, though.

She hadn't killed anybody.

Poor Gail had gone from one mess to another.

Poor Gail. Poor Abe. Poor Sythe.

She looked out through the peephole in Abe's front door at the reception area of The Beresford. It was undeniably quiet. Eerily so. Her own apartment could be seen across the hallway. She could make a run for it and surely nobody would see her. But perhaps it's exactly those kinds of risks that would get her caught. She gazed for another thirty seconds, looking over at Mrs May's place and up the stairs to the new lady, Aubrey. Then she became annoyed, because that would have been more than enough time to make a dash for home. If it could be called that.

Then she got to thinking about mistakes. The ones she had made in her life. Had they led her to this place? She fought hard to remember a time before the beatings had started, but her memory kept warping back to that image of her husband's foot above her head, ready to stomp down on her brain with all his might, undoubtedly cracking her skull and killing her. That moment had led her to The Beresford, to a broken vase, which she would use to stab through the eye of another attacker.

Where would this latest mistake lead her?

Down Abe's hallway, Gail stopped at a trio of paintings on the wall. She ran her finger along the bottom of the canvas on the right, jumping it over the gap to the next section, until she had spread her DNA across the length of Sythe's donated triptych. She had no idea what it meant or represented, but it was beautiful. Thought-provoking. Problem-hazing.

Dismembering a neighbour is physically demanding. Gail made her way to the kitchen for food. On the countertop, next to the microwave, was half a bottle of red wine. She searched the higher cupboards for a glass and found one behind the third door she opened. The glass was big enough to fit the entire contents of the bottle inside. She had just killed again, her baby would have to forgive this moment of weakness.

In the fridge she found butter, pastrami, salami, breaded ham and mayonnaise. She laid it between two slices of brown bread with a thick wedge of cheddar and placed it on a plate. Normally, she would cut the sandwich in half from corner to corner but she couldn't be bothered to search for a knife, now that the food was in front of her. She took her snack and drink back down the hallway and into Abe's bedroom.

It smelled like the bedroom of a man who lived alone. The bed was not made. There were clothes on the floor in the corner of the room next to an overflowing laundry bin. Three half-empty deodorant cans adorned the windowsill, and there were five separate glasses on the bedside table that hadn't been taken into the kitchen to be washed up. Still, Gail sat herself on the edge of the dead man's bed, balanced her wineglass on the table with the others and took a bite of her sandwich.

A sandwich. The abuser's snack of choice.

Everything in that room, in that apartment, suggested that Abe was nothing remarkable. A normal guy with a healthy interest in books and an enviable quest for knowledge. He was normal. He was quietly spoken and helpful and gracious. No way would anyone suspect that he would raise his hand to a woman. What had Gail missed? What had he been hiding?

Nothing in that room was giving her a clue, and the sandwich was being washed down by a middling cabernet already. She pictured his kind face when she had arrived, and then the image flash-cut to the top of her body-parts pyramid.

She was tired. Tired of waiting for help. Tired of thinking about what she had done. Tired of overthinking what she should do next.

Gail laid back on the bed and pulled the crumpled cover over her legs. She thought about her husband. How he would have a drink, knock her around the lounge for a bit before eating a sandwich and going to bed. What did he think about? Did he feel guilt and shame? Or did he feel the way that Gail felt in that moment?

Alone.

Justified in her actions.

Tired.

And unapologetic.

She wasn't like him. She wasn't like herself.

The room was silent. Outside, the trees whistled as the wind rushed through branches. To Gail, it sounded like they were laughing at her. She was scared. For herself and the baby inside her, now the size of an avocado. But, while she was thinking of herself and her undoubtedly doomed child, she was not worrying about the police or her husband or the Jewish guy she killed that day. With the light still on in the bedroom, Gail closed her eyes and, within a minute, fell asleep, for the first time, as a murderer.

She did not wake once in the night, as is often the case for the guilty.

EIGHT

Counting backwards from five when you want to get your child to do something that they don't want to do is an incredibly useful technique. It is nothing to do with fear, it is to do with the unknown. Your child does not want to know what happens if you get all the way down to one.

Yes, there are those who will push you all the way there, but most will get themselves moving at three or two.

As a parent, you don't even know what happens if you manage to count all the way down. Somehow you have all the power but you share the fear because neither of you really wants to know. That's why it works.

Mrs Conroy uses the same technique on herself in the morning. As soon as her alarm sounds, she switches it off and starts to count.

Five ... four ... three ... two...

Then she sits up. She gets straight out of bed. No need for the snooze button.

She never gets to one.

Mr Conroy has a different technique. When his wife's alarm sounds, he wakes up but does not open his eyes. He listens to her count backward then feels as she gets up off the mattress. He then pulls the quilt in tightly over his shoulders and curls his knees into his chest. Often he will drift back to sleep. A few minutes later, his wife arrives with a cup of tea and a kiss to the forehead. He sits up, asks her how she is feeling and whether or not she slept well.

He always tries to take a sip of his tea too soon and it is always too hot.

That day was no different.

'It's at least two hours in the car, we need a good breakfast.'

She always makes a good breakfast but she couldn't stop herself from saying it.

Neither of the Conroys had received a message back from Blair in weeks, which was odd because she had been dead for months. Both of them had tried their hardest to take the lack of contact as a sign that their daughter was growing up and being busy in the city. They didn't want to appear pushy or overprotective so they'd held out. But even when Blair had ignored messages from her mother, she always responded to her father.

Always.

He had seen four messages go by without an answer. Two hadn't even been acknowledged as being read. And one of those was an offer of financial help. He told himself that he was probably stepping on her independent toes so backed off, though it had plagued him.

Mrs Conroy was beside herself with worry. She hid the depth of her panic from her husband, but her mind wandered towards alcohol and orgies. To drugs and sex cults. She knew how absurd she was being but had no idea she was the closest to the truth.

And while she hid her anxiety and outlandish theories, her husband kept quiet the recurring nightmares he had been experiencing, where the Devil manifested Himself in a manner of guises. They concealed their insecurities from one another and delved deep into prayer for the safety of their daughter, like the good, ineffectual Christians they were.

Our thoughts and prayers go out to the family of the woman who was stabbed in the throat and burnt into a fine powder.

They set off early because they wanted to get back home early. Before it got dark, if possible. Mrs Conroy didn't want to be in the city at night. It scared her.

The car journey was longer than either of them expected. Mr Conroy could only get close to the speed limit in his hometown, where he knew all the bumps in every road. Anywhere else, he was overly cautious if the car hit thirty-seven miles per hour. They tuned the radio to an easy-listening station, which kept them from having to converse too much.

'Look how high those buildings are.' Mr Conroy was in awe as he pointed ahead over his steering wheel.

'Keep your eyes on the road. The next turning is on the left in two hundred yards.'

'Are we close?'

'It says seven more minutes.'

'That's close.'

Mrs Conroy nodded.

'Here it is. On the left.'

Six and half minutes and they would see their daughter, their wonderful, kind-hearted Blair, in the flesh for the first time in half a year. Mrs Conroy's stomach was starting to turn. Nerves. Excitement. She wasn't sure. Blair would have no idea that her parents were coming to visit. If she was alive, she would have hated the surprise.

Blair was so lucky to be dead.

Both parents were shocked at the majesty of The Beresford as they drove up to the building. It was just far enough away from the taller buildings in the centre of the city to be classed as suburban or perhaps almost rural, Mrs Conroy thought. This pleased her, it wasn't such a crazy adjustment from the town where they still lived and had brought up their daughter.

They could see life behind the twitching curtains and there were lights on in each corner of the house. They hoped one of those lights was Blair's.

'You're sure you don't want to ring her to say we are here rather than rocking up to the front door like a pair of gate-crashers?' This was how her father showed his nerves.

'It wouldn't be much of a surprise if we announced it, now, would it?' This was how her mother hid her excitement.

'I guess you're right.' He turned the key to cut off the engine, and they spent a moment leaning forward and looking up at The Beresford, wondering which room belonged to their special girl.

They looked at one another, and Mrs Conroy suggested that it was time to get out the car, stretch their legs and give Blair a huge hug. They both knew their daughter would be shocked, perhaps even annoyed at the impromptu visit, but they were past the point of caring. They needed to see her. They needed to look into her eyes and ask her how she was getting on with her life. They wanted to witness the way she was carrying herself now that she was independent and earning money and fending for herself on every level.

They wanted to tell her, in person, that they loved her. Without making her feel bad.

The Conroys stopped in front of the main entrance. Before pressing the doorbell, they took a deep breath, and Mrs Conroy counted backwards.

Five...

Four...

Three...

Two...

NINE

She never got to 'one'.

'Hello.' A tall, angular woman – handsome, rather than pretty – opened the door before Mrs Conroy's trembling finger managed to hit the button for the bell. 'Can I help you?' She stood there with her red hair caressing her shoulders and a book in one hand. 'I was just getting a book from the library when I saw you through the window.' She smiled, her eyes flitting between both Conroys, not giving either of them more time with her gaze than the other.

'Ah, yes. We are here to see Blair.' Mrs Conroy, obviously, took the lead.

'We're her parents,' Mr Conroy chimed in, seemingly proud of his achievement.

Aubrey didn't know how to respond, what to say, so she opted for the truth.

'I'm sorry but I don't know a Blair. But then I have only been living here for a day. There's Gail and Mrs May and Abe, but I have not heard of a Blair. I could be wrong of course. Why don't you come in?'

They wiped their feet on the outside mat and went to step over the threshold when Mrs May appeared from nowhere.

'Hello. I'm Mrs May, I own the building. Is there a problem here?'

The old lady knew that there was no problem, there was going to be a problem soon, but at that point, she could see their eyes. The hope, the wonder, the trepidation as a parent struggles to let go of their child and does not know whether they will be different from the person they once were, whether they will be pleased to see their parents.

The hope was the worst thing.

'Oh, no. Not a problem. We are just here to see our daughter.'

Mrs May let the end of the sentence hang uncomfortably.

'Blair,' her mother continued. 'Blair Conroy. She moved in around six months ago.' Mrs Conroy knew exactly how long it had been. Being aloof did not suit her.

'Yes. I know Blair. A lovely girl. Always reading or running.' Mrs May smiled. This relaxed the Conroys as they recognised their child in those two activities. 'But I am afraid that she no longer lives here.'

'What do you mean?' Mr Conroy seemed angry.

'Well, it was maybe six weeks ago, she just upped and left. No word. Very unlike her. At first, we thought she had gone home to see her family, but a week or two passed and there was no word.'

'You didn't think to call the police?'

'She is an adult, Mr Conroy. She can come and go as she pleases. She chose to go. Anyone who lives at The Beresford can choose to go. I'm not responsible for her decisions. I provide a roof for those who stay here and pay their rent on time. Your daughter forfeited her deposit, and I used the money to clear the apartment for the next tenant, who kindly answered the door to you moments ago.'

The agitated parents look at the tall redhead next to the old lady. She looks uncomfortable, awkward. Nothing like their sweet Blair.

'Where the hell did she go?' Mr Conroy was taking charge of the situation over his wife, who balked slightly at the mention of *Hell*. 'She didn't leave a forwarding address? That doesn't sound like Blair at all.'

Mrs Conroy cycled through those words and images in her mind that had been tormenting her lately.

Sex. Drugs. Drinking. Rape.

Aubrey didn't know what to do. She felt like she was intruding on something that was not her business, but it would be rude to just walk away. She stared at Mrs May, hoping that the old woman would come up with some adequate reasoning behind Blair's sudden exit.

'I'm sorry to say that this is more common than I would like. I keep the prices reasonable, as well as the up-front deposit, and it means that people often don't mind forfeiting it. They pack a bag in the night and leave. It's become so common that I don't even think about it anymore.'

'I don't give a damn about your business practices, I care about where my daughter is right now.' Mr Conroy raised his voice. His wife seemed embarrassed.

First Hell, then damnation.

'I would appreciate you not coming into my home and raising your voice at me, Mr Conroy.' There was a quiet spite to Mrs May's tone. Her eyes bore into the old man to let him know that she meant it and that this was his last chance to back down.

He couldn't see that. He was too riled. Too worried about his only child. But his pious wife was rattled in a different way. She saw a darkness. In front of her was an evil. The way the old lady turned was unholy. Ungodly.

She was not as she appeared.

Mrs Conroy pulled on her husband's arm to drag him out of there. He was steadfast in his slander and blame. She yanked harder, seeing the venom rise within Mrs May. There was something in those eyes.

'Come on.' She used all of her strength to pull her husband away. 'There's nothing to be done here. She left without a word. She's not here.'

He slumped. A human sigh.

'But she sent me a message last week.' He looked as though he might cry.

Mrs May was confused. She allowed her own ire to evaporate as she listened in on the Conroys. Somehow, Blair had sent her father a text recently. There was no cause for concern. She seemed happy enough. She had mentioned Abe.

It couldn't be true. Mrs May knew that Blair was gone. She was never coming back. She could not have sent those messages. She did not get out of The Beresford alive. There was no way.

It distracted the old lady. She was bored of The Conroys now. There was no sympathy for any of the parents who came plodding to her door, hoping for answers, their faces downturned and melting towards the floor with sorrow and dismay.

'Your wife is right, Mr Conroy, there is nothing for you here. I'm sorry that your daughter did not contact you to say that she was moving on, but she must have had her reasons. I wish you luck in your search.'

Mrs Conroy was now back in charge. She ushered her husband through the door and pushed his lower back in order to force him in the direction of their car. Before the door closed behind her, Mrs Conroy turned back and looked the owner of The Beresford in the eyes.

'I see you, demon.'

Then she pulled the door closed and followed her husband.

Aubrey was dumbfounded by the drama. What was going on? Why had the woman said that to Mrs May? What did she mean? Where had Blair disappeared to? And why did Mrs May seem not to care? It was all very suspicious.

Mrs May tried to push it all to one side. Hogwash.

'Blair was here to escape the life her parents had set out for her. She was escaping *them*, dear. It's no wonder that she didn't tell them where she was going.'

Aubrey wasn't entirely convinced.

'We do attract the occasional drifter. Nothing to concern yourself with. How are you settling?'

'It's lovely, Mrs May. You really could charge a lot more, you know. It would stop people skipping out on their deposits, I'm sure.'

'Oh, no, dear. I like to keep the rooms filled. I think the pricing helps turn things around quickly when somebody moves on.'

'That's your prerogative. I only answered the door to those people because I was waiting around for a delivery and was looking at the library.'

'A delivery?'

'Yes. Just some furniture and my new computer. To set up an office.'

'My, you do work fast.' Mrs May was genuinely impressed.

'No rest for the wicked.'

At that, Mrs May remembered that she had left Gail in Abe's apartment.

TEN

Gail was confused. She awoke to the sound of a key turning in the lock. It took her a few seconds to realise that she was not in her own apartment. Then she realised that she had fallen asleep in Abe's place and gone through the entire night.

Then she panicked.

She was in Abe's bed, and the door was being unlocked. He was coming home. He would catch her.

Then, wait...

Abe was dead. Abe was in the bathroom in a body-parts pyramid. Wrapped in black bin liners.

Deep breath.

Then Mrs May was shuffling down the hallway. Gail could recognise the old woman's trademark heel scuff.

'What are you doing?'

'You left me here on my own.'

'Yes. But why are you still here? In Abe's bed?'

Gail explained that it was hard work sawing a man into pieces. And it was harder to then clear up afterwards on her own. With no help. (She laboured this point.) She had waited and waited, but she was tired. She was pregnant and dealing with the fact that she was now a murderer. She needed to lie down for a second. To take stock. She must have closed her eyes for a moment.

'Where is Abe?'

'In the corner of the bathroom.'

Mrs May summoned Gail to get up and follow her with a sharp, almost undetectable nod of the head.

It was sparkling in there. Almost sterile. Abe was exactly where Gail had said, neatly piled up.

'Are you sure this is your first time?' Mrs May quipped.

Gail did not know how to respond.

'How many?' Mrs May pointed at the pyramid.

'Sorry?'

'How many pieces did you cut your neighbour into?' It was somehow matter-of-fact and blunt.

'Oh, I don't know. Twelve? Maybe fifteen.'

'Okay. So here is what you are going to do...'

The old lady had Gail where she needed her. What she was saying was in no way a suggestion, it was instructional. It is what Gail had to do. No questions. No quibbles.

Gail was told to take three of the packages, it didn't matter which ones, get in her car and drive. Drive away. One road, one direction. Keep going until it was time to refuel. Then she had to get rid of those packages. She could bury them, burn them, throw them in the trash. They could be disposed of together or separately, they just needed to be as far away from The Beresford as she could get.

The next day, she would take three more packages and a different road in the opposite direction. It didn't have to be the exact opposite, just not the same. If she went north on day one, she could go west on day two.

Repeat until the bathroom was Abe-free.

'Are you sure this isn't *your* first time?' Gail gagged back in her landlady's direction. Both comments were out of kilter with the situation. Gail was not herself.

Mrs May joked about her age once more, saying that she was 'a hundred-and-fifty years old, there's not much I haven't done before'.

They stood in silence for a moment, staring at the pyramid of body parts, then at each other, neither knowing what else to add to the conversation apart from a slight shrug of the shoulders.

Gail was given a key to Abe's place and told to keep her comings and goings as discreet as possible. Because Aubrey was new and she seemed different to them.

Them. Like they were the same kind of person. Killers and conspirators alike.

'It shouldn't take you more than five days to shift everything. But don't get cocky. Don't get careless with haste. If you are left with four pieces, you don't get rid of them all. You take three pieces one day and then you drive the final piece in another direction on the last day. It will stop you getting caught. Okay?'

Gail agreed.

Mrs May told the pregnant murderer that when she is finished, she is to drop the key back immediately, though she is more than welcome to take the three-part painting in the hallway as it could be worth some money one day.

'Now, if you don't mind, I will leave you to it, because I need a drink.'

It was only partly true, Mrs May was going to have her midday tipple but the truth was that she had to conserve her energy because she had to make an important prayer.

ELEVEN

Mr Conroy was the safest driver on the planet. Too safe, in fact. Sometimes he would drive so cautiously, it put him at risk. But, after visiting The Beresford and learning of his daughter's apparent disappearance, that God-fearing, law-abiding, rearview-mirror-checking man found out what it felt like to push his foot down on the accelerator a little more.

Back at The Beresford, Mrs May was in the dark, her candle lit, her red wine poured, her focus honed. This was going to be exhausting. She would not be crying for compassion as she did with young Abe Schwartz, nor would she be cathartically spitting vitriol as she had with Sythe, though her anger was ready to overspill.

This was not about catharsis or compassion. It was something else altogether.

It was worse.

A call for destruction.

She rang her bell.

'What is wrong with you.' Her knuckles white from gripping the sides of the passenger seat, Mrs Conroy yells over the engine – in the wrong gear – as her husband speeds around another bend. He was driving more erratically than usual but he was still too cautious to take the car on the motorway, preferring to stick to the back roads where traffic was sparse.

'I'm getting us home. We need the community right now. They will help us to find Blair. They know her. They care for her. They won't stop until she is back home safely.'

'I agree, but we need to get home safely ourselves, first.'

'Oh, behave. I'm not breaking any records here.'

'What did you say? Behave? What has gotten into you since that house?'

'Do you want Blair back or not?' This was most unlike Mr Conroy.

'Want her back? I didn't even want her to leave. You're the one who said that she needed her independence. You were so sure she'd come back to us.'

'Oh, so it's my fault she's missing?'

He had to hit the brakes harder than expected, having misjudged the severity of the chevrons on the next corner.

'She's not missing. Nobody said that she was missing.'

Her husband rolled his eyes as he screeched around another corner.

Mrs May was sweating and breathing heavily. Working herself into mania.

Hiss. Spit. Roar.

She held the image of her enemies clearly in the forefront of her mind. She did more than just spew her hatred. Her soliloquy was direct in its intent. She wanted injury, pain, sickness or even mutilation.

Mrs May prayed with everything. She was deliberate and calculated in her wording. Her enemies were fools. And she would not stand for it.

Bile. Wheeze. Crackle.

The old lady was tired and fading. She was sick of the relentless cycle. One in. One out. Death and secrecy. Nobody able to leave. She was bored of the visits from naive families. She was angered by the disillusioned parents knocking on her door and blaming her. How dare they?

Mrs May was aggrieved by almost everyone, but it was the parents that enraged her, and that was her focus. They were the ones who would revive her venom and feel her wrath.

It built into movement. Her arms and legs flailing, her voice a warble with frustration. It developed into uncontrollable shaking until it seemed she was vibrating on the spot, heating up. Everything amplifying into a crescendo of noise and movement and revulsion.

Building. Always building.

Mr Conroy misjudged another bend in the desolate back roads. When he skidded, he panicked, and instead of hitting the brake, he pushed down harder on the accelerator. He overcorrected the skid to the left, then the right, then the left again.

When the Conroys hit the tree, the driver took the worst of it. Mrs Conroy's legs snapped at the femurs as the seat on the old car flew forward just as the dashboard crumpled back into her lap. She also suffered a heavy concussion from the windscreen.

Mr Conroy was not so lucky. He wasn't made of the same material as his wife. He was softer. The impact on his side of the car as it hit the tree, causing a sudden stop, was not strong enough to counteract the effect of physics on his body as his organs continued to move forward into the ribcage that was halted by the seatbelt.

Luckily for the old man, the whiplash cracked the top of his spine and knocked him out so that he could not experience the pain of his broken ribs, serrated organs and internal bleeding.

A small mercy.

Mrs May fell back against her sofa, covered in sweat and panting. It was done.

She finished her drink.

Mr Conroy stopped breathing.

TWELVE

Things are different.

One day, you are producing television sermons for your father, a pastor in a small Christian town. The message is received beyond the borders of your home and you are content with helping. The next day, your father dies and you take over his position. You have no formal religious training but you have some drive and some ideas.

Soon, you are performing the sermons yourself. And the message is being broadcast to more than one hundred countries. You have millions of people watching you each week, and you have many more millions in your bank account.

And a bestselling book about positivity and living life to your full potential.

And public-speaking engagements to go along with your publication.

And television talk-show appearances.

And breakfast meetings with world leaders.

You praise God for your substantial wealth and do not believe that you should feel guilty about it. You believe that Heaven must be the most amazing place because, if this is what being alive on Earth is like, you are in for a fucking treat when you die.

Then there's the other angle.

You get out of bed at three in the morning. Twenty-three minutes later, your wife finds you down the hallway, screaming, 'Pray for me, pray for me, the Lord is taking me to Hell.' You decide to take this story around the globe. Share your experience with other Christians.

Before you know it, you are flying to a country you have never been to, and there are a thousand people waiting to hear you speak. You tell them that it was an out-of-body experience, not a near-death experience. You come up with lines like, 'You cannot live in this body with memories of Hell.' And it doesn't really mean anything, but it gets the crowd onside. You can follow it up with something like, 'The Lord took away the fear from my mind but left me with the memory so that I could share the story.'

You are very clear that it was a vision, because only in a vision can a true Christian see Hell.

Tell the crowd that there is a lack of fear of the Lord today. People are no longer God-fearing. They push the boundaries, they play with the rules. Remind them that God hates sin. That there is punishment for sin.

Back this up with an encyclopaedic knowledge of the Bible. Quote scripture by chapter and verse. Keep throwing out names and numbers.

You've drawn them in.

Now scare them.

You were pulled from your body and ended up in a cage in Hell. This is not metaphorical or allegorical, you were there, fully awake. The walls were filthy and there were bars. The Bible mentions the bars. There is a tremendous heat. You should be dead. You can't move. You are face down.

You are not alone in that cell. There are two demons. Twelve feet tall and reptilian in appearance. They pace around you, cursing God. One of them picks you up like you weigh nothing and throws you into a wall. The pain should have been excruciating but God blocked it. Though he let you feel some so that you could return and tell your story.

They cut you with their claws but there was no blood because there is no life in Hell.

Keep saying Hell. And Demons.

Say Mark or Ezekiel or Revelations, then add some numbers. This backs it all up.

Two more demons walk in. One crushes your head flat but you can't die.

God was there. He was a light in the darkest of all darknesses. A place that is totally evil. A place with no love. They try to rip off your arms and legs, but God pulls you out and sets you down next to a pit of fire one mile wide. Brimstone rains from above. There are screams. Millions of deafening screams from within the pit. The sound penetrates your very soul.

Remind the audience that it is real fire. You were there in Hell. The real Hell. Not the metaphor. And people can believe you because you describe it the way it is described in the Bible. Forty-nine verses talk of Hell and nineteen of those mention fire. So there must be fire.

So it must have been real.

Pad things out with the horrendous smells of sulphur, because that is what everyone thinks. Say that maggots fed on you.

Get your book deal. It is not a self-help book, but it brings everyone around to the same message.

You get wealthy, too. And like the televangelist, you should not feel guilty about that. If your words are true, you should feel no self-reproach.

Only if the truth of that night was that you got up at three, drunk out of your mind, went to go to the toilet, collapsed in the hallway and shit yourself, only to be discovered twenty-three minutes later by your wife, only then should you feel guilty.

Perhaps then, if you believe in Heaven, you will understand where you are going.

The problem is, Hell is not fire and brimstone. Hell is not south of Heaven. It is not demons and cages and scalding and whipping. Not for everyone.

Hell is loss and isolation and the inability to talk.

Hell is repetition and indolence.

Hell is war and intolerance and disease.

Hell is here.

Hell is now.

It does not have to be a pit of fire filled with thousands of people, it can be another person or a bad decision or a building.

This person. This decision. This building.

THIRTEEN

Mrs May's music was driving Aubrey insane. She was playing a list of songs she had put together and named, 'Jazz and Reading', because it was so inoffensive to the ears that she could work while it played in the background, and even read a book if she wanted. But there was a tinny noise coming up from the landlady's place that took the jazz to an avant-garde place that was detrimental to progress.

Aubrey smoked when she was stressed. She was cerebral and scientific and God-fearing, but nobody is without vice and Aubrey's was the cancer sticks. Her father's had been junk food and expensive red wine. Her mother's was the pills she popped to regulate her mood and appetite and irritable bowel. Her brother took a little bit from each pile.

She didn't know that the best place to smoke undetected was out the back by the burn can. If Abe had won the battle with Gail, he'd be out there right now, setting fire to some metatarsals while numbing himself with weed. That's how his events had panned out.

Kill someone.

Burn them in the garden.

Meet your next victim while you're disposing of the last one.

But Abe lost. His story was over. He was now in the lobby. Part of him, at least. His left arm, right shin and entire pelvis had been stuffed into one of the local supermarket's bags for life and some blankets had been laid across the top. Gail was carrying them out to her car, ready to take the long drive north as had been suggested.

Aubrey came back inside, calm but smelling of cigarettes.

'Hi Gail.' Gail was startled, she had hoped to get out with nobody noticing. She stopped. 'Where'd you put the rest of the body?'

'What?'

Panic. Sweat. Stutter.

Aubrey laughed. 'The bag. Looks like you're hoiking around a dead body in there or something.'

'Oh. Ha, ha,' she faked, awkwardly.

'Did I just see you coming out of Abe's place?'

'Er ... yes ... I ... I just ... I'm doing a goodwill run, you know? Taking some things to the charity shop. I told Abe, and he asked if I could take a few things for him.' She pulled at one of the blankets as though it would prove something.

'Well, that's very kind of you.'

'We try to help each other out here at The Beresford.' Gail had no idea where that sentence had come from.

'I shall bear that in mind. Maybe we could go for a coffee sometime. You could let me know a bit more about what it's like around here.'

'I'd like that, yes.' She picked up the bag, trying to make it look as though it wasn't heavy. 'But, you know, just got to get rid of this body first.' And she forced out a laugh, which Aubrey reciprocated.

'Good luck with that.'

Aubrey dragged her slender frame back up the stairs to her apartment and sat back down at her desk. Mrs May's music had stopped, and it gave Aubrey the headspace needed to get on with her work.

Gail took the bag outside and heaved it up into the boot of her car. She had done what had been asked of her. Three body parts only. She had murdered somebody and now she had to try to get away with it. She flicked the engine on, and the fuel gauge said that she had three-quarters of a tank. More than enough.

She belted up and took a breath before putting the car into gear. The Beresford was supposed to be her escape. She was about to drive a hundred miles in one direction but somehow she still felt trapped inside that building.

FOURTEEN

When the old lady awoke from her nap, the first thing she did was open the blind to the front of the house and check to see whether Gail's car was gone.

It was. She was somewhere out there, thinking up the best way to dispose of three death packages, and that meant Abe's room was vacant.

Something hadn't sat well with Mrs May about the Conroys' visit. She found the people abhorrently rude and had prayed hard as a result to let that frustration out, but it was something they had said that really niggled.

Blair had been texting them. Recently, too. Those screens were difficult enough to navigate in the cold or rain, but Mrs May knew that it was impossible for Blair to tap her finger against the phone glass when her bones were dust in the wind.

It had to be Abe. Good old reliable Abe, with his awkward smile and the benevolence of his time for others. He had been messaging the parents of his dead almost-lover. To keep the pretence going that she was still alive, no doubt. But perhaps some perversion, some pleasure, moved him.

There was a light jazz beat falling from upstairs, so Mrs May knew that Aubrey was inside her apartment. She glided over to Abe's and let herself in with another set of spare keys she had hanging by her front door.

Sythe's painting in the hallway made her snarl. As much as she had been fond of Abe, she had never really warmed to the artist. He had not found out who he was supposed to be. He was trying, desperately. He could have been at The Beresford for another fifty years and he still would be no closer to the truth.

Mrs May could see that Abe's place had had a woman's touch. And it had been recently. It wasn't an after-effect of his relationship with Blair, it was Gail. The kitchen was spotless. No crockery on the sides, no rubbish in the bins, the recycling had been taken out, and the work surfaces were disinfected. No way was that Abe. That was a desperate woman trying hard to fill her time and distract her mind from the heinous crime she had committed.

Blair's mobile phone was in a drawer in Abe's bedside table. Gail was happy to stab Abe through the eye and give his apartment a spring clean, but she still respected his privacy.

There was no code to unlock the screen, and the top two contacts in the texting app were Mum and Dad.

Mrs May did not respect Abe's privacy. It was her building. If you tried to hide something, she would find it.

She scrolled through the texts. The ones to Blair's mother were short and to the point, almost dismissive. As far as she scrolled, the words were like that. Abe knew Blair and he knew about the complications of the relationship with her parents. He mimicked Blair's style. She wouldn't be able to tell that it was not her daughter responding to messages.

It was the same with her father. The texts were warmer. Abe would have had to instigate some of them to keep up the deception. He spoke warmly about himself.

Abe is a great guy.

Abe always helps me out with that kinda thing.

Sorry I didn't text back but Abe and I went out for dinner.

Mrs May shook her head. She'd been so wrong about Abe. She imagines him lying on the bed in the same way Gail was that morning, and he's laughing to himself as he hits send. And she tells herself that you can never really know anybody. She'd always had such a soft spot for the kid. He made one hasty decision with Sythe, it was instinctive, self-preservation, and it altered him. Abe had never been mean or malicious, and he certainly was not stupid. So what did he get out of tormenting the Conroys with those messages from beyond the grave?

Nobody would ever locate Blair Conroy, Abe had made absolutely certain of that. There was nothing, no evidence whatsoever. Apart from that phone. He should have burned it in the same way he had burned Gail's. He could have left it all behind him.

How could she possibly know somebody who didn't even know themselves?

And now she had to get rid of that phone. Her. Mrs May. The woman who never left the building. These devices are always listening, they can always be detected.

Stupid Abe.

Dumb, impulsive Abe.

Perverted Abe.

She shut the front door, locked it and cursed that boy.

In her haste and maddened mind, Mrs May had forgotten to check the peephole before exiting. She turned around from Abe's door, one hand on the keys, the other on a dead girl's mobile phone, and Aubrey was back in the lobby, watching everything.

WHAT DO YOU WANT?

If there is a God, where is He? And what is he playing at?

And, while we're talking, what's the deal with child cancer? And Onchocerca volvulus? Whose idea was it to have parasites? And parasites that burrow into people's eyes and eat them away from the inside, causing blindness? Who creates something with that kind of life cycle?

Why should man not lie with another man? What's the deal with slavery? Why do women get raped and families get murdered and countries get bombed? Who, being all-powerful, would allow that to happen?

Why create whisky and cirrhosis of the liver?

Sugar and obesity?

The wondrous beauty of the orgasm and AIDS?

All-loving, you say?

What if a person has devoted their life to you, prayed every day, been Christian in everything they do? What if they have loved their neighbour and offered charity where needed? What if they never committed adultery or coveted another man's wife? Why, then, are they rewarded with a cancer of their own? What's the great plan behind allowing another believer to watch as their mind disintegrates with Alzheimer's disease? What was their fault that you gave them such a feeble reward?

Why do you not answer their prayers?

Why are you silent?

Is the world not as you want it?

Would you like the chance at a do-over?

Mrs May, you know what you want.

Time. I want more time.

Then do not ask God.

I have seen that He does not answer. He will not cover up your indiscretions. He will not punish somebody who has mistreated you. He will not get you out of paying that speeding fine. He wants your undivided attention and complete devotion.

But he does not answer your questions.
I know what I want.
I'm not going to ask anyone. I'm going to tell them.

FIFTEEN

What was he going to say?

My wife has been gone for weeks now. I think she ran out on me because I keep getting drunk and beating the shit out of her. Anyway, here are the details of the registration plate on her car.

Gail's husband couldn't even admit that he was an alcoholic. He was still ambivalent about whether the beatings were provoked and deserved. So he wasn't going to call the police and explain that.

Maybe she would get a speeding ticket or accidentally drive in a bus lane, and he could get an idea of her location from that when the fine turned up at his address. Otherwise, he would continue to drink and he'd have to beat himself up about something.

Since arriving at The Beresford, Gail had hardly used the car she had arrived in. She was a city gal now. She walked into town. She might ride the train, but she rarely used her car. And with her baby thriving inside her, she felt uncomfortable about strapping a seatbelt across her waist; the steering wheel was also a threat should she get into an accident. So, everything about the journeys she had lined up for the rest of the week was filled with added peril.

She was sweating, driving to nowhere. The navigation app on her phone was open but she wasn't using it to follow a route, it was to keep her heading in one direction. There was quarter of a tank left but she wasn't going to risk running it too low, despite what Mrs May had told her.

The roads had been dark and winding for ten minutes, but that eventually gave way to the lights of a small village. A church on the left as she entered looked immaculately cared for, as did the driveways and front gardens of any houses she passed. A stark contrast to the world she had left behind her.

Three miniature roundabouts later and she arrived at a petrol station. Quaint. Two pumps and an outhouse. She filled her tank, bought a bottle of water and asked whether the toilets were open. She rubbed her stomach to indicate her condition. The guy behind the till was half interested, half watching a video on his phone. He waved one of his hands in the direction of the building she needed.

Gail used the facilities, expecting them to be as disgusting as any roadside café she'd ever visited, but they were as pristine as anything she had passed in that place. The only thing that was dirty in their beautiful little town were the large metal bins around the back of the toilets. They were for work use only, not for patrons – a sign said so. But Gail tried her luck and the chained lid could be lifted a little way.

She went back to her car, nobody else was around, and the employee inside was taking no notice of her. She casually looked around for any cameras but didn't want to draw undue attention to herself, so got back in, started the engine and drove forward, out of view.

That gap, it was big enough to get something through. She didn't want to put all three packages in one place, that would be irresponsible. Abe's pelvis was flat enough to squeeze in there. And if for some reason it was discovered, it wouldn't give anything away, surely. It would cause a stir, obviously, but authorities would look around that village – too perfect to be perfect, in Gail's opinion – for the rest of the body. And they'd never find anything because Gail was going to put the arm and the shin another fifty miles north. The remainder would be scattered so far and wide nobody would be able to link two pieces together.

There was a rush of adrenaline as the justification formed in Gail's mind. She stepped out of the car, leaving it running with the lights still turned off, and approached the back. She took the wrapped pelvis from beneath one of the blankets, pushed the lid of the bin up as high as the chain would allow and dropped her first package off. The stench of whatever else was rotting inside hitting her immediately.

She dry heaved. Twice. Then ran back into the toilet and threw up. Perhaps it was the smell, perhaps it was the pregnancy, perhaps it was the gravity of the situation, Gail had no idea, but whatever was inside her had to come out. She washed her face with water and stopped outside.

The employee was waiting for her.

No.

Her eyes widened.

She stopped in front of him and said nothing.

'Is everything okay?'

What had he heard? Was she too loud when she lowered the lid? She couldn't get caught. Not now. It was her first package. Would she have to kill the young petrol attendant, too?

'I ... er ... I...'

'I'm sorry. I wasn't listening or creeping up or anything. I remember when my older sister was pregnant, she was sick all the time. I just noticed on the monitor that you'd left your lights off and I didn't want you to drive off like that when you'd finished.'

Gail could not disguise her relief.

'Oh, yes, the lights. Baby brain, eh?'

'Quite. My sister used to say that, too.' He smiled and bid her a good day, said he'd see her again soon.

Not a chance in hell.

SIXTEEN

'That's Abe's room, right?' Aubrey knew exactly what it was, she wanted Mrs May to explain herself.

The Beresford was *her* building. As far as the old lady was concerned, she could go wherever she pleased, she did not have to justify herself.

'That *is* right.' She shut it down.

'It just looked as though you were locking up.' It hung in the air.

The woman who did not have to explain herself decided that the best course of action was to explain herself.

'I was locking up. Gail had taken some of Abe's old things on her charity run. She called me, from a payphone of all things, frantic that she had lost her mobile phone. She thought she may have dropped it at Abe's when she picked his items up but didn't have his number.'

'But she did have yours?'

'The Beresford is in the directory, dear. I called Abe and he said he had found it and left it on a table in the hallway and that I could get it for Gail.' She held up Blair's phone.

Her story had a million holes, but she'd given more than she believed she had to.

Mrs May started to walk off.

Aubrey could have left it there, gone on with her business and pondered over the alleged plot, but that was not the kind of person she was.

'Why do you need to go in there and get it if Gail isn't even here?'

Mrs May stopped, took a breath, and turned around to the inquisition.

'There are a few reasons, Ms Downes. Firstly, Abe won't be back this evening. Gail will. But she is overly stressed about losing her phone because her ex-husband was a physically abusive man, and it leaves her feeling paranoid. She is calling me back in ten minutes and would like to know that I have the phone in my possession. Now, that may not be the reason but I didn't want to ask too many questions because it isn't really my business. I was just trying to help.'

She had laid it on thick, talking about the abusive ex to elicit some guilt, adding in a dig about not asking questions and being a busybody.

Aubrey didn't care.

'That all makes sense apart from the bit where you got into Abe's apartment while he wasn't in.' She raised her tone towards the end of the sentence to make it sound like a more playful enquiry.

'With a key, dear.'

'You have a key to Abe's apartment?'

'It is my building, Ms Downes. I have a key to every lock in this place, of course.'

'I'll be honest, I don't know what I think of that, Mrs May.'

Aubrey's computer held a lot of personal information about herself and her clients. She also kept physical records of policies and transactions – they were locked in a file that Mrs May did not have a key to. She wasn't worried that Mrs May would go snooping in her apartment while she was out, trying on her knickers or using her toilet, but she didn't explain that. Instead, she said, 'I don't know what I think of that.'

'Check your terms and conditions. I have to have spare keys for safety. Also, people lose keys or forget keys. It's a lot cheaper for me to let you in rather than paying a locksmith. I don't use them without permission. There's nothing to worry about.'

'No. No. I wasn't saying … I just have sensitive information about work. I guess I understand Gail's phone paranoia now.'

The conversation was left on a friendly note. Aubrey went outside to smoke a cigarette, and Mrs May went back to her apartment with Blair's phone, content that Aubrey was walking off with her tail tucked firmly between her legs.

But Mrs May had been at The Beresford for longer than anyone could remember, she had seen all kinds of people pass through her doors, so she knew that Aubrey Downes was not right for the place, she didn't fit. The old lady would give her the benefit of the doubt on this occasion, but she knew that her new tenant's suspicious nature would eventually get her into trouble.

At some point, she would have to deal with Aubrey Downes.

She'd have to go.

It wasn't like it was with Abe, Mrs May wanted him to leave. She wants Aubrey to go. And, at The Beresford, that is not the same thing.

SEVENTEEN

Gail received a text from Mrs May that told her, briefly, what had happened with Aubrey and that she should seem a little frantic about her phone on arrival at The Beresford, just in case she was being watched.

She was on her way back to The Beresford at that point. The text had interrupted the on-screen navigation, which she now had to use because she had driven so far out of her way that she no longer knew where she was. According to the application, she was an hour and forty-five minutes from the place she now called home.

And the boot was empty.

Abe's pelvis was locked inside a large bin, filled with half a tonne of stinking rubbish she hoped would be collected and shoved into landfill within the next day or so. She had made a note of the name of the town so that she could look up the local news for the next week.

His arm and shin were buried deep into the woods sixty miles further north from his pelvis. Going into those woods with the light on her phone and a small garden trowel was terrifying but also told her that she needed to be better prepared for the next trip. The trowel was easier to hide beneath the blankets in her bag, but the effort to dig deep enough to bury two body parts so that they would degrade, rather than be uncovered by an animal or dog walker, was far more than she wanted. And she was already sweating profusely due to anxiety.

It was a relief to see The Beresford. The driver's seat was soaked in sweat, as was Gail's back. She stretched her arms to the sky as she got out of the car, then locked it.

Comfort soon gave way to fake panic about the phone she had never misplaced. She unlocked the front door, there was no sign of Aubrey but Gail kept up the pretence.

She knocked on Mrs May's door and the old lady answered within seconds. She handed Blair's phone to Gail and told her to take it and get rid of it tomorrow with whatever packages she was taking.

'And be careful. Your new housemate seems very inquisitive.'

Gail nodded. She felt disgusting and she looked worse. She just wanted to be back in her place. Her light and airy apartment that didn't have any body parts stacked in the corner, in a bedroom that didn't smell like crisps and masturbation.

Mrs May looked over her shoulder into her own apartment as though she might have company, then whispered to Gail, 'Everything went okay?'

'Yes. Fine.'

'No hiccups?'

'No,' Gail lied.

'So, it is done.'

It has started, Gail thought.

She left her landlady to whatever she was doing before Gail had knocked and went back to her apartment, clutching Blair's phone in her right hand as though it were her own and she had missed it like she had once missed her husband while he was overseas serving his country.

Aubrey wasn't watching.

Gail stripped and showered. It was hot. Too hot. The entire room was filled with steam. She needed the heat to cleanse and she needed the power of the water to hit her back, stiff from sitting in the car for so long.

She wrapped a small towel around her head and a larger one around her body. Her face was pink and she wondered whether she was so hot that she was actually sweating again. Once out in the hallway, the cold air hit. She felt refreshed. She lay on her bed and shut her eyes for a moment.

The next day, she would head west with an arm, a thigh and a spine.

EIGHTEEN

Gail woke up early, still wrapped in the large towel, the smaller one had come undone and was beside her on the floor. She'd been sleeping better than ever since becoming homicidal.

The sneaking around was not her favourite part of being a newly minted killer, and she wondered about those psychos she'd read about and seen in documentaries who seemed to thrive on destruction and gained some kind of gratification – usual sexual – from taking somebody's life. What they didn't show you was the work that goes in after the event.

The tiptoeing.

The lies.

All that digging.

It was no fun.

Murder was not as glamorous as it looked.

Her alarm clock read just before 7:00 am. If she got up and got dressed right away, maybe grabbed a piece of toast, she could go down to Abe's place, pick up three pieces of his body and drive west. It probably wouldn't take her as long as it had yesterday because she had more of an understanding of what hiding a body entailed.

She could get back to The Beresford by lunch, butter another piece of toast, drink a vat of coffee, grab a few more limb pieces and head out east.

Get the whole thing over with.

She managed to eat, dress and straighten her hair by 7:20. A coffee would have been ideal, but Gail decided to get one on the road. Caffeine would be her fifty-mile reward and would keep her motivated. She was also limiting herself due to the avocado-sized life in her womb.

It was probably too early for Mrs May. She was a woman who drank wine throughout the day and had an afternoon siesta; it didn't seem right that she was also an early riser. Besides, she'd given her orders, it didn't seem like she wanted Gail to run everything by her, just give Abe's key back once he was gone. There shouldn't be any need to sneak around The Beresford at that time in the morning.

Get in. Get out. No looking back.

Aubrey was downstairs. Gail could see her on the porch through the window.

She was completely made up. Her hair was perfect. Not a crease in her skirt, jacket or blouse. She was flawless. Apart from the cigarette hanging from her lips. Gail thought Aubrey worked for herself from her office in The Beresford, so why the need to look like she was heading into a boardroom. Maybe it was to feel the part. Dress for success. She'd heard about people who made their bed every morning. Somehow it made them more successful. She couldn't remember why. But she guessed that her perfectly coiffed housemate was also sporting a flat bedspread you could bounce a penny off.

It was a spanner in Gail's plan. Aubrey's back was turned, one foot resting against the wall for balance, she looked out towards the skyscrapers and blew plumes of smoke in their direction. It wasn't one of those idiotic vape things that Gail didn't understand, either, it was a good old-fashioned cigarette. Gail could have snuck into Abe's undetected but how would she get out and past Lady Lung Cancer with the body parts? The charity shop story wouldn't work again.

Haste and panic get you caught.

'Morning.'

'Jesus Christ, you scared the shit out of me.' Aubrey took a long drag on her cigarette, presumably to calm her nerves.

'I'm sorry, I just thought I'd come and say hello. I wasn't expecting anyone up at this time.'

'The early bird and all that. I'm sorry, I should move away, you shouldn't be breathing this in, in your ... condition.'

Gail spotted that Aubrey had her bag and a laptop case with her. She must have been going somewhere.

'That's very kind, but don't worry, I'm heading back in, just wanted to pop my head out for a second. Are you heading out to work?' It all felt very natural to Gail, she should have been worried at the ease with which she managed to slip into deception, but she wasn't analysing her own behaviour, she was getting the skinny on Aubrey.

'To be honest, I've something of a brunch planned. I just thought I'd take some work into the city, get a read on the place, you know?' Gail nodded as though she knew. 'You don't happen to know a place that does good coffee?'

'I know two places. One does pretty terrible coffee but it's friendly, the other does coffee that costs more than a hardback book and is pretty intimidating.'

'Well, the second one sounds right up my alley.' Aubrey spoke without a hint of irony and the complete absence of a smile. Gail gave her the details of the cafe then watched her stub out her cigarette and flick it out onto the wet grass. 'Wish me luck.'

'Good luck.' Gail had no idea what that was in reference to.

She watched the red hair blur into the distance then disappear around a corner. Then she ran inside, picked up three pieces of Abe and threw them into her car along with a bigger shovel, just in case.

At fifty miles, she drank a coffee. She buried all three pieces in one hole this time, the shovel meant that she could go deep. She buried one piece, covered it with a few inches of soil, then placed the next piece on top and repeated. She was back by lunchtime. Toast wasn't enough, so she opted for pitta bread and hummus. Then it was back to Abe's, three more bits in the car and a journey in another direction. That affable little pervert was being spread far and wide.

She was back before dinner and only felt half as worn out as the day before.

Probably because she'd made her bed that morning.

There were four pieces left, including Abe's head, which she had been most worried about and had put off until the end.

She felt like punching the air when she stepped back into The Beresford, but Aubrey, always-around Aubrey, was on the chair in the library. And she was drunk out of her mind.

NINETEEN

It felt like a set-up. Like some old white guy wanted to teach a young woman a lesson about business and how it should be conducted. He did this by conducting himself in a heinous and vengeful manner. To make his point as clear as possible.

Aubrey had reached out to one of her father's long-time clients, Joseph Kirkly – Joe to his friends, Kirk to his closest friends. Her father made a lot of money from Kirk's business and he'd also taken a fair amount in their monthly poker nights over the years. Kirkly had known Aubrey since she was a young girl in school. They'd arranged to meet for a brunch, as he was in the city on business, anyway.

Things started off well enough. Small talk and pleasantries. Kirkly said something complimentary about Aubrey's father and offered his condolences again, and she told Kirkly about The Beresford and the quirky old lady that ran the place. She also filled him in on how her mother was getting on. Boring and predictable stuff to break the ice.

She explained that she was grateful for everything her father had taught her but wanted to make something on her own, see what she could accomplish without throwing the great Downes name around.

'People will just be nice to me because I'm John Downes' daughter, and I want to make my own mark, you know? Be respected for what *I* do, what I have achieved.'

Old Kirkly turned. 'He's not even cold yet.'

'I'm sorry?'

'Your father, an honourable, hardworking and honest man, you've only just put him in the ground. And you want some advice on how you can poach his best clients so that you can dismantle his organisation and call it your own?'

'Wait. What? That's not what I'm saying at all.'

'What are you saying, then, Ms Downes? What are you going to do differently to your great father? What's the USP for Aubrey Downes that is going to have people running in your direction? It sounds like you just want to set up the same company again and have it run alongside your father's.'

'No. I just wanted an informal chat. Pick your brains a bit. Catch up.' She was flustered. She never should have used the word 'chat'. She didn't want to catch up. It was all falling away.

'It feels underhand, Aubrey. Dirty. I could talk about this. I could make sure that nobody gives you a second thought.'

'Is that a threat?' His comment had snapped Aubrey back into her hard-nosed self.

'It's a damn promise. My advice to you is to stop trying to be something that you're not. Don't try to emulate your father. Don't try to beat him. He left you a company. Sit at the top of the table and play nice. Take the money. Let people be nice to you even when they can't stand you.' The venom in his eyes was frightening. Aubrey couldn't understand what she had done so wrong.

But she was not about to let some jumped-up little golf buddy pretend that he knew anything about her or her father.

'Like my dad did to you?'

'What?'

'He couldn't fucking stand you, "Kirky". Thought you were dry and boring and God-awful at poker. He pretended to be your friend so we could hike up your premium every year, you fucking joke.'

He was gobsmacked. And Aubrey could see that he looked hurt. Good.

She couldn't stop herself.

'I know you're tied in for another five years. My father was happy enough to do business over a handshake and a promise, but I made sure you signed a contract, because you're slippery. My dad was a good guy, so now here is my promise to you: if you go around bad-mouthing me, you are going to see just how different I am to my wonderful dad, because I don't care about you, "Kirky". I don't care for your character and I don't care about your business. I'm going to do something of my own. But the next time you set foot in my father's building, I *will* make sure that I am at the top of that table, and you can kiss my feet and pretend that you fucking like it.'

Aubrey stood up, finished her drink and threw a few notes towards Joseph Kirkly.

'Who said there's no such thing as a free brunch, eh?'

She left him at the table, agog. There was no way for him to reply. People on neighbouring tables were laughing at him. One group even cheered.

Aubrey had either made the perfect power play, showed she was the boss, or her name was now dirt from here to home and beyond. She expected a call from her mother that same day.

She'd lied. Her father and Kirkly went way back. They were friends. Close, even. She'd destroyed that twenty-five-year relationship with one false sentence. Aubrey looked to the sky and apologised to her dad. Then she told herself that what she had done was right. If she'd have backed down, if she'd have let that man bully her into submission, she'd have had no chance.

Her response was a risk but risks have two outcomes.

Surrender only has one.

Then she lost four hours to a bar nearby and a whisky that only somebody with Downes money could afford to quaff.

Still, she made it back to The Beresford but could not stomach the idea of climbing the giant staircase to her apartment. So she took a seat in the library and dropped her chin onto her chest.

Two days and it was possible that Aubrey Downes was already dead in this town.

TWENTY

Mrs Conroy needed something to keep her on track. She was plugged into a morphine drip for the pain in her snapped legs, but there was only one thing that was going to soothe the pain in her heart at losing her husband so abruptly.

She needed to hear a voice or see some kind of vision or witness words leap off the page of her Bible. It was not enough to have the thoughts and prayers of her friends. It didn't hold up that her Lord worked in mysterious ways. Suddenly, that sounded like a cop out. What had Mr Conroy ever done that he would be taken in that way, never finding out what happened to his beloved daughter.

The only part of her Christian faith about which she had remained sceptical was the idea that God would speak to a human. The only people she had ever seen say such a thing did not come across as genuine, or they were killers on trial stating on that holy book that God told them to do what they did. Even the greenest of Christians knew that God would never do such a thing.

He would never tell a man to go out and murder fifteen prostitutes. That advice went against everything sacrosanct. Besides, God would not waste his time on one man's killing spree when he had so many wars to handle.

Thou shall not kill.

An eye for an eye.

If Mrs Conroy was not going to renounce the Lord, she would have to hear from Him directly.

She remembered a sermon given when she was a similar age to Blair. One that had stayed with her. It regarded how a person would know that God was speaking into your heart, how you would know that it was God's voice and not your own, or even *the enemy*.

There were five questions that you had to answer yourself.

1. *Are His words in line with scripture?*

Mrs Conroy knew that if God were to talk to her, He would never ask her to do something that did not adhere to his Word. That's why she didn't buy what those serial killers were selling when they tried to blame her Lord for cutting someone's head off or raping a swan.

The trick was to read through scripture and see whether certain phrases jumped out at you. This may be His way of trying to communicate directly. Of course there is the danger that a person may pick out sections of the Bible that fit their situation. This is common in times of desperation.

Nothing was jumping out at Mrs Conroy. They were printed words. Ink on a page. Nothing more.

2. *Is your heart open to God's answer?*

This is more a question of how deep your love and faith for God goes. If you are ready to move in whichever direction God leads, you will hear Him. If you are still trying to provide the answers yourself, then this may be acting as a blockage. You have to check your heart and ensure that you are fully surrendered to God's will rather than your own.

The whole town was devout, on the surface at least, but Mrs Conroy lived by a strict Christian code. She had surrendered to the Lord from a young age. And she did not need to check her heart because she could feel that it had been broken. The only thing it had ever been open to, besides her husband and her daughter, was God.

Where was He now?

3. *Is it confirmed through Godly counsel and others around you?*

If you feel that a message is possibly coming through, it is worth finding someone in your life and community who holds faith as strongly as you do. It is also helpful if they are known for speaking wise words. Take your local pastor, counsellor or spiritual director. If you are finding it difficult to discern what God is trying to communicate to you, they may be of assistance. Share your story. Work together.

Mrs Conroy's problem was that the members of her community had already been in to visit. And they all had the same advice and whispered their words of hope and support. They told her that God was listening, that there was meaning behind this. Mrs Conroy was starting to realise that these were worthless platitudes. Worthless, still, because God wasn't saying a fucking thing.

4. *Is it confirmed through other circumstances in your life?*

The third question feeds nicely into this one. It hints at the fact that God is all-knowing and his plan is greater than one incident. Mr Conroy overdosing on tree bark and his lungs tearing open against the inside of his splintered rib cage is but a footnote in this ongoing narrative. He sees all of our lives from birth to death, and His plan is vast and wide; it is more than we could ever imagine.

That's the spiel.

So, the big guy might be placing a dream into your heart, and that is him working in your life to enable His plan. You have to be aware of the places where He is opening doors. There may be new people being brought into your life. The clues and the confirmations are there if you are open to the Lord.

The problem was that Mrs Conroy's dreams had been about her daughter getting drunk and high and raped and killed. And there was nobody being brought into her life, they were only being taken away.

5. *Will it require you to trust God?*

The final question.

God doesn't call on what is comfortable. He pushes us beyond our capabilities. He makes things painful and unbearable. That way we are forced to place all of our trust in Him and His great plan.

Mrs Conroy pondered on this final question as she looked down at the pins protruding through her thighs to clamp the bones in a way that they could eventually heal. Then she looked in the chair next to her hospital bed where Mr Conroy should be sitting. And she thought that last part sounded spiteful and capricious. And an easy get-out for Him.

Obey or you're screwed.

She'd obeyed Him all of her life. She had loved Him and feared Him, and what had he done? Taken away her family. How could that be part of a great plan? And now she had to bend over and take that and find trust in Him? No fucking way. Not again.

She went through those questions in her mind, and there were two conclusions to why a devout woman such as Mrs Conroy had never heard the voice of the Lord: He wasn't there. And, if he was there, he was a judgemental little dick.

God hates us all. And Mrs Conroy hated God.

The problem was that these same five questions could also be asked of the Devil. He had been appearing to Mr Conroy in his dreams. He could have been speaking to him. Perhaps He could have led the Conroys to their daughter. God's plan sucked.

If there was a Devil, then there must be a God. Right?

Mrs Conroy didn't know what to believe.

She'd had it wrong her entire life. Those lazy little thoughts and prayers that were so often floated out into the world made no difference at all. They were weak and regular and too routine. If she had prayed hard enough as she looked at her husband's mangled body, if she had given everything inside her, if she had sweated and cursed and cried and been completely exhausted with effort, if she had pushed those thoughts in the right direction, who knows, she may have been given another year with her husband.

TWENTY-ONE

It smelled strongly of whisky in the Beresford Library. That smoky, peaty smell that turns so many away from the drink.

Aubrey looked as though somebody had taken a young Katherine Hepburn, crumpled her up and thrown her at a chair.

Gail looked at her watch, it was too early in the day to be that sozzled. Even Mrs May didn't start slurring her words until after six. She was caught in two minds. There was a chance Aubrey was so drunk that she hadn't even noticed Gail walk in; she could creep past and head to her room for a long bath, wash the day out of her.

But she was tired of creeping and sneaking. She was bored of the subterfuge and the obfuscation. She was sick of being the bad guy, the killer. She could do something good, help another person.

She could be herself. Something she hadn't been allowed to be for so long.

'Aubrey?' She took a step closer.

Nothing.

'Aubrey, it's Gail. Is everything okay?'

Nothing.

Gail crouched down to see whether Aubrey was awake. Then she peered over at Mrs May's place. Where was she? Normally she'd be all over something like this. Gail didn't want to involve her. This was her thing. She was going to help Aubrey.

She knelt down beside the heap on the chair and spoke softly, putting a hand on her shoulder, calling her name and shaking her.

'Fuck. Gail. That's good. Means I got home.'

'You are home. But you're not in your room. Did something happen?'

'I got drunk.'

'I had noticed. Is it a happy drunk or a sad drunk?'

'It's a pissed-off drunk. So, I guess it's somewhere in between. I'm hungry as hell now.'

'Was it the meeting? Did it not go well?'

Aubrey pushed herself up on the arms of the chair. 'Nothing I haven't seen a million times before. Some pencil-dicked neanderthal trying to put a woman in her place. I'm usually a little more gracious and articulate, but I lost it this time. Gave off at the guy.'

'Well, good for you.'

'Yeah, but I lied and told him my dad never liked him, which was awful now I've had time to think about it.' She kept trailing off. Tired. Drunk. Overthinking. 'I've probably fucked it.'

Gail didn't know what to say.

'I just need to go upstairs and fucking sleeping this off, deal with it tomorrow. I have to get some water. And eat something. A sandwich or ... something.'

Gail had put hundreds of miles on her car already that week, and there was already another hundred or so between herself and her husband, yet, somehow, she was still trying to get a drunk person upstairs to bed while they asked for a goddamned sandwich.

She tried to help Aubrey to her feet, but she was too proud and independent for that. Gail stood close to her, though, because she looked unsteady.

'Come on, it's not that far. Let's get you up those stairs.' Gail was trying to sound enthusiastic, in the way that you would talk to a child in order to cajole them into something they didn't really want to do.

She stayed behind Aubrey all the way up the stairs, holding on to the bannister and keeping herself braced for the fiery Amazon to fall back into her at some point. Gail noticed that her left hand was still a little dirty from the digging, and her thoughts went immediately to Abe's head, which she was planning on distributing the next afternoon. There were four packages left in the bathroom. It was no longer a pyramid. There was a ball and a few twigs, which Gail assumed were parts of Abe's scrawny arms, and something else she could no longer remember.

The nightmare was almost over. She could get back to growing her avocado into a pear or bell pepper.

At the door, Aubrey didn't thank Gail for her supervision, instead she asked, 'So what do you think of the old lady? You know, Mrs May?'

Gail had to be careful how she answered.

'I think she's rather sweet. Very helpful...'

Unless you need to clear up the blood from the body you've sawn up.

'Sure. But ... weird, right?'

'Eccentric, maybe. Idiosyncratic. But not weird, per se.'

'You're too nice, Gail. She's weird. I feel like she's up to something. Don't you think she might be up to something?'

Gail needed to not talk about this. The old lady may well have been up to her own 'somethings', but Gail wasn't aware, all she could focus on were the somethings Mrs May was making her do.

Aubrey was leaning against her doorframe with her eyes closed. Gail couldn't help but stare. There was something captivating, even alluring about her. She was unconventionally sexy. Gail was used to an overweight drunkard breathing in her ear from behind as he lowered himself into her. There was nothing sexy about that. She found herself wanting to touch Aubrey's pale face.

'And you' – Aubrey opened her eyes suddenly – 'you are a little bit sneaky, too. Lurking around. Don't think I haven't seen.' She was smiling, but the words still hit Gail as accusatory. 'I've got my eye on both of you.'

She stumbled into her apartment, smashing the door against the wall behind, but stood straight up and carried on walking, mumbling as she went, 'And where in the hell is that Abe guy, anyway? I mean...'

The door shut behind her.

Gail was still outside.

She waited for a moment, and then a moment longer. Aubrey didn't re-emerge. That was it. Help over. Gail had done her good deed for the day, helping her drunken neighbour back to her flat. It didn't quite cancel out the murder and the burying of body parts, but it was a start.

Aubrey's suspicions were a worry. Perhaps they could be taken with a pinch of salt, as she was so desperately inebriated. But, often, that is when the truth can come out. She'd lived with that. Her husband wasn't aggressive because of the booze, the beers made him feel like himself, the real man he was. He was a true drunk.

Maybe everybody was.

And did Aubrey really have her eye on what Gail was doing? Why was she asking about Abe? Should Gail tell Mrs May? It didn't seem right to rat Aubrey out for a drunken comment, and it would only upset the old lady.

Gail decided to keep the information to herself. Mrs May didn't need to know what had been said. She didn't even have to know that Aubrey had drunk a bucket of Scotch and passed out in the library.

Nothing went on in The Beresford that Mrs May did not know about.

WHAT DO YOU WANT?

When you think of entrepreneurs, you think of the bootstrappers. Those who have pulled themselves from the lower classes by means of their intellect, drive and limited resources. Maybe they are working a full-time job then spending the evenings in their garage, inventing the next must-have product or service.

In truth, the most commonly shared attribute of these self-starters is access to money. Family wealth or an inheritance. Yes, they are the big-ideas people, the blue-sky thinkers and the risk-takers. But it is that access to money that allows them the freedom to take those risks.

They are privileged.

They start ahead.

If you managed to get yourself through university without taking out a loan, or you had your loan paid off by someone else, or you moved back home with your parents and rented out the apartment that was gifted to you in order to make the repayments yourself, you are automatically in a better position to be entrepreneurial than most others.

Everyone else is playing a sport where they start the game fifty points behind.

And it's okay to have this privilege. A person cannot help the family they are born into, or the generosity of their parents, or that they are handed the beginnings of a property portfolio or a position within a business. What's important is that you acknowledge your start, where it came from, and empathise with those who do not share your blue blood.

Privilege is not your fault. But entitlement is.

Aubrey, it looks as though you have everything you need. But what is it that you want?

Respect. I want to be treated as an equal. And not because of my father's reputation or standing in the industry. I want it to be because of the person I am, the businesswoman I am and the results that I get.

I want a seat at the top table to be obtained on my own merit. One day, I would like to be at the head of that table. I want to be in the room where it all happens. I want responsibility and culpability. I want the pressure and I want the rewards.

I want the success that my father earned in his work and his private life. I want that same ability to separate both of those worlds. I want everything he built but ten times more.

Is that too much to ask?

Try asking.

TWENTY-TWO

Paranoia levels had been at an all-time high when Gail left with Abe's head in a supermarket carrier bag. The morning had been fine. Not a stir from Aubrey, who was doubtlessly sleeping off a hangover from Hell. But there were certainly stirrings and creaks around lunchtime when Gail returned for the skull.

Now, she was done.

Abe was gone.

She couldn't even remember if that face was buried in the south-east or the north-west, she'd been a hundred miles in every direction that week. If the authorities wanted to find all of Abe, they would have to comb through 31,000 square miles of land.

She felt safe again. The same way she had felt that first night at The Beresford. And it was with great pleasure that she knocked on Mrs May's front door, holding the keys to Abe's apartment up in front of her magnificent grin.

She didn't let Mrs May speak.

'All done,' she said, dropping the keys in the old lady's skeletal hand.

'Everything?'

'Every last bit.'

'That's great. You can get back to focussing on the baby.' She pointed at Gail's bump.

'That's exactly what I plan to do. Put all this behind me.'

'You go and rest, dear. I'll go in and clean Abe's place up. We will have somebody new moving in tomorrow.'

'Wow. That was fast. You didn't even know I'd be finished by today.'

Mrs May brushed past the comment.

'You want that painting in Abe's hall?'

'Er, yeah. Sure.'

'I'll drop it over tonight.'

She shut the door.

And that was that.

TWENTY-THREE

Aubrey's brother had called to talk to her about the conversation he'd had with Mr Kirkly that day. It was odd. Kirkly had called to confirm how much longer he was tied into his policy. He'd never done it before. It had always just rolled into another policy, and if his premium had increased, then he would not argue, he'd just stump up the cash.

'He and Dad have been friends forever, it just seems weird that he'd call now that Dad is ... gone. It's like he's going to take his business elsewhere.'

'So?'

'So? What do you mean, "So?"'

'I mean, he's one client. If he was only with us because he was friends with our father then that's ridiculous.' Aubrey couldn't tell if Kirkly had mentioned their meeting. She was playing the waiting game.

'I understand that, sis, but the company was built on relationships. Relationships that Dad made. What if more clients decide to go the same way. That's when it will start to matter.'

'It's not going to matter for five more years. He's tied in for that long, isn't he? I remember writing that contract.'

'Well, yes.'

'Then we have a lot of time to start building new relationships that can cover the ones that might leave in half a decade.'

'You are a hard-nosed bitch, sister. I probably shouldn't let you near old Kirkly, eh? You'd tell him he didn't matter or something.' And he laughed. And Aubrey was still unsure whether her brother was subtly telling her that Kirkly had mentioned what she had said over brunch.

'I've never really liked the guy, to be honest.'

They both laughed. Whether complicit in what was being unsaid or completely oblivious, it was a nice moment between the two siblings. There was some relief for Aubrey, perhaps Kirkly wasn't going to tell the entire industry what a bitch John Downes' daughter was and get her blacklisted. Maybe he was going to keep his stupid mouth shut. Maybe he realised that he couldn't push her around just because she was a woman. Maybe he had learned something.

Maybe not.

She would learn more in the coming days and weeks about whether the conversation had been relayed and misconstrued. If it had, she would receive more calls from her brother, each with a less friendly vibe. But talking with her brother had left Aubrey feeling buoyant. There was no use in sitting back and waiting for a tidal wave, she had to get out there and chase one down. The day before had been a write-off. She'd slept in and done no work. She had wanted to speak with Gail to thank her for being so helpful, but her head seemed to be affected more by gravity than the rest of her body.

Whisky hangovers were the worst.

But that day was on the upswing. She switched on her computer, made a coffee and plugged her headset in to make some calls. If nobody picked up, then word had spread, but Aubrey wasn't thinking that way. She had moved to The Beresford to make a new start, to carve her own way and create the impact she desired.

It was a new day.

She had a plan.

This was the fresh start she wanted.

That's why people came to The Beresford.

Whether they knew it or not.

TWENTY-FOUR

Saffy Long had been selling her homemade jewellery online to friends for six months. Her social-media presence had exploded recently through no reason that she could find, but she was happy to accept the exposure and the raft of orders that followed.

She had found an office in the city at a reasonable rate, which had the space for her to deal with the increasing demand, and The Beresford was an absolute steal of a price, and so perfectly placed that she could live nearby and work longer hours without having to commute.

It was the step she had been hoping for.

She hadn't been featured in any magazines. No bloggers had reviewed her favourably and caused a stir in the retail sector. No celebrity had shared one of her posts. One day she was in her bedroom gluing earrings, the next, she needed a studio space and had ordered her logo to be printed and placed on the door so that it appeared to be etched into the glass.

It was a whirlwind.

It can happen in the world now. You could be sharing some of your fan fiction on your blog and get offered a six-figure publishing deal. You could be singing songs on your YouTube channel and get noticed by a media-savvy A&R guy, who signs you up to a record label and takes you out on tour supporting a huge group. You can even make your millions by filming your life every day. Letting strangers invade your personal business. Living your life through a lens, being someone you're not or being who you really are.

You don't even need talent.

It can kick off.

Saffy had the talent. She had the product and the logo and the branding and the look. And she had the attitude and work ethic to make it a success.

What these overnight successes often do not have are the right people around them. The ones to tell them when they are becoming a diva. The ones to keep them grounded. And, most importantly, the ones who will keep them protected.

Saffy had it all.

But she wasn't protected.

TWENTY-FIVE

Mrs May handed the painting to Gail and said, 'I'm going to need you to kill Aubrey.'

Gail said nothing.

Mrs May said, 'Here's a knife.'

It looked unused. Sharp. Silver. A bone handle.

Gail was frozen for a moment, three parts of a picture under her right arm, a gleaming blade in her left hand.

'Did you hear me?'

'Yes. I think you said that you *need* me to ... kill ... Aubrey.'

The old lady went on to tell some truths and some lies and make some subtle threats along the way. It wasn't something that she wanted to do, either. She just wanted things back to the way they were at The Beresford.

She told Gail that, earlier that day, Aubrey had been returning a book to the Beresford library – *Outliers* by Malcolm Gladwell. A reread, she had said.

T r u t h.

They had made polite conversation. Aubrey had then gone on to ask Mrs May a plethora of questions about Gail.

Where she was from. Why she came to The Beresford. What were her plans for work when she had the baby? Apparently, it all came across as concern. Mrs May had answered the best that she could and as diplomatically as her old brain could handle.

H a l f truth.

Aubrey had mentioned Gail with affection. She had appreciated what had been done for her when she'd decided to use a twenty-five-year-old McAllan to wash away her troubles. It was small talk only. Aubrey wasn't trying to dig into Gail's past or her future plans.

Then came the l i e.

Mrs May told Gail that Aubrey had said something like, 'What do you think about Gail? She behaves in quite an odd way, don't you think?' This struck a chord with Gail, because Aubrey had said something similar about Mrs May while inebriated. The same sentiment. It rang true. As the best lies often do.

Aubrey told Mrs May that she had spotted Gail going in and out of Abe's apartment. And she'd noticed that Abe hadn't been around from the day she had moved in. She'd never seen him. She'd heard so much about him, but he was proving to be fairly elusive.

Mrs May had regurgitated her story about Sythe and how he would often not be seen for weeks. It was the nature of his job and the essence of The Beresford. It accommodated everyone. They could come and go as they pleased, as long as they paid their rent.

More lies.

And everything that followed was manipulation. Mrs May wanted Gail to believe that Aubrey was far more suspicious of her than she actually was. That she wanted to keep an eye on her – as she had said while drunkenly leaning against her doorframe a couple of days before.

She had asked Mrs May whether something was going on between Gail and Abe.

She wondered where Gail went for three hours at a time during the day, taking her car and bags of blankets.

She had knocked on Abe's door several times to introduce herself, but he was never there.

It had made Aubrey think of the Conroys and how they were looking for their daughter who was suddenly missing. Did Gail know her?

All lies to unsettle the young, pregnant woman.

Pepper in some not-so-subtle messages about prison and giving birth in a cell before having your baby ripped away from you so it can be given to an abusive, alcoholic father or dropped into a system that does not put child safety anywhere near the top of its priorities and it's clear to see the grip on the paintings release and the knuckles on the hand holding the knife whiten.

Gail didn't want to kill anyone. Abe had been an accident. It had been self-defence.

It wasn't her.

To premeditate a murder was a different story.

To look Aubrey in the eyes and know that you were going to take her last breath from her was so different to what had happened with Abe. Gail didn't remember his eyes – even though she had stabbed him through one of them with a broken piece of vasc. She could hardly picture his face anymore – even though it was the last part of him that she had buried. It happened so quickly. A flurry of colours and limbs moving.

This would have to be calculated.

It wasn't her.

After returning the book and talking about Gail with Mrs May, Aubrey had left The Beresford to go into town with her laptop. She wanted a change of scenery, and the coffee machine she had ordered for her apartment had not arrived yet.

True.

She had told Mrs May that she planned to power through until six then buy a bottle of red on the way home and have a slow evening, maybe even read a book.

Also true.

This meant that Gail only had another thirty minutes to wind herself into knots about what Mrs May had asked her to do. She could spend that time running through everything the old, scheming woman had planted in her mind. She may even conclude that killing Aubrey was not a viable option because it could get Gail into trouble and uncover what had happened to Abe. But it wasn't really about that. She would kill Aubrey to protect her baby.

Protect it from the horrors of the world.

She would kill Aubrey to end the nightmare.

End the sneaking around by tying up the final loose end.

She would kill Aubrey to preserve the building.

Gail would kill Aubrey.

And Saffy could move in to The Beresford one minute later.

PART FOUR

ONE

Jordan Irving was passing through. He had six weeks of work near the city and The Beresford was going to be his crash pad. The trip was worth a lot of money, and he'd paid two months up front with ease.

In and out. That was the plan. The place was a bed for him, that was all. He didn't care about the garden space. He had no need for the library. There would be no obligation to get to know his neighbours or fraternise with the friendly but eccentric landlady.

He packed light – enough clothes for the week and his all-important laptop. He wanted to walk in, go to his room, get his work done in that month and a half, then leave the way he arrived.

He was one of three people heading towards the great building that evening.

Aubrey had placed calls to several historical clients, and it didn't seem that her name had been sullied. There was a sense of enormous relief.

She shut her laptop as soon as the time changed to 18:00 in the top right corner of her screen. So many people she knew would keep going. They'd stay late at work, not to do more, but to seem like they were doing more, hoping the boss would catch a glimpse of them still at their desk when they should be home to eat dinner with their partner or help get the kids ready for bed.

For Aubrey, the people who stayed late were either brown-nosing or they hadn't managed their time well enough throughout the day to complete their tasks. She also believed in the sanctity of the work/life balance. It didn't have to be 50/50, it just had to be balanced.

Get your work done.

Get your life done.

Get some sleep.

That's what her father had taught her.

After her outburst at Kirkly, her scales had tipped too far into the life column. An hour of meetings followed by four hours of hard liquor was pushing towards hedonism. But today, Aubrey had it right. She shut the laptop at six and closed the work away. She bought that red wine she wanted and she planned to go to her room and drink it all while slouching on the sofa in front of some form of entertainment.

The bone handle of the knife, crashing down on the front of her skull would be the last thing she would ever feel.

Mrs May had the idea to let Gail into Aubrey's apartment where she could wait and pounce at the right moment. It would be simple and unexpected. The knife was sharp enough that Gail could attack from behind and slice through the spinal cord. It would probably paralyse Aubrey. Gail could leave her to bleed out or finish her off.

Gail did not appreciate how cold and removed Mrs May suddenly seemed but reasoned that it was her way of dealing with things. That the old lady was trying to help herself, of course, but was also on Gail's side.

Mrs May dealt with things by completely removing herself from them, emotionally. Gail did the opposite. Thinking everything through. Experiencing the panic and the dread. Thinking of things she would never have contemplated before she had arrived at The Beresford.

She had killed once but it had been on instinct. She had spent years protecting herself from her husband and now she had to protect her baby.

That's what it was. She had killed to protect her baby. And, if it came to it again, that would be her only reason.

Maybe she would start to like it. Enjoy it.

Maybe that's what happened with Abe.

No, Gail. That's not you.

The plan did not work for Gail.

You can't reason murder. Not the premeditated kind, anyway.

She was sure that she would either lose the nerve, waiting in

Aubrey's apartment, or she would pass out with anxiety while hiding in a wardrobe or something.

No. It was a terrible plan. Gail needed to know where Aubrey was at all times. She wanted to be near the entrance to The Beresford to leave as little time as possible to pull out from the idea altogether.

Aubrey needed to get home and get killed.

That was the only way it would work.

TWO

The removal guys had taken most of Saffy's things to her new warehouse location, but she threw a couple of boxes of beads and jewels and string into her car with her soldering gun and pyrography kit, so that she could still create at her new home. Nothing for work, just for fun.

She drove an old, noisy Volkswagen Beetle her mother had owned in the sixties. Even with a sudden influx of cash and investment opportunities arising around her sudden success, she never planned to get rid of that car. It was perfect. It fit her in every way. And, though to look at it, one might consider it ready for scrapping, the vehicle was reliable; it started first time, every time.

The only way it had been updated was to be fitted with a CD player.

She rifled through a wallet of music and pulled out the album *Let It Bleed* by The Rolling Stones. She skipped to song nine, looked in her rearview mirror and set off for The Beresford.

In an unintentional act of sick symmetry, Gail slumped herself down in the reading chair of the library area. The knife was in her hand, covered over by the book on her lap, and her eyes were closed enough to look as though she were asleep but open enough to see when Aubrey was close enough to hurt.

The key turned in the front door, and Mrs May slithered back into the shadow of her apartment. Aubrey used her shoulder to push the door open. The wine bottle was in her right hand and a laptop bag was slung over her left shoulder. She put the keys in her left coat pocket and entered.

She didn't see Gail at first. She wanted to wipe her feet and make sure the door was closed properly behind her. She called Gail's name when she finally noticed her on the same chair she herself had been found in a couple of days prior.

Gail did not respond.

'Gail? Are you okay?'

Normally, Aubrey would have assumed Gail was asleep or too engrossed in her book, but as Gail had taken the time to check up on her when she was drunk, Aubrey felt obliged to reciprocate.

She nudged the laptop bag strap higher onto her shoulder and made her way towards the library. Quietly, Mrs May came out of her doorway in order to witness what was about to unfold. She checked her watch. In a couple of minutes, one of them was going to drag the other around the corner so that the new tenant did not see whoever's body didn't quite make the cut.

'Gail?' Aubrey asked again.

One step closer.

'That must be some book,' Aubrey smiled as she reached the chair, seeing that the pages were left open and had sent her new friend into a peaceful sleep. Aubrey looked down at Gail the way a parent looks at their baby in a crib.

Gail knocked the book to the floor. As Aubrey's gaze followed it, Gail brought the blade upward and into Aubrey's stomach. She was surprised at how easily it seemed to penetrate. Gail gripped the bone handle hard and twisted.

Aubrey released her grip on the wine bottle and it smashed on the floor, followed by Aubrey herself, who landed on her laptop. Gail held the knife in place and followed her second victim to the floor.

'Shh, shh, shh, shh,' she instructed, tears rolling down her cheeks. 'It's not me,' she whispered.

Gail was pressing her weight down on Aubrey. Pressing down the way her husband used to press down on her. This is why he did it from behind, he didn't want Gail to look at him. He didn't want to see that she hated it, that she didn't want it.

'Don't look at me.' There was shame in her voice. But Aubrey, feeling the sensation of the knife continually twisting in her abdomen, all strength now released from her limbs, was still as stubborn as ever. She stared down her killer.

Gail pulled the knife out of Aubrey's stomach and the blood

pooled out of her, turning the cold wound hot. She screamed then turned her eyes back to Gail's.

Gail's shame morphed into anger. Her weight still pressing Aubrey into the ground, the blood staining her skirt as she moved up her victim's body. She brought the tip of the knife around to Aubrey's chest and rested the sharp point over her heart.

'I have to protect my baby.'

Aubrey garbled something but Gail could not understand.

She moved her ear closer to Aubrey's mouth, hoping she would repeat it.

'Your child is the Devil,' she whispered again. Even in her dying moments, Aubrey managed to use her words to devastate her adversary.

Gail leant her weight on the handle and the knife pushed through Aubrey's heart.

They laid there for a moment until Gail was sure Aubrey was no longer moving, then lifted her head to see that she was dead.

Aubrey was gone, but her eyes were still open and directed at Gail. The now two-time murderer pulled the knife from her second victim's chest and smashed it down onto Aubrey's forehead four times.

One hit for every word.

'Don't. Look. At. Me.'

She stood up, the knife still in her hand and blood down the front of her skirt. Opposite her was Mrs May, who had seen everything unfold.

'There you go, old lady. Are you happy now? Are you?'

'You need to hide her. You have sixty seconds.'

THREE

Jordan Irving was twenty-one and hadn't passed his driving test. But Jordan Irving had never taken a driving test. He hated cars. He hated the way people spoke about cars, particularly men. He hated that they were considered a representation of wealth or success. But, mostly, he hated the idea of travelling somewhere and the only thing you can do is drive.

Sure, you can make a hands-free call but you still have to concentrate on the road so you don't end up killing yourself or somebody else because you're distracted by a conversation. You can't look at your phone if it vibrates to indicate that somebody has sent a text or email.

One time when he was still at university, his friend pulled over because he wanted to change CDs safely. The police pulled up behind, questioned them both and still made them take a breathalyser test – though he thinks they would have been waved on their way had their skin been the same colour as the cop's.

Irving was a workaholic. He loved the film industry and he had worked on some great movies with talented casts. One day he hoped to become a producer. But not just a money man, a hands-on creative force behind every project he was involved with. Writers and directors had had their day, it was a producer's medium now.

Before he got to that position, though, he would have to work, and he would have to work hard. He'd been tasked to spend six weeks in the city on a location-scouting assignment and had been granted permission to attend some of the read-throughs while there. Not every filmmaker was as encouraging when it came to nourishing enthusiasm or talent.

Irving would take all of his opportunities.

That's why he didn't drive.

He loved public transport. Especially trains. He'd book in advance so that he always had a seat with a table, a power socket and his back facing the direction he was travelling. The first thing he would do after sitting down was take out his laptop, plug it in to the charger – unless his mobile phone was low, then that took precedence – throw his giant headphones over his head and start typing.

If there was work he could be doing, he would do that, but, in between, he was working on his own projects. He'd built enough contacts in the industry to know how to get a screenplay seen, or at least put onto the right desk, so he was writing that whenever he could. And, while creative industries were, on the whole, a lot more liberal and open-minded, Jordan Irving still felt that he had to put in more than the next white guy trying to do the same thing as him.

He had turned up so early for his train that he could have got on the one that left before his, but he'd booked his seat and didn't want to go through the rigmarole of changing his ticket, so Irving found a bar, ordered a large glass of red wine and wrote three pages of his script.

Even when he was finally on the train he had paid for and it stopped for twenty minutes because there was somebody on the track three miles up – a suicide he presumed – he was happy to tap at the laptop and listen to music that was drowning out the moaning commuters who were pissed off that some selfish idiot had killed themselves during rush hour.

It was lucky his train pulled into the city later than it was scheduled, otherwise Jordan Irving would have arrived at The Beresford before Saffy.

FOUR

'Why did you say sixty seconds?'
'What?'

'Why did you say sixty seconds? That's so specific. You would say "about a minute" or that it needs to be done right away, but not "sixty seconds". Why is it sixty seconds? You said it last time. I'm sure you did.'

Gail automatically brought the knife up from her side as though she was ready to do something with it.

Mrs May did not look shocked or scared by the movement. Gail couldn't hurt her.

'I don't know what you mean. Look, I just know that the new tenant taking over Abe's old room will be arriving soon. That's all. And we don't want this mess here. All I meant was that we need to get this sorted *quickly*. It's right by the front door.'

Time was ticking by. Mrs May knew that she had spoken for too long. She didn't need to be explaining herself to Gail. She just needed her to listen and obey the instructions.

'You're lying. You are LYING. I remember it. You told me when Abe was dead that I had one minute to get rid of his body. You're doing it again. What is going on in this house?'

Saffy's Beetle was loud. Mrs May and Gail both heard it in the distance. It was getting closer to the house.

'Please, Gail. She's here. The new tenant is here. We have to move Aubrey. I can't do it alone.'

'If that doorbell rings in sixty seconds, so help me God I will fucking lose it. Tell me what is going on here!'

A car door slammed out the front of The Beresford.

'I don't know what you mean.'

'Liar!'

'She's coming. She's twenty seconds away at the most.'

'Then you don't have much time.' Gail pointed the knife at Mrs May as though telling her to proceed.

'I can't explain it, Gail.'

'Try.'

Through the window, Mrs May could see a deliberately scruffy-looking bohemian type walking up the steps.

'You are going to have to trust me. That's all I can say. We can talk after. Just move the body around the corner for now. The new girl is here.'

Gail paused for a second. She didn't want to trust the old lady, she couldn't even trust herself. From the corner of her eye, she could now see the woman approaching. She was holding a cardboard box with both hands.

'Please, Gail. You've just tied up the loose ends. Don't create more.'

Gail shook her head, bent down, grabbed the neck of Aubrey's blouse and started pulling. She dragged her around the corner and left her lying in front of one of the bookcases that was out of view from the front door. Then she dropped to her knees in front of the spilled red wine, covering the blood that had spilled on the floor. She pretended to be picking up the broken glass and let the red wine stain over the blood on her skirt.

The doorbell rang and Mrs May took a deep breath to compose herself before opening the door.

Gail thought to herself that it had been around sixty seconds since Aubrey last breathed.

Not a minute.

Exactly sixty seconds.

FIVE

He had managed to add another ten pages to his script on the train journey. He wasn't sure they were any good but he was pleased with the volume. He'd read somewhere that Bukowski didn't have a word count, he just tried to write ten pages a day. Jordan Irving wasn't even a fan of Bukowski but he did like the way that he worked.

The story concerned a young blues guitarist, sitting in a grubby apartment, playing along to a Robert Johnson record when a citywide power cut drops the area into darkness. When the power comes back on, the record starts to play in reverse and he hears a voice telling him to murder everybody in the building.

Irving wasn't sure how it was going to end but he was writing his ten pages each day and hoping that the answer would come to him as he got deeper into the story. It went against everything he was taught at film school, but he believed he was on to a winner. Commercially, it ticked the horror box, crime box and the public's fascination with the occult. And, if he was lucky enough to get his first project off the ground, it would provide a lead role for a young black actor.

He was dreaming big and working hard.

The city station was busier than the town where he had started his journey and it was colder. He wrapped a scarf around his neck and kept his headphones on, partly for the music, partly for the warmth. And he walked.

His phone was fully charged, but the navigation was telling him that he was less than ten minutes from his temporary home. He kept his hand on his laptop bag as he walked. If some city street urchin wanted to take it from him, they would have to prise it from his cold, dead hand because the information on the hard drive was irreplaceable.

It was his life.

His life's work.

Eight minutes later, he was outside The Beresford. There was an old-fashioned Volkswagen Beetle parked outside and an old woman clipping flowers by the front door.

SIX

'Mrs May, I presume.' Saffy put the box down for a moment, and the old lady spotted a rainbow of plastic beads. Thousands of them, she guessed.

'That's right, come in.'

'I'm Saffy. Saffron is my real name but nobody has called me that in literally forever, not even my mum.' She seemed nervous. Scatty. She hadn't even noticed Gail down on her knees, picking up broken bits of wine bottle, at that point.

'Saffy it is, then.'

Gail was stewing. She felt like a dog or a puppet. Mrs May could just turn it on and off whenever she felt like it, it seemed. She was over there small-talking the new girl while Gail was on her knees in a puddle of blood and red wine.

Paranoia kicked in.

She felt like Mrs May was laughing at her. She always seemed to have a favourite. It was clear that she never liked that Sythe guy, but she never said anything horrible about Abe, even though he'd slapped Gail around the face. She wasn't damning about Blair, but she wasn't complimentary either. Gail had moved into top spot once Abe was gone, and she was sure the old lady had wanted her to triumph in the battle with Aubrey.

But now there was Saffy. What a ridiculous name.

And why was she so happy?

'That's Gail over there.' Mrs May pointed, and Saffy looked over and gave an awkward smile. 'She accidentally dropped a bottle of red wine on the floor. A good bottle, too.'

'Oh, no. It looks like it has gone all over your outfit, too.' Saffy feigned concern. She used the word 'outfit' instead of 'skirt' and that was enough to annoy Gail.

Saffy turned back to Mrs May and they mumbled more inanity. Gail had reached her limit. She stood up, knife still in her right hand, and moved over behind Saffy. It was too quick for Mrs May to intervene.

Gail held the whacky jewellery designer around the neck with her left arm and placed that sharp, bloodied blade against the front of her neck.

'What are you doing?' Mrs May kept her movements small so not to spook Gail.

Saffy wriggled. She wasn't trying to free herself, it was more to get into a position of comfortable surrender.

'Be careful, dear. She's pregnant.'

Gail took Mrs May's words as concern for her and her unborn child. That she didn't want Saffy to throw an elbow back or something because it may hurt the baby. It softened her rage a little.

But not enough.

Saffy froze.

'I want to know what happens if I run this blade you gave me across her neck.'

'You gave her the knife? What is this place?'

'Be quiet, girl, the grown-ups are talking.' Gail did not sound like herself at all. Her eyes looked different. Her mind kept going back to Aubrey's final words about her child being the Devil. She couldn't understand why she had said that. Was it just to hurt her? Was it to fuck with her mind? Because it was working.

'You know what will happen if you cut her neck. She'll die, Gail. More blood on your hands.'

'More? What are you two?' Saffy was outspoken in life, and it appeared she would be outspoken in death if it came to that. 'Is that why it's so cheap? So you can lure people in and kill them, you fucking psychos.'

Gail ignored her.

'I know what happens if I cut her. What happens after? What happens sixty seconds after, Mrs May?'

There was a back-and-forth between the old lady and the pregnant woman in which the question was dodged and then asked again in a different way. Dodged again. Asked again. All the while, Mrs May was calm and collected, and Gail grew more and more tired of her politician-style rhetoric.

'I don't know what the hell you two are talking about, but if you're going to do it, just fucking do it.'

Maybe Saffy was playing a risky game here, calling their bluff, hedging her bets. The women seemed the most unlikely of killer duos. Maybe it was a game or a prank, or some kind of initiation gone too far. What were the chances that a two-hundred-year-old and a frumpy woman in her second trimester were a couple of slashers.

The thing was, Saffy couldn't see Gail's eyes, because she was behind her. Also, she had never seen Gail's eyes when she was frightened and alone and vulnerable, and trying to escape her own horrible, abusive home life. So she couldn't tell the difference.

'Just fucking do it,' she had said.

Gail just fucking did it.

She pushed the silver blade into Saffy's annoying neck and pulled it quickly across to the right then let go of her third victim.

Two thousand coloured plastic beads spilled out across the floor of The Beresford, reaching out to every corner, as Saffy dropped her cardboard box and instinctively grabbed her own throat in a futile attempt to stem the blood flow.

Neither of The Beresford Two paid her any attention. Their focus was on one another. Mrs May looked resigned, while Gail held up her side with anger and frustration.

'Why did you have to go and do that?'

Saffy was still alive, gurgling from the slit in her neck as she lay on the floor. She looked on in disbelief as the old woman spoke so matter-of-factly. She seemed more irritated by the broken wine bottle than the almost-murdered tenant on the ground.

'I want to know what's going on here.'

'With what?'

'Stop it. Just stop. You know what. What is this place? Why does this happen? I'm not a killer.'

'I'm sure this girl with the stupid name would disagree. As would Aubrey over there, by the bookcase.'

'What is going to happen in sixty seconds? Is that doorbell going to ring again? Because there are a load of beads to clear up if that's the case, and not a lot of time.'

'I've told you that I can't give you all the answers.'

'Bullshit.'

'I can't. Honestly.' Mrs May looked around as though somebody might be listening in on her. 'We can sit down once this is cleared up, dear—'

'Don't "dear" me.'

Mrs May did not take orders.

'We can sit down properly when this is all over, *dear*, but until then, this needs to get cleared away.'

'There's someone else coming, isn't there?'

'I will tell you this much, we should get a head start on these beads, your sixty seconds doesn't start until she finishes breathing.' The old lady pushed her foot against Saffy's hip to see how weak she was. 'I reckon we have another minute or so before that kicks in.'

Gail fell right back into her place, doing as the old lady instructed. She was to take Saffy's phone from her pocket in case she tried to call anyone, then go to the cleaning cupboard near the library and take out the large broom to sweep all the beads into one pile, and the pruning shears so that Mrs May could head off the new tenant out the front of The Beresford to buy a little extra time.

She made Gail feel like they were a team. In on this together. Co-conspirators, even though Gail was doing all the dirty work. If one of them went down, the other would have to follow.

So she did as she was told. She took the broom from the cupboard and started brushing all the beads back towards the box, which had been flipped so that the coloured plastic balls could be pushed inside. She swept up the broken glass, too.

Every ten seconds or so, one of them would prod the girl with the claret smile across her neck to see if she was still holding on.

They cleaned around her.

She choked.

Mrs May sprayed something on the spilled wine and sticky blood.

Saffy tried to speak.

Gail didn't want to hear any more last words. Her baby was no devil. It was innocent. Like all babies. Whatever the dying girl was trying to whisper, she could keep to herself and the Gods.

Most of the beads had been swept back into the box, but Gail plugged in the vacuum and chased some of the stragglers down. Mrs May had a scourer in her hand to scrub the wine and blood but gave Saffy one last kick before getting on her decrepit hands and knees.

'Gail!' She had to shout over the sound of the vacuum. 'Gail!' She did it again, and Gail pressed the button to stop sucking up the bits of plastic. 'She's gone.'

The timer had started.

Jordan Irving would be there in sixty seconds.

The old lady dropped the scourer, picked up her secateurs and stepped out the front to pretend that she was tending to her roses. It could buy some much-needed time.

Gail wrapped a clump of Saffy's scraggly hair around her hand and dragged her over to Aubrey. She was petite and easy to move. Her oversized cardigan probably weighed more than her body. Gail managed to pile her on top of Aubrey's body. And she wondered whether Aubrey had said all of those things that Mrs May had told her. She did have a wicked tongue.

'Devil baby,' she muttered under her breath, shaking her head, trying hard not to spit on a dead woman, then picked up the scourer that Mrs May had dropped and got to work on the stains.

Thirty seconds later, she could hear a man's voice, and then the old lady joined in.

Gail was so close to having everything cleaned up. Not perfectly, but enough that somebody who had never been to The Beresford would not notice things were out of the ordinary.

When she had that knife to Saffy's throat, all she wanted were answers. Why she could feel herself changing. What was so special about that building? What did Mrs May know? How long had it been happening for? Who the hell was she becoming?

She hadn't thought any further than threatening to kill the tenant in order to gain this information.

Of course, it would always end in her death, because you can't be held up by someone you live with and not alert the authorities. How would you sleep at night?

Once she realised that Saffy would definitely become her third kill, Gail had the notion that she would continue to murder someone every sixty seconds until Mrs May opened up and told her the truth.

The doorbell would ring and Gail would stab.

While on her knees, wiping the last bit of blood off the wood, she caught a glimpse of the newest of new tenants to The Beresford. He was over six feet tall. Black. Beautiful. And built like a tree. She would not have stood a chance against him.

Mrs May had opened up enough for Gail to abort that idea. And for that, she was grateful.

The latch to the door clicked, and Gail ran over to the dead bodies and sat on them. There wasn't much space around that corner but it seemed the best option because she was still covered in her victims' blood.

Their introduction could wait.

He seemed eager to get to his apartment, and Mrs May was not in her usual hurry to give a tour of her famous garden and library.

Gail peered around the corner as the new guy walked off towards Abe's old place. He was athletic and muscular. If it came to the point where Gale had to take his life in some way, it was going to take some real effort to saw through those limbs afterwards.

WHAT DO YOU WANT?

Nuclear families. Remember those? Two parents. Married. A man and a woman, just like it says in the Bible. 2.4 children. Mating for life. Like penguins. Or Catholics. Job done. Exist until death.

And that works. For a third of the population. They can cruise until the end, just like that.

That's okay.

Maybe that husband steps out whenever he feels the urge. His wife knows about it but it isn't hurting anyone. Only her. In fact, after he's cheated, he's often nicer than usual.

Your sex was purely procreation, not recreation, anyway.

Sure, sometimes the dinner isn't on the table at six and that can make him angry. He doesn't know why, he just knows that he should be and he can be. He walks over to you, his knuckles dragging on the floor, and he pushes you. Maybe a slap. Maybe you feel the back of his hand.

It's nothing, right?

Just the way things are.

Nobody gets hurt. Only you. The kids don't see anything. And he's still providing for them. For you. You have food and shelter. You want for nothing. Nothing but some tenderness or compassion or help with the kids. But you stick it out. You are a unit. A family.

You don't want a divorce.

You don't want to have to share your kids.

You don't want to have to think about finding someone else now you feel stretched out in all the ways you were warned would happen.

But you don't want to be alone.

So you stay. And maybe he comes home late from drinking with friends and he climbs on top of you in bed, his full weight pressing down on you, and he has his way. You don't like it. He's hurting you.

Maybe you never got to that point of 2.4 children. You found it difficult to conceive and he blamed you or felt like less of a man. A push turns into a slap, which mutates into a punch, and that ends in a beating. You miscarry early. You lose another when you're almost at the finish line.

He treats you better for a while. Until you fail him.

You know you don't want this anymore, but there seems no alternative.

What do you want, Gail?

Escape. I want safety. Security. And a baby that doesn't die.

Vengeance? Justice?

Walking out will have left him angry, self-destructive, embarrassed and defeated. He will torture himself and drink to a hastened demise. There is no sense in asking for vengeance when somebody is their own worst enemy. His loneliness is enough justice. I made that happen.

I am a mother. I do not ask for myself.

It seems only worthwhile to ask for the things that I cannot guarantee myself.

SEVEN

Like everyone who entered their apartment for the first time at The Beresford, Jordan Irving was amazed at the space, the quality of the finish and the original architectural features. Unlike the others, he didn't care.

The kitchen would only ever be used for a morning coffee, if he had the time. He would grab his lunch from somewhere in the city and most of the time he would eat out for dinner. He had no qualms about going to a restaurant and asking for a table for one. It didn't bother him that some families or couples would stare at him and either think he was weird or pity his apparent loneliness.

The lounge had enough space, if he pushed the sofa over a few feet, for him to perform a few body-weight workouts in his first few days. He could find a gym in that first week and get a month-long membership. That way he could be out of the building at 6:00 am, before anyone else was up, and he wouldn't return until late most nights, meaning that he would never get caught in a situation where a neighbour might ask him about his day or his work or, God forbid, his writing.

It was painful for him to have to explain the writing. He was lucky that he worked in the film industry because it lent a little more credence, but people would often comment that it was 'just a hobby, then'. It was infuriating. Even more so for Irving because he was so focussed and determined. But he was certain that he could get through the next month and a half without having to explain that to anybody – bar the friendly old woman who had rented him the place.

The bed was huge. He'd need that for sleeping and masturbating – when he could be bothered – but that was it. There was a wardrobe for his clothes, which he hung up immediately, and the ironing board had been placed inside like they do in hotels.

Toilet.

Shower.

Perfect.

Victorian, clawed-footed bath tub: superfluous.

Abe's old flat had everything its new tenant needed and a little more. When Abe was disposed of, the apartment was cleared of possessions that were unique to him, but all the furniture remained.

Irving was a simple man with simple requirements, and he lived a minimalist existence. Almost all his clothes were packed into that one bag. He used to keep all the books he read, but they were now gone and had been exchanged for an e-reader, which contained more than he would ever be able to read and took up the bookshelf space of half a novella.

He had done the same with his films. Even though it was the area he wanted to work in, he sold them all and bought as many as he could in a digital format, which were stored in the cloud and backed up on a hard drive the size of half a novella.

Pictures were scaled back. He had two of each piece of crockery in case he had a guest over. There was no drawer in his kitchen that contained *stuff*. Nothing could distract him. Some would think that it took all the personality out of his apartment, and others believed it was zapping the personality out of Jordan Irving. Both some and others were correct.

He was so single-minded in the pursuit of his dream and success that he had forgotten how large the world can be. And that there are other people along that journey.

And that not all success can be measured with a number.

What it did mean, though, was that Jordan Irving was the perfect neighbour for a couple of women who were trying to get rid of two dead bodies.

They wouldn't have to sneak around. He wasn't interested in them. That was great, because if Jordan Irving became suspicious, if he evolved into another loose end they had to tie up, the knife wasn't going to cut it.

Six weeks.

By the time he was due to leave, Gail's baby would be the size of a papaya.

Maybe even a grapefruit.

EIGHT

'What are you doing?'
'I'm waiting for you to finish.'

'You're sitting on two dead women.'

Gail was pregnant and she had been on her feet all day. Aubrey and Saffy wouldn't mind, they were dead. It was strangely comfortable. That's what she wanted to say, but instead she just stood up.

Mrs May explained that the new tenant had told her he'd already had a long day and was planning on finishing some work before freshening up and going to bed early.

'I've seen his kind before. He's one to stay in that room and hardly ever come out unless it's absolutely necessary. So you've got a decent window to get these two over to your room.'

'My room?'

'I'm not having this in my apartment. You can drag them up the stairs to Aubrey's if you like, but it's a huge effort and you're pregnant. Get them out the way. I'll sort out the library.'

Mrs May liked Gail. She knew her backstory and she could see that her future was all going to be about the baby. But Mrs May did not want to be involved in this side of things. She didn't want to have to mop up the blood from a businesswoman's stomach or an entrepreneur's throat. It was easier with the Sythes and the Abes of this world, because they tried to hide things away. They got rid of the bodies in secret. They did all this crap by themselves.

Those were the days.

Gail performed her minion duties. She placed a bin liner over Saffy's head and another over her feet, then taped them together around the middle. The idea was that she wouldn't spread any more blood. But it made her awkward to move so she made a slit in the top of the bag where Saffy's head was and wrapped her hand around the bird's nest of hair of the young designer who would never see the faux etching effect on her city warehouse window.

She watched Irving's door as she dragged the package across the lobby.

Nothing.

Aubrey was so tall that the bags did not meet in the middle of her body, so Gail had to wrap another one around her waist and tape both ends to it. She used the hair winding technique again to drag that tall redhead, who could have easily become her friend.

Mrs May was good to her word. She mopped up the streaks that led from the library to Gail's room and, when she'd finished, the library looked as it always had. Tidy but dusty.

Gail sat on the floor in her hallway and cried. What had she become? Why was this happening to her? She was a good person. Or, at least, she thought she was. She had escaped an abusive partner. The evil piece of shit had managed to knock her up with one of his soft rape sessions, and she was determined to change her life and the life of that baby. She would show it what love really was.

That child would know that his mother would do anything for them.

It wouldn't know about the three people she had killed to protect them, but she would ensure that her child would understand what being a mother meant to her.

That is what kept Gail going.

That is what she was clinging to.

But she couldn't help wondering if there was a way to get out of her current predicament. She thought about her parents and her friends and whether there was a God. It didn't seem right that there was some higher power, because she appeared to have gone from one hell to another.

What was her way out?

Was her new life actually worse than the one she had left?

And was there anything she wouldn't do to get to the place she wanted to be?

WHAT DO YOU WANT?

Descend, for a moment, if you will, into the backstabbing, cutthroat world of beauty pageantry. Young girls, too young for make-up and with no need to wear it, painted to look like a filtered photo, and hairsprayed within an inch of their lives, all in the pursuit to understand their individual beauty, by making them all look alike.

And all sound alike.

What makes you different from the other girls competing today?

Nothing. We are all caked in foundation and our hair is scraped back.

Why do you think you are the best candidate for this title?

My mum wants it more than the other mums. She said we have to win because Mrs Pearson is a real bitch.

Where do you see yourself in five years?

I'd like to be doing well at school, but my parents are both chronically overweight, and if I don't start winning some pageants so that my mother can live vicariously through me, I'm afraid she's going to hit the crack pipe again and I'll be left trying to care for her. My dad drinks too much.

This would never be said.

It seems there is no beauty in truth.

With no truth, there's no trust.

If you could only have one wish, what would you wish for?

Please form an orderly queue, step up to the microphone and say the words, 'I. Would. Wish. For. World. Peace.' Then smile like you mean it. Like you've given it some genuine thought.

What do you want?

We want truth, honesty and trust.

Nobody wants world peace and everybody knows that. But do you really want truth?

If you have one thing that you can ask for, you have to word it correctly.

You ask for world peace, and the simplest way to make the world entirely peaceful is to erase all human life. Imagine the quiet. The serenity. But that is not what you want. You want things to be better. You want to feel safe at night on your own as a woman when you walk home. You don't want to have to fear walking past a man because he is more than likely going to say something derogatory or flirt or force himself on you in some way.

You want to trust that your military are fighting to keep you free and not taking part in conflicts that serve the self-interest of a faceless few.

You want your police force to be honest and uphold their oath to protect you, no matter your gender, age or race.

Asking for world peace can solve all of these issues, but the only option for true peace is the extinction of humanity. What you really want here is education and discussion. That is what you must ask for.

Saying that you are eating bacon distances you from the fact that you are eating pig. It is further distanced by not referring to the animal as 'a' pig. Buying bacon that was once a local pig only means that the pig was killed closer to where you live.

The only farmers in the world are the ones who grow vegetables because anything to do with meat is a factory. Run in the same way a factory for cars or televisions is run. Only they're covered in shit and blood, and there's nobody taking the remote controls away from the televisions as soon as they are made.

And bacon gives you cancer.

Sometimes you want the lies because the truth is as inconvenient to you as a world at peace would be.

Besides, bacon is delicious and you probably won't get ill because you're invincible.

You walk into a bookshop and you are not 'discovering' anything in there. It is carefully marketed and orchestrated for you to buy the ones that need to be bought. You are being told what to watch, who to vote for, which team to support and which God to believe in.

You want the truth?

All of these things serve to obscure the greatest lie of all.

The fruit and vegetables are placed at the front of the supermarket because the colours draw you in. Everything behind is bad for you.

But you just see the colours.

You buy into them.

You believe them.

It's easy to do as you are told.

You are not where you think you are.

PART FIVE

ONE

The devil baby was the size of a large artichoke and The Beresford was silent.

It had been another busy couple of weeks for Gail. She had travelled north, south, east and west again. This time a little further than before, never visiting the same place twice, though she did pass through the village where she had filled her petrol tank and dumped Abe's pelvis. She didn't stop this time. There had been nothing in the papers, so that bone must have been in landfill somewhere, slowly decaying.

She'd seen enough thriller movies to know that a killer can never return to the scene of a crime, it's a sure-fire way to end up in handcuffs.

Gail had also travelled north-east, south-east, south-west and north-west. She'd even discovered some of the compass points between those. Towns nobody had ever heard of. The kinds of places you only find because you are lost in the woods or have taken a wrong turn. What better place to do something horrific than the setting for every late nineties horror movie?

Most of the parts had been taken into wooded areas and buried deep. Gail had gone so far into the undergrowth on occasions that she figured she could have left a hand or shoulder on the floor and it would have been devoured by animals. But she wasn't an idiot. And she wasn't lazy. There were no risks to be taken. She couldn't afford it. She would not lose her baby, no matter how many holes she had to dig.

Out in the woods, in one of the directions she had travelled, Gail was approached by two people as she was burying a hand.

Fuck. This is it. Undone by a couple of doggers.

All she had was a small shovel. She could hit one, but the other would get away. If it came to it, she'd take the man out first and take her chances with the woman. She was a mother now, she was stronger.

'Ahoy there,' the man said, waving a hand, his other holding on to his partner.

'Evening,' Gail responded, surveying the area around her. She had her shovel and a shopping bag that still contained a limb that needed burying. With her foot, she patted down the earth of the hole she had recently filled in.

'Everything okay up there?'

Gail had the higher ground, which she knew was beneficial.

Castle, that woman-beating, verbally abusive bully of a husband was about to save his wife.

'All good, thanks.' Gail tried to look away, hoping they would just move on to whatever car park they were hoping to have sex in.

'What are you doing up there? Digging?' The woman joined in.

'Foraging. Mushrooms.' Gale dug the shovel into the bottom of a tree, bent down and grabbed a handful of flat brown mushrooms, seemingly stuck together to resemble a hen's splayed feathers. 'Hen of the woods,' she announced, proudly.

Her military ex was fascinated by this sort of thing. She remembered him saying how you should never eat a foraged mushroom unless you are absolutely certain what it is. A shaggy ink cap is perfectly edible but a common ink cap could lead to convulsions and death if consumed with alcohol.

Useless information until one is found burying a body in woodland.

Gail placed her haul into the bag so that it covered the remaining limb.

'Wow. Impressive,' the woman responded, nodding at her partner.

They weren't moving.

'Yeah. You can find them in the day but they can be quite camouflaged by the tree and leaves. At night, the torch illuminates the white edging so they're easier to spot.' This was a lie. Gail was thinking on her feet, trying to recall any information she could about fungi. She droned on about anything until she knew she had bored the couple enough for them to move on with their evening.

Castle: he knew how to survive in the wild on food that was stuck to the bottom of a tree but he couldn't make himself a god-damned sandwich.

On one occasion, Gail had travelled so far in one direction that she hit water. She thought about a boat, dropping bits of body over the side, maybe weighing them down somehow, and letting a thousand fish nibble at the flesh only to be eaten themselves by some apex predator. But it was getting too elaborate.

Forget the perfect crime.

Cut the body up. Drive somewhere far away. Dig a huge hole. Drop the body part inside.

Repeat until empty.

Somehow, it had become her daily routine. She'd hoped to be working part-time or doing something creative from home. But her days had been filled with driving, digging and burying.

There was no time to discover who she was, only who she was not.

A killer.

A friend.

A mother.

Abe's head had freaked her out. She had left that part of him until last. She'd done the same with Aubrey. But with Saffy, it was different. Just the thought of her smug, little face filled Gail with rage. The poor girl hadn't done anything wrong other than turn up at the wrong time. Still, Gail found a degree of pleasure in sawing her head off.

She liked the sound of the saw biting its way through the vertebrae in Saffy's neck. She did it quickly and roughly. She just wanted that bitch's head off. She wanted to call her 'bitch'. She wanted to spit on her face as the back of her head slammed to the tiled floor. She tried not to smile.

Anger and pleasure.

Who she was and who she wasn't.

She'd had the box in the corner of her bedroom for three days now but hadn't wanted to open it until Aubrey and Saffy were completely gone. Gail was trying to be sensible with the money she had saved, especially as she wasn't drawing in a wage just yet. The crib was basic. White wood. Wheels at the bottom of the legs so she could push the baby into the corner once it was asleep or rock the thing back and forth to help it sleep.

She'd ordered the modular version because it was a little cheaper, and she'd saved the job as a reward for herself once she had disposed of her two latest victims.

She rubbed her stomach.

The baby was the size of a large artichoke.

And The Beresford was silent.

She still hadn't seen Jordan Irving. It had been two weeks since he had arrived.

Mrs May had kept herself out of the way. The only thing she had really achieved was placing the advert for Aubrey's apartment.

She needed a new tenant.

TWO

There was something about the old lady that Jordan Irving just liked.

He'd been staying at The Beresford for a fortnight, and he had not had to introduce himself to anybody else who lived there. Work had been demanding but rewarding. He had located an old club called The Crowley that had been shut for two years. There were still flyers in the windows for upcoming shows that had long since passed.

The place had been a real boho hangout for decades. Famous comedians would go there late at night and test out ten minutes of something they had been working on to see where it was getting laughs and, more importantly, where it wasn't working. They had poets and songwriters and performance artists. If you had something you wanted to show, you could get on the stage and give it a shot.

Some big names had passed through there on their way to the top, and a few had even graced its one-person stage on their way back to the bottom. It had a reputation. It was a giant maker and a dream breaker and it died.

People don't have to go out anymore. They don't have to make small talk or have a conversation that lasts more than 140 characters if they don't want to. You want to be a comic, you want to make people laugh, you can prop your phone up against that book you're never going to read and film yourself telling a few jokes or performing a 'bit'. You can upload that for free and, if more than sixty-two people see it, you're reaching more people than you ever would on a busy night at The Crowley.

It's not the same, though. You can't feed off the audience. You can't respond directly, in the room, to the feedback. You can skip a horrible comment online and go on believing you're the next Dave Chappelle because you only grade your worth on likes and views.

And that's why places like The Crowley are dying.

And comedy is dying.

And humanity is all but dead.

But it gave Jordan Irving a ready-made dive-bar club for the film. The producers loved it. The director loved it. The actors thought it was authentic. And Irving caught a glimpse into that world he wanted so badly. The producers didn't want to have to build a set, so they saved money, especially as the rent was so cheap after three years of being vacated. The director was always looking at things artistically, and the actors were always striving for authenticity because they made money pretending to be somebody they were not.

Jordan Irving imagined himself on that stage, a bright spotlight burning down on his head, sweating, trying not to look nervous as he pitched his idea for a screenplay.

Maybe someday.

All of this had kept Irving out of The Beresford. He had found a gym that had some heavy bars he could throw around in the morning, and the showers were always clean. At the other end, he was getting back during unsociable hours, wearing his headphones and ducking his head as he bolted to his apartment to seem even more unapproachable.

But he couldn't escape the old lady in the mornings. It's like she knew when he was going to leave. Whatever time he was heading out the door, she would be up and in the lobby, or with her flowers or just coming out of her apartment.

As much as Irving didn't like small talk, he had been raised in a way that told him to respect his elders. He couldn't be rude to Mrs May. The morning chats started to become a regular thing. He was a creature of habit so he made them part of his daily routine. He even started to leave the building five minutes earlier so they could talk for longer. It didn't matter what time he left, she was going to catch him, anyway.

She seemed interested in him and didn't look at his writing as a pastime. She was encouraging. She told him how she used to have an artist who lived there, started at nothing and became toast of the town. Irving pretended he'd heard of Sythe to be polite, but painting wasn't really his thing; he was more into the magic of the moving image.

'There's no reason that can't happen for you if you want it enough.'

Nobody ever said things like that to Irving, not with the genuine belief that Mrs May showed him. Of course his mother spoke that way, but he could tell that, deep down, she would prefer it if he were bringing home a cheque every month from work.

Steady and reliable. Which is exactly what Jordan Irving was, but his career choice was not.

Day by day, Mrs May learned a little more about the new tenant yet he never found out anything about his landlady. She wasn't giving anything up. He wasn't asking the questions. It felt good to talk openly about his passions and not have them shot down.

He felt heard and he felt interesting. Which is the way most people feel when they do not realise they are being groomed.

Mrs May always had a favourite.

THREE

Mrs May's ritual remained unchanged.

You would think that the events that had occurred in her building over those couple of months would have worn her down. She was a thousand years old and still had all her mental faculties and physical mobility. She could have been scared by things. It could have been too much to handle mentally.

But she still got up early every day. She drank her cup of cold black coffee. She ate her eggs. She walked around the garden. She listened to her music. She danced. She drank wine after noon and slept the first two glasses off.

She kept being Mrs May.

Perhaps it was an age thing. She'd lived through a lot. Wars. The death of the man whose soul matched hers. She could take it. It was the generations that followed that would have struggled. Each one growing more and more brittle. More needy. More self-absorbed. More entitled.

For Mrs May, life went on. It had to.

So she kept her days the same.

Coffee, eggs, garden, music, wine, siesta.

And then she would always pray.

For weeks, her focus had been on Gail. As with Abe, she called for compassion on the young (almost) mother. She prayed that Gail would level out, and understand who and where she wanted to be. Above all, she prayed for the health of that unborn baby. That it would make its way safely into the horrible world they all lived in.

The old woman had seen it all before and could tell that Gail was built from tougher stuff. Whether it was anything to do with Mrs May's daily rituals or Gail just had that mettle, it was clear that she could handle difficulty. Sometimes, the ones who have been constantly beaten down in their lives are the ones who prevail. It should make them weaker, but it does the exact opposite, whether they realise it or not.

So Mrs May turned her attention elsewhere. To the softly spoken, muscular black giant that now occupied Abe's pit.

She prayed for Irving's success.

'Allow no misfortune to allay his path.'

She sweated and swore and exhausted herself as she did whenever she delivered her pleas.

With compassion covered, Mrs May moved on to straight passion. Irving was focussed and driven but too buttoned up. He needed to let loose. Get laid. Get the poison out.

She howled at the moon for Irving to sweat, to graft, to fuck, to win.

Pray. Collapse. Freshen up. Drink more wine.

This wasn't a new thing for Mrs May. Sythe and Abe, and the trio of women who had perished recently were not a shock to the old lady's system. This type of thing had been happening since she moved herself into The Beresford. The death and the darkness were part of the routine.

There were subtle differences but, essentially, it was almost predictable.

Every day the same.

Repeat until the end.

FOUR

It was difficult to place the aroma.

Gail had been given some essential oil by Mrs May to go in the aromatherapy diffuser she had placed in each of the apartments at The Beresford. Leammas Root. Gail had never heard of it.

'Also known as Yellow Rock,' she had said. But Gail was none the wiser.

Apparently it would take out the scent and the essence of the dead bodies that Gail had gradually disposed of but had started to decompose in her flat in the meantime.

It was difficult to know which was worse, the death or the scented oil. It wasn't terrible but it wasn't appealing. Gail leant into it for a day or so then reverted to her favourite patchouli oil. It smelled like home again.

The crib had taken forty minutes to erect. There was a section that the instructions said was a two-person job, but Gail had got around that by using the wall and her feet to hold two sides upright as she screwed in the third.

It felt real. This was the bed where her son or daughter would rest and, hopefully, sleep. She had read about nesting, but that was supposed to come nearer the time of arrival. Her apartment had hardly been a home since she arrived at The Beresford. Yes, initially, there was some relief to be away from her husband, but the independence was short-lived upon the confirmation that she was pregnant.

From then it had been a muddle. Holding on to every penny she had saved in her getaway fund, she stocked up on furniture gradually, treating herself to a soft furnishing or candle when she could.

She thought about the small room opposite hers, the one most residents used for storage or an office, and she pictured decorating it for her baby. It was definitely big enough for a baby.

Once the bump started growing her clothes became more uncomfortable. She would undoubtedly get to a point where she required some maternity jeans.

The last few weeks had been hectic. Heinous. She was now a three-time killer, though she preferred to think of herself more as a serial *protector*. She had kept her baby safe, now she wanted it to feel loved. She wanted that boy or girl to emerge into this world with a crib and a musical mobile and cute baby grows and bobby hats and teddy bears.

The loose ends had been tied. There was only one other person living at The Beresford, and she hadn't seen him since the day he walked past her as she sat on two dead bodies, hiding.

She could not see any trouble in her immediate future, unless a body part was unearthed, or her husband located her. Gail could focus on staying well, eating right and keeping active, to ensure that she gave her baby the best chance.

Her baby. Her child. That oversized artichoke with no personality. Gail loved it. She couldn't understand how she could love somebody so much that she had not even met. But she did. And she had shown that. She felt that she had demonstrated that she would do anything for them. She would kill another human being. That is how strong her love was.

But murder is not the full extent of the effort that one can go to in order to exhibit their undying love for another person.

No. It can go much further than that.

To show how much you care, to ensure everything will work out, to guarantee your success, fame or fortune, to get a little extra time with a sick loved one, to be appreciated in your own time, it does not have to involve taking something from others.

You have to completely give yourself.

FIVE

The garden at The Beresford had always been a feature. At least to Mrs May. She kept the flowers pruned and the foliage clipped. She'd provided the burn bin that Sythe and Abe had used so much. The logs that one of the shelters housed were all chopped by her, because she liked to remain active. And it was her idea to install the brick barbecue at a time when The Beresford was occupied by a younger clientele, who liked to stay up late and made her feel like she hardly drank anything in comparison.

The courtyard was her design, too. A rectangle split into four quadrants of shingle with a stone cross pathway. In the summer there was a wooden table, some benches and a couple of wine barrels that doubled up as drinks tables.

That night was the first time Jordan Irving had been out there.

The day had been long. An early-morning gym session after his now customary talk with Mrs May. She'd asked him what Tinseltown had in store for him that day. He'd quietly informed her that it wasn't that kind of movie. Not a huge blockbuster with an unlimited budget. Those were hard to get onto. It was more of an independent project. But it was still a feature.

He sounded like he was justifying his efforts, which is what he always did to his friends and family because they thought it was funny to ask him when he was going to get a 'proper job'. He hated that.

But that wasn't Mrs May.

'Well, it sounds like a big deal to me. You must be excited to go into work every single day. That is rare. You should be very proud.'

He wasn't. But he wanted to be.

The old lady had managed to pick him up a little, and he worked the rest out at the gym. He showered and went for a lonely breakfast. That day, he did not have to be at work until after lunch. Most people would think about having a lie-in but Jordan Irving saw time as precious. To him, it was an opportunity. He finished his breakfast and had two hours to work on his screenplay.

The more he wrote, the more he believed he could do something with it. Yet, somehow, the more he wrote, the less he believed in himself.

He wanted to be considered an artist.

Was that too much to ask?

Three hours later, he had his ten pages. The words had flowed. He'd made some corrections and edits to the previous day's work.

Then it was over to the abandoned Crowley club. The director thought it might add something to the read-throughs and rehearsals if they were done in an authentic space. And the club was so integral to their story.

It was the same thing over and over. A slight tweak here and there. Asking the actors to perform a single line in a different way seven times. To some, it would look laborious. To Irving, it was fascinating.

He had some time between scenes to speak to the actors. He tried not to look nervous. They were open and honest. They laughed about some of the awful roles they had played and some of the low-paying gigs they'd had in places not too dissimilar to The Crowley. They were hoping the film was a springboard to more work.

They were just like him.

Paying their dues.

They ate take-away Chinese in the theatre and went for drinks afterwards. The director spent a lot of time bitching about the industry. He'd been shit on a couple of times and was having to prove his worth again. The actors didn't seem to care, but it dragged Irving down. This movie was a huge step up for Irving, and the director was making it sound like the film was a means to an end.

He walked home in the dark, didn't feel like the train that night. Without thinking, he opened the door to The Beresford and walked straight past his apartment and into the garden for the first time.

Maybe he felt like supporting Mrs May. She'd been so good to him, and he knew how proud she was of the outdoor space. He wanted to reciprocate.

Maybe he was in a daze, deep in contemplation.

Maybe something else entirely.

But he was there, standing in the middle of that paved cross. The sky so vast.

What was out there?

Was it really opportunity?

'Irving?' A voice came from behind him. An old-lady voice. She had called him Jordan, and he had said that he preferred using his surname.

'Holy sh— ... Mrs May. I'm sorry but you just scared the heck out of me.'

'I'm sorry. I didn't mean to. I tried to be quiet because you looked pensive. Busy day? It's kind of late.'

'Kind of late for you, too, I'd imagine. What are you doing out here?'

Cue the lies.

She told him that it was just about her favourite place to be. Sometimes at night, she came out and looked around, just as he was. She would think about how large the world was out there, and how she never left The Beresford. Because she had travelled far and wide with her husband before his death.

The sentiment was true, but she was out there because Irving was out there.

'How was work, dear?'

Irving was just so pleased that she had referred to it as *work* that he felt obliged to open up to her.

Mrs May gazed into those beautiful brown eyes and drank in every word he was saying.

'It's just such a hard slog, you know? I'm hopefully on my way up but I'm passing others who are on their way down. And it makes you realise that you can't always make it or that you can make it high but not to the top, and even then, there's always a drop, it's just a matter of how long that fall is.'

'That's true of any line of work. I think that people can get lazy and complacent. That's when the ball drops.'

'Maybe you're right. I guess I just had it in my head that if I worked harder than everybody else, I'd be in a better position. And I do. I work like a dog almost every day.' Irving looked out at the stars and they made him feel even more insignificant. The old lady spotted it. For the usually stoic individual, his emotions were written on his face.

'You know what, Irving? There are a couple of things, when it comes to personal success, that people don't understand. One: you need luck. You could be the greatest writer/painter/guitarist/footballer or whatever in the world, but if you are living in the rainforest, you're not getting discovered. You'll need luck. You need your work to land on the right desk at the right time. You need to be heard by the right person in the right place. That is nothing to do with talent. It's luck.'

'Of course,' Irving chimed in. He was listening.

They both nodded in agreement.

'And secondly?' he asked.

'Secondly, that luck means shit if you aren't willing to continue working hard. Too many of these lucky bastards get given the golden ticket and they think that's enough. You can't just stop. That's when the real work begins. That's how you stay at the top. The people who fall back down the ladder are the ones who take it all for granted.'

'You are a wise woman, Mrs May.'

'I've been around for twelve hundred years, I've seen a thing or two.'

They both laughed.

'Well, rest assured, I'm working hard until that luck comes in, and I'll keep going if it does. I'm doing everything I can other than selling my soul for success.' He rubbed his face with one hand. He was tired.

'Okay. But if you ever feel like going that way, I know a guy.'

They both laughed again, heartily.

'Good night, Mrs May.'

'Good night, Irving. See you in the morning.'

SIX

Mrs Conroy had buried her husband. She had to sit in a wheelchair with a black blanket covering her legs because she wanted to hide the pins. The priest had committed Mr Conroy to the ground.

Earth to Earth.

Ashes to ashes.

Dust to dust.

'In sure and certain hope of the resurrection and eternal life.'

She wasn't buying it.

Why would you want to go to Heaven? To be with a God who would take a beautifully kind, generous and pious man as Mr Conroy? Who would rip him from life with so much left to go, so much left to do.

She was in danger of becoming bitter.

Though He had hurt her in a way that nobody else could, Mrs Conroy was finding it difficult to give up on her God. She wanted Him so desperately to talk to her, to confirm that it was all in His great plan. That her husband was taken for a reason. A reason that her small human mind was too simple to fully comprehend.

She was reading her Bible, hoping some words would jump out at her. That God's words would reveal themselves.

She found herself at Isaiah. One small passage stood out from the page, as though it were written in bolder letters, as though it were raised from the page as the other words lay flat and blurred.

'Because you have said, "We have made a covenant with death, And with Sheol we are in agreement. When the overflowing scourge passes through, It will not come to us, For we have made lies our refuge, And under falsehood we have hidden ourselves."'

Mrs Conroy was one of those people who could quote the Good Book at will. She could almost always think of a chapter or verse to fit any point that she was trying to make. But for some reason, it felt as though she had never seen that particular paragraph.

She had been sentimentally flicking through her husband's Bible

– a New King James version. Her own standard King James Bible was slightly different in that the first 'you' was a 'ye' and 'Sheol' was 'Hell'.

A passage concerning a bargain to cheat death and dodge the grave. She thought her eyes were deceiving her. That surely this was not her God communicating with her. This felt like a darker force.

The other Him.

What was He trying to tell her? Something about her husband? Had he made a deal? Where was Blair? What had she done? Had she entered into some kind of pact? It was all starting to make sense. Her dreams were messages, too. She had been told to listen for God's message to her in her dreams.

It felt as though she had not blinked for a long time. Her eyes were wide, taking in the world anew.

'No. No,' she said out loud.

They were devout. They never did anything to let *Him* in. Their lives were simple. They did not want for anything. They were financially sound. God had given them a daughter, when medically it had seemed that they were not destined for parenthood. She would not believe that any kind of agreement had been made in order to receive such a gift.

'No.' And Mrs Conroy slammed her husband's Bible shut.

She wheeled herself out of the front door, leaving it open behind her. Down the garden path, she muttered to herself. Left out of the gate, whispering, 'It's rubbish. Utter rubbish. There's no such thing. Voodoo. Hoodoo. Ha! Never. He was a good man.'

Mrs Conroy was picking up speed in her wheelchair as she hit a straight section of path. Shaking her head in disbelief all the while.

She knew the stories. They all did.

An average harmonica player takes a guitar down to the crossroads where Highways 49 and 61 intersect. He waits there until midnight, when a strange figure emerges from the darkness. Some accounts refer to a large black man, some to a dark demon, others to Satan Himself, while many believe it to be one of the Devil's underlings, as the big man would see this as beneath Him.

The average musician hands over the guitar. The demon, or whatever guise has been taken, tunes in the guitar, plays a song and hands it back. The next day, that average harmonica player is an accomplished guitarist who stuns the world with his skills.

But it comes at a price. This new-found talent is an exchange for a soul.

That's what they say.

Those Hoodooers.

There seems to be no great detail on how this occurs, but the person will often meet an untimely end. It is thought that the soulless individual spends eternity in a pit of fire, and that is adequate recompense for the fifteen minutes of fame or fortune they had in life.

Mr Conroy didn't buy it.

There was no way her husband gave his soul for them to have a child, and his reward was a face full of tree and windscreen followed by everlasting lashings and brimstone. That was preposterous.

Because that would mean the Devil is real.

And if the Devil was real, then so was God.

Mrs Conroy knew there was no God.

Her wheelchair had picked up pace and was heading for a main road. The Devil was in her mind, still. She grabbed the right wheel hard, not because she wanted to turn out of the way, because she wanted the thing to flip.

The car hit her before she hit the floor.

Her head crushing under the weight of the bumper accelerating into her skull, damaging her brain.

But it was not going fast enough to finish her off.

The Lord works in mysterious ways.

SEVEN

Gail hadn't killed anybody for a month and her baby was the size of a grapefruit. She could've found out the sex but opted out, increasingly certain that it was a boy.

Her boy.

And he was going to break the chain of abuse. No way he would be like his father or his grandfather. It may have gone back further. These things often do.

'It is crazy that this is the first time we have met.' Irving's work had slowed that week and he was around the building a little more. He was going for a midday workout, and Gail was coming in from town with a bag of food shopping.

'I know. I don't think I was even pregnant when you first got here.' She found herself laughing heartily at her own joke.

'And how is it all going? How far along are you now?'

They made polite and comfortable small talk for a while. She told him that she loved the feeling of being pregnant. It was so empowering but also she had never felt such a feeling of love. It was gushing and perhaps a little sickly, but Irving was captivated. He was young and something of a loner, but the few friends he had and still kept in touch with were in a different stage of their lives, which did not involve settling down with one person. Not yet.

Gail explained that she didn't know the sex, she was a bit old-fashioned that way and wanted to be surprised. Irving told her that he would just have to know, even if it helped with which colour to paint the baby's room.

He was not suspicious of Gail, she could tell that much. If the old lady wanted her to kill him at some point, she'd have to be a hell of a lot more convincing than she had been with Aubrey.

Then it kicked.

'Are you okay?' Irving looked worried. Like he thought she was in pain.

'Oh, my. Absolutely. This started happening a week or so ago.' She reached out for his hand, and he let her take it. She placed it on her stomach, and they both waited in silence.

The baby kicked.

Irving was nervous to respond too quickly in case it was something else, but the look on the mother's face told him that he had just felt a human kick another human from the inside.

'Isn't. That. Glorious?' She was beaming. Her cheeks were not flushed but there was a healthy rouging. Irving could completely understand the idea that pregnant women glow. There was something so feminine about it. Gail looked so happy and strong and beautiful.

His hand was still on her stomach, and her hand was still on his.

He was staring at her.

And Gail was staring back. This beautiful specimen of a man. Tall and dark, and so muscular. Her husband had a large frame and always felt threatening, ominous, unpredictable, but Jordan Irving was soft and considered and genuine. She was as captivated with him as he was with her.

Mrs May was staring at both of them from the corner, rendered in a tableau of harmony.

'Well, it's about time you two met. I had a feeling you'd hit it off.' She wandered towards them, and Gail released her grip on Irving's hand. 'I wanted to invite you both to dinner this weekend.'

For somebody living away from his home, his family, his friends, Irving was still a little reticent about accepting such an invitation, but Gail set him at ease.

'Oh, Irving, Mrs May's dinners are legendary. You'll have to have a small lunch that day, I can tell you.' Her warmth seemed to set him at ease.

'So, you're going to cook? I was going to suggest a restaurant I had been to recently. It's a lovely offer, Mrs May, are you sure?'

'It would be an absolute pleasure.'

'Well, I think the pleasure will be mine to spend an evening with you two lovely ladies. Count me in. Now, if you'll excuse me, I have some energy to burn. Are you okay with those bags, Gail?'

'Yes, yes. I'm fine. Thank you.'

'Until the weekend.' He smiled, placed his headphones over his ears and left with a spring in his step.

The two women of The Beresford gave each other a look that suggested they knew exactly what the other was thinking.

They did not.

Gail took her bags of shopping to her apartment and sat on the sofa with her feet up.

Mrs May went back inside and prayed hard for them both.

EIGHT

The repetition was not always exact. Though Mrs May was living the same day over and over and over for what seemed like an eternity already, certain events would pepper their way throughout those days at different times.

People left and people died. Sometimes in the morning and sometimes not. But they always did eventually.

Romances often bloomed but never worked.

The thing that always happened, and it was the one part that Mrs May could do without, was the arrival of the frantic parents. It was usually a mother. Although last time, both the Conroys had stuck their noses in where they were not wanted.

She could empathise, of course. Why would a parent not go completely insane at the disappearance of their child? But it infuriated her, all the same. Like they were somehow trespassing by dropping in unannounced.

The old lady had been awake for an hour after her midday siesta, and the wine was flowing. Then the bell was ringing and she was ambling. Just a glimpse through the glass at the tall, angular woman on the other side of the door was enough to see that this could only be one person. Aubrey's mother.

Mrs May rolled her eyes.

Another one.

Mrs Downes was once a real powerhouse of a woman. Intelligent. The right level of sass. Confident. But she had been dampened after marriage. Not that she could blame her husband, he was supportive and they were a content family. She found that she fell into a role and never really emerged again as herself. She liked her position. She was not unhappy. But the spark was missing. Though it had clearly been passed on to Aubrey. That's why she had allowed her to leave and pursue her own ideas before she got settled into her father's company and never made it out alive.

Her stature belied her timidity. She was polite to Mrs May and explained the situation and her worry. She even managed a little self-deprecation in there. Mrs May answered as she always did. That people often left without settling up their rent and, therefore, surrendered their deposit.

'It happens more often than it should, if I'm honest.' She always said that but she wasn't always honest.

She went on to say that she did not think that was the case with Aubrey, though, and that it seemed her business strategies were working, which kept her away from her apartment. And she had been travelling a little more lately.

Mrs May rarely let the parents inside. It was morose.

She promised to talk to Aubrey whenever she returned and ensure that she got in contact with her mother to let her know she was safe.

Mrs Downes appeared to accept that. It was all she was going to get on this occasion. The old lady could see it in her eyes, though. The fire was still in her. She would be back and she would be angry. That was one of the ways the parents arrived. They were furious, or they'd lost hope; they felt foolish, or – as Mrs Downes had exhibited – numb.

Some had looked into things. They saw that the building was a couple of hundred years old and that this brisk turnover had been happening from early on. To which Mrs May would always respond with the fact that she couldn't be held responsible for things that happened at The Beresford over a hundred years ago.

Nobody ever pushed on that point.

It was a simple avoidance for Mrs May, who shut the door on another mother and returned to her apartment to check her messages.

There was only one.

The confirmation of a new tenant.

An older lady.

She would be arriving at the weekend.

In the evening.

After The Beresford residents' dinner.

These things didn't always happen at the same time. But they always eventually happened.

NINE

Luck. That's what she'd said. If you really wanted to reach the top of your game, whatever profession you chose, you needed that strong work ethic, of course, maybe even a little talent, but that wasn't always necessary. In the end, it came down to luck.

But it's not always the good luck that can shape your future.

Take a look at those Silicon Valley tech heads, starting a small company in their garage before making a splash with something innovative like the computer mouse or an operating system. They've got that hard work nailed down. They're studying in the day, and they're soldering and coding at night. They get some investment and roll out a product. It doesn't work properly, so they patch it up and improve it.

The hard work pays off and then they get a little luck, which sends them global. Every computer *has* to now have an operating system. And it's even more intuitive if you can use a mouse to click and drag things like you never did before.

One path is the operating-system guy. Good luck, followed by hard work, followed by more hard work eventually culminating in good will and charity.

But what about the bad-luck guy. What about the guy with the mouse, who now wants a better operating system, who wants simplicity for the end user? His path is similar.

Hard work.

Good luck.

More hard work.

Bad luck.

Because the board he put in place that would allow him the freedom to express his creativity and vision have voted him out. He's gone. From the company he made out of nothing. He is gone.

And this is a crossroads.

He can begin his descent, passing people who are not as good as he is, as they rise above him. Or he can continue to work hard, create a new company, sell it, get his old one back – the one he loved – and create something else that every person on the planet cannot do without.

That's how bad luck can affect success.

It depends what you do at the crossroads.

Sink.

Swim.

Or sit there, playing your guitar, waiting for somebody else to come along and tune it, play it, then hand it back to you.

The film had to shut down. They couldn't say whether it was indefinite or just a delay. These things happened. Writers strikes and political movements and global epidemics…

Jordan had turned up at the club in the late afternoon. The door wasn't open. He banged against the glass a few times and peered through a gap in the paper that was covering the windows. There were no lights on, no movement. No sound.

He waited a while, occasionally looking around the corner to see whether the actors were turning up. He checked the diary on his phone to make sure his schedule was correct and he was in the right place at the right time.

He was.

The right place for bad luck.

The right time for failure.

After five attempts, the director finally picked up.

'Sorry, Jordan, I've been trying to get through to you. It's no biggie, okay? The project isn't dead. Just delayed. The club you found is perfect, and it isn't going anywhere. It's been derelict for years. So we shall reconvene in a month or so. You okay?'

'I guess so. I mean, yeah, if it's all still going ahead at some point. It's a great project.'

'I agree. And I'm confident it will.'

He wasn't.

'Look, Jordan, it could be a blessing. You're still getting paid for the next couple of weeks. Use that time well. Get your arse in a chair and finish that screenplay you were telling me about.'

'I will. Yeah. That makes sense. Thanks.'

'I'll be in touch. Hang in there.' Then he hung up.

Irving stomped his foot backward into the metal portion of the doorframe and heard something crack. A wall of cold hit his face, and he decided to walk into it.

Walk home.

Home to The Beresford.

Home to a dinner with his temporary housemates who will want to ask him questions about the film and how his day went. And he'll have to say that it's all gone to shit, and maybe his mum and friends were right about it not being a real job.

If he was on his way down, at least he didn't have that far to fall.

It was not going to be a good night.

TEN

Nobody wants their life anymore.

There was a time when people would feel a pang of jealousy at somebody else's outfit or car or the size of their kitchen. You wouldn't see that they had baked cakes with their daughter or prepared a sweet potato Katsu curry from scratch. You would not know that they had just finished a session at the gym, one minute after that session ended.

You'd have no idea that their child was exceeding in maths or had scored three goals on the weekend to mark a memorable comeback for the team.

Or that their husband was the best in all the world because he'd bought flowers for no reason, and booked a spa weekend for his wife and mother-in-law.

If you don't see all of this, you don't want all of this. You don't question why you don't have all of this.

The problem is that these people don't have it, either. They are making you feel like shit because your husband hasn't bought you flowers and you're not best friends with your mother and your kid hasn't just got the lead in the school musical. But they are only showing you that because they have seen somebody else who just turned fifty and has a six-pack. And another person who has been giving daily updates on the progress of their home extension where they plan to host large family gatherings and parties for all their thousands of friends.

What you don't see is that the extension is causing great tension in the household. The kids hate the mess and upheaval, and there's a strain on the marriage as the budget blows out of control. You just see that the dado rail has gone in and the oak floor has been waxed.

And you don't witness Mrs New Conservatory starving herself or shouting at the kids because she's tired and can't cope.

Because then Mr Buy-Flowers-For-No-Reason-Other-Than-Infidelity wouldn't want the new conservatory life. And Ms Katsu

Curry wouldn't want to be bought flowers. And Mr New Porsche wouldn't feel the need to let you know how smart his kid was.

The result of all that is maybe somebody would then want their own life. Or at least appreciate what they have rather than what they do not.

But that is not the case.

Everything is so transparent. It's not honest but you can see through it.

That means Gail doesn't want to be a good mother, she wants to be the best mother. She wants to breastfeed because all the real mums do that. She has no idea whether it will happen, whether the baby will latch on, but she knows that she has to do it, because she has been told that it is the healthiest thing for a new child and that it is natural. And that people can't be offended if she pulls out her breast in a coffee shop, for that very reason.

And she will never hit her child or raise her voice. Instead, she will get down to their level and explain things, just like it says in the books. She will make snacks from scratch so that her child doesn't have a reliance on sugar. She will do all the things that she sees other women, who are not in anywhere near the same predicament as her, do.

And when she can't, she will feel like a failure.

She won't share that, though. Nobody wants to see that.

Irving can't make documentaries, there's no money in that. He can't make a small arthouse movie, either. His friends would still tease him about not having a proper job. And his mother had already posted pictures of his graduation online. He needed a blockbuster with big names. He needed an award. He needed to be the guy who took his mother down the red carpet.

Producing great art was not enough, because everybody could see the box-office figures and that is how they measured success.

He could be content with independent cinema distribution if he couldn't see the life of multiplex movie directors, who in turn could see the life of the producers.

Esse quam videri.

It is better to be than to seem to be.

Mrs May was hoping for a civilised dinner party. Good food and better discussion. She wanted to know who her guests really were, not who they seemed to be. More importantly, she was interested in what they wanted from their lives and how much they truly wanted it.

ELEVEN

Dinner had started well. Irving had pulled himself out of the funk of being temporarily unemployed, and Mrs May had guzzled down half a bottle of Chatêauneuf-du-Pape before her guests had arrived. She had even found a 0.5% red wine that Gail could have that would not affect the baby.

'I don't feel like such a leper now.' Gail raised the glass and took a giant gulp.

Mrs May had prepared her customary three courses with accompanying alcohol. They had passed through the awkwardness of Irving's description of his current work situation and the obvious lie that he was telling himself in order to keep his spirits up.

Gail was feeling looser after three glasses of almost alcohol-free wine, but that had more to do with whatever it had been spiked with rather than good vibes or the placebo effect.

And then it came.

'Tell me what you want, Irving. And don't bullshit me. I want to hear an ideal-world scenario. If you could have it, exactly, what would it be?' Mrs May was serious, severe.

Irving was about to speak when she interrupted him.

'Exactly!'

'Ideal world, I would like to create movies that are critically acclaimed while also being successful enough at the box office to afford me a lifestyle that is comfortable beyond my means and allows me to take care of the ones I love so they do not have to struggle.' He sounded like he'd given it some thought.

'And why can you not have that?'

'Ha.' He laughed. But Mrs May was deadly serious. 'Mrs May, that is not how art works. The great writers live in hovels while the hacks are in mansions. It's the same with music. I like hearing the stuff you play, but I don't know the names of any of the acts. I hate what I hear on the radio but I know who they are. Every last overproduced, auto-tuned one of them.'

'Cheers to that.' Gail seemingly wanted to be heard.

The other two looked at her, said nothing, then looked away.

'I had a young Irish kid in here one time, Aidan Gallagher was his name. Sweet kid. Dreamt of becoming a painter. I asked him that same question that I just asked you. He told me he wanted to lose the Irish farm-boy thing, just ditch it. All that rich history, he wanted to trade it in and become someone else. A painter. A real artist. The toast of the town. Wanted his work to be worth money. Always. You know what I said to him?'

'No.' Irving was captivated by the old lady's story.

'I said, "How much do you want it?"'

Irving was waiting for the next part of the conversation, but Mrs May turned her attention to Gail.

'And you, young lady.'

'Me?' Gail put her hand against her chest coquettishly.

'Yes, you. What do you want? Above all else. Anything. The thing you truly want with everything that you are.'

'I am afraid my dreams are not so grandiose as our friend Mr Irving's here.' She put her hand on his for a moment. 'I worry every day about my baby. I'm scared it could be born with a hole in his heart, or horns on his head or not breathing at all. I wish I could guarantee a safe arrival and a long and healthy life, free from complicated illnesses and heartbreak.'

'I understand that, dear. Though I think heartbreak is essential for everyone. It is the one pain that can make us stronger. Now tell me, why can you not have that guarantee?'

'Because it's out of my control. I can eat the right foods, and I make sure that I exercise enough – but not too much. I only drink wine that can't make me drunk, although this one feels like a very strong 0.5%, if you don't mind me saying. Maybe a 0.52%.' She did that thing where she laughed at her own joke. 'I can follow the advice and take my female pills or whatever, but there are no guarantees.'

'I had a young man who lived here for quite some time. Kind and thoughtful, very well read, he had a great thirst for knowledge. But he was a little shy, perhaps. He was skinny. Timid around women. The kind of guy that always ends up becoming a friend.'

'The friend zone.' Irving rolled his eyes.

'He wanted to guarantee that the next woman who moved into The Beresford would fall for him. If he was sure that would happen, he could be at ease around her from the off. He could be cool or charming. He wasn't an idiot. He wasn't a virgin. It wasn't about sex. The guy wanted love. And he deserved it. He was lovely, a good guy.'

'Sounds like Abe.' Gail was slurring.

Mrs May ignored her for a moment.

'He wanted love and he got it. For a short time, but he had it. The one thing he wanted more than anything.'

'And you think he somehow made that happen? The artist?' Irving knocked back his wine, and Mrs May refilled.

'Do you both believe in God?' Mrs May asked, ignoring the question. 'I'm not asking whether you are religious, just whether you believe.'

'I do,' said Irving.

'I like the idea of it but I'm not sure, with everything that is going on in the world,' Gail answered. She sounded naive.

The old lady continued. She was going to say the same thing whatever their answers had been.

'Have you noticed how many people are absolute about His existence? And they live their lives by Him. They are devoted, fearful they give everything to Him. And what does it get them? What does giving yourself up to God mean? It does not guarantee you health or success.'

'So you don't believe?' He wasn't offended, he just wanted to understand the point.

'There are two things I am certain of: God exists. I am sure. But He has checked out. He was asleep at the wheel but He is not here anymore. He has given up. So there are millions of people around the world giving up their soul to Him for nothing. For no reward. For no eternal life in Heaven. Their souls are worthless.'

Irving thought it was a bleak way of looking at things. Gail was listening but felt the edges of her vision begin to ripple. Mrs May continued with her rant, saying that your soul was the most valuable thing you have, and that you should never give it up so easily to a God who is no longer present and will do nothing with it.

It was as passionate as one of her prayers.

She told them that giving up your soul for anything other than the one thing you truly wanted above all else is foolish. Because the price is high and is only worth it if you receive your dream.

Irving chimed in. 'Outside in the garden that time, you were joking with me. You said that you knew a guy that could help me if I wanted to sell my soul for a successful film career. You were joking, right?'

'You're scaring me a bit, Mrs May. I don't think I like this.'

'Aiden. That Irish farm boy. He dropped his accent, he changed his name to Sythe.'

'I've heard of him,' Irving added, continuing the pretence to stay a part of the conversation.

'Yeah, I have one of his paintings.'

'He gave it up for his success.'

'Oh, now you're being ridiculous.' Gail stood up at the table. 'Just stop. It's not funny anymore.'

'And Abe found love straight away with Blair. It didn't work out in the end but he wasn't done. There was more love out there for him. He was going to find it.'

What happened next was chaos. Gail took particular umbrage to the mention of Abe. And it was worse that the old lady was suggesting something so disgusting as him selling his soul for love. Mrs May insinuated that Blair came to the same fate as Abe. That Abe helped Sythe to that end.

And Irving was confused by this.

And Gail was frightened that the loose ends she had tied up were about to become untied.

And the old lady pushed and pushed. And her passion riled Gail more – her drink was not helping matters, giving her some courage and bite.

Jordan Irving tried to calm them down. Eventually they were all standing up around the table.

'Don't you dare. Don't you dare bring all that up. You're mad.'

'Why don't you stop trying to protect your baby and be a mother? Guarantee its safety and happiness.' The old lady had some spite in that tongue of hers.

'You don't talk about my baby. You're mad. You're mad.'

Mrs May grabbed Gail's wrist to steady her. To calm her. Perhaps to goad her. Because the mother-to-be felt instantly threatened. And when she felt that way, she lashed out.

Gail grabbed the carafe from the table by the neck. There was only a little wine left in the bottom. She picked it up and struck Mrs May across the side of the head with the heavier glass at the base. It hit her square on the left temple, and she released her grip and dropped straight to the floor.

Irving grabbed the carafe out of her hand as Gail pulled it back towards her. Maybe to take another swipe.

'What are you doing?'

'She grabbed me. You saw. It burned me.' She showed him the marks on her wrist. But he wasn't interested. He had already run around to make sure the old lady was alright.

She wasn't moving, and there was blood trickling from the side of her head, down her cheek. Everyone was small in comparison to Jordan Irving, but he thought she looked even tinier than usual.

He put his cheek above her mouth but couldn't feel any breath. Gazing down her body, there was no movement. He checked her pulse.

Nothing.

Gail just stood there watching.

'I think you fucking killed her.' He looked horrified.

'Oh, shit. That means we have sixty seconds.'

TWELVE

Gail had some explaining to do.
And fast.

'Sixty seconds? What the fuck are you talking about? You just killed this sweet old lady because she disagreed with you.' Irving was stood over Mrs May's body. He wasn't sure what to do. He could detain Gail, pin her down so she couldn't get away while he called the police.

But nobody ever called the police at The Beresford.

'Old, yes. But sweet? She was talking about making our wildest dreams come true if we sold our souls. You get that, right? She wanted our souls.'

'Come on, Gail, that's just an old wives' tale. She couldn't really do that. It was drunken dinner chat.'

'You don't get it. There's something about this place, and there's something about Mrs May. Things happen here. People have died.'

'Yeah. You probably killed them.'

'I did. She made me.' Gail pointed at the corpse. 'And every time she made me kill someone, a new tenant would show up exactly sixty seconds later.'

'Horse shit.'

'It's true. Sixty seconds before you got here, I slit the throat of some ditzy jewellery designer. I dragged her to the library and you walked straight past us.'

'What are you saying to me? You're confessing to a murder?'

'We don't have time for this, Irving. I didn't mean to kill Mrs May. She was frustrating me. I think she put something in my drink.'

'You know what you sound like?'

'Paranoid. I know. But in about twenty seconds, the doorbell is going to ring and a new tenant is going to want to see Mrs May. I guarantee it.'

'You sound as crazy as she did. Selling souls. Cursed houses. You're out of your damned minds.'

A minute had almost passed. Irving wondered how Gail could believe in this one-minute-later superstition but not buy the whole selling-of-souls idea. Gail started walking towards the door.

'Where do you think you're going?' He sounded threatening.

'Someone is going to have to let the new tenant in.'

Irving was about to roll his eyes. He was going to tell Gail that she had to stay in that apartment otherwise he would make her stay. He was going to run to the door and block her exit. He was going to call the police. He was going to try CPR on the old lady.

But the doorbell rang.

THIRTEEN

Irving was at the mercy of Gail, who now seemed confident and sober.

She was the one in control.

She'd done this before.

She had seen this all before.

Gail strode ahead of Irving. She wanted to get to the door to see who the new tenant was, so she could say, 'I told you so.' It seemed that they had both forgotten about the old, dead lady bleeding in her apartment. The poor woman who had run that building for more years than she could remember. The one who had prayed for compassion for Abe and a million other Abes throughout the years. That spritely pensioner who drank all day and tried to help every single person who was lucky enough to pass through The Beresford to reach their dreams. She was lying motionless on her dining-room floor, dead for a minute, and already forgotten.

Neither Irving nor Gail performed the customary look out of the window to catch a glimpse of their new housemate. It was always Mrs May that answered the call of the fresh tenant.

Gail took a deep breath and opened the door.

The smiley greeting soon fell away from her face as she inhaled through her mouth again, this time in fear, taking three slow steps backward. Irving could see how wide Gail's eyes were, but the door was blocking his view of the person she was looking at. Then they stepped inside.

The old lady.

Mrs May.

Alone as ever. No blood on her face. No sign of any head trauma.

'Right, dear, let's not go through that again, okay?'

FOURTEEN

It should have been much worse.

Gail was expecting some kind of attack, either verbal or physical. Some sort of onslaught. A tirade of abuse. It was the least that she deserved after cracking the formerly dead Mrs May around the head with a heavy-bottomed carafe.

Irving was mumbling to himself, pointing at Mrs May then at the apartment, then back at the old, alive woman.

'Yes. There is a body in there, but I am here.' She pointed down at her feet. 'It's not the first time it has happened. Some idiots get it into their heads that they can't leave if I am still alive.' Her eyes roll. 'They think that, if they kill me, it will somehow break the curse. I don't even know where they get that idea from. And they realise sixty seconds later that it doesn't work.'

The young tenants were gobsmacked. Irving a little more so because this was the first time he had witnessed the phenomenon she and Gail had spoken of.

'It's cold out there. I could do with a drink to warm up. Shall we go back inside? And perhaps you could stop smashing things over my head, Gail.' Mrs May shut the front door behind her and urged Irving to lead them back into her apartment.

They found themselves standing around the table once more, as though that minute had never happened, and they were midway through their discussion, but clearly they were not. They had Mrs May in front of them twice. Once on the floor dead and the other decanting a bottle of red wine.

'I'll tell you, this carafe was worth every penny. Very sturdy to stand up to the blow you gave me.' She itched her temple where the other version of Mrs May had been hit.

Gail was somehow embarrassed.

'She wasn't lying to you about the one-minute thing, Irving. It may be difficult to swallow, but it is true. You have seen it for yourself, now. And I was not lying to you about your dreams. They can become a reality. You can have what you want.'

'So, what, you're going to tell us that you are the Devil, are you?' Feisty Gail was back in the room.

Mrs May laughed heartily.

'Of course not. I'm really not that important. A minion at best.'

She went on to explain that she was a collector. Some people have cupboards filled with paperweights, or they buy a thimble from the different towns they visit, or it's teddy bears, old books, classic cars, jazz vinyl ... Mrs May had none of that clutter. She collected souls.

It was her job.

She had given hers up a long time ago. God had forsaken her as he so often did. He was not answering her prayers, so she prayed in a different direction. Hoping her cries would be heard.

'You'd be shocked at how many people have literally no idea what they want in life. You ask someone for their favourite film and they falter, instead, giving you a list of ones they do not like. People want things: smaller thighs, bigger breasts, their mother-in-law to contract a mysterious wasting disease. But a soul is worth so much more than that. It must be the thing you absolutely desire the most.'

For Mrs May, it was simple, she wanted more time. Her husband's illness had progressed too quickly and there was no time to do the things they had always dreamed about doing together.

So Mrs May had begged for time.

She was given an extra year with him. In return, her soul was no longer her own, and her eternity would be spent at The Beresford, collecting the souls of others.

'It was worth it. I swear to that.'

Gail and Irving found themselves buying into it, believing everything the old woman said. She had reappeared a minute after her own death and was now standing next to her dead self. Was it so much of a stretch to accept that she had convinced Sythe to relinquish his soul in exchange for artistic notoriety?

The fact that she was so calm about everything only made her seem more credible.

Most people are more upset to have been murdered.

'Listen, I don't want you to give me an answer right now, too much has happened. What I want is for you both to go back to your apartments. You have a few minutes. Imagine the building is engulfed in flames and you can only take one thing. I want you to grab that one thing and bring it back to me.

They both left without saying a word.

Irving was intrigued.

Gail was starting to feel the control that Mrs May seemed to have over her. Though she had not used the unborn baby as leverage yet.

Once they'd left, Mrs May kicked the dead Mrs May to roll her forward and underneath the dining table. She pushed her chair beneath the table, too, so that she did not have to look at herself.

Gail returned with a bunch of keys, and Irving had his laptop slung over his shoulder.

'That was quick. But the good news is that you both seem to have the capability to choose the one thing you need or want the most.'

'So, in return for my soul, you can guarantee my son will be born safely and thrive throughout his long, illness-free life? That's what you're saying? And for that, I get to spend forever in Hell.'

'Well, as you're already here.'

'What? What are you talking about now?'

'Oh, my dear. You think the greatest trick He ever pulled was convincing the world that He didn't exist? It was convincing the world that they were living on God's green Earth. God is defeated. He's checked out. And His Earth is now our Hell.'

The old lady persisted with her final explanation. She told the young pair that it was the great lie that somebody invented Hell. Fear is a powerful tool. If you tell the world that they will end up in a pit of fire for all eternity if they are not good in life, if they do not worship a good Lord, if they are not fearful of a God, then you have created something evil, something to avoid. But the truth was that had never occurred. What had been created was the idea that humankind lives on Earth, it was a more positive message. A solid marketing campaign.

That way they would never question or realise where they really were.

'Sell your soul, don't sell your soul. Live at The Beresford, live somewhere else. Wherever you are, you're in Hell.'

FIFTEEN

Turns out that it was as simple as signing a contract.

'Just like the one you signed before you moved in here. The kind that says that I get to keep your deposit if you stop paying what you owe me.'

There was no crossroads. No ritual. No blood-letting or human sacrifice. They would not be surrounded by men in cloaks or branded in any way. Again, these were the lies perpetuated to obscure the truth that there was no Hell after Earth and there was no Hell on Earth.

Hell was Earth.

And it was getting worse with every passing day. So why not make the most of it?

Mrs May had sold this story a thousand times before. Sometimes she would use a person's desperation, like she had with Sythe. And it helped that he drank a lot, too. With somebody like Abe it was a longer game. She could have done it faster but there was no sense of achievement with obtaining an easy soul. It was worth more for the person to dig deep and find their desire.

Irving had stayed quiet throughout the explanation. He had only been at The Beresford a little over a month. He had not seen anything out of the ordinary. He had been endeared to the old lady and was warmed by Gail's apparent optimism.

He had not strangled a neighbour or melted their flesh or slit their throats. He knew nothing of that. He was a simple man with a complicated vision of his future. And he found himself looking towards Gail rather than the soul collector.

Mrs May took a step back. She had made Gail kill for her unborn child. She would let her reel in Irving.

'Look at me,' Gail said. 'You hear everything she is saying. You have seen what you have seen here tonight.'

The old lady almost smiled, Gail was going to do the work for her.

'Look at the choice you made. You could save one thing in the world and it was a piece of technology. Your laptop. Because that is where you keep your dream, right? That is where your life's work is. That's your screenplay. It's your music and photos. It is who you are.'

Irving nodded at her.

'And I grabbed my keys. Because the thing I want most is my son's safety, right?'

'Right.' Irving nodded his head like he was psyching himself up in his agreement.

'Wrong.'

The old lady's eyes widened in the same way that Gail's had when she walked back through the front door of her building. Not dead.

'I want to get out. I want my fucking freedom. And my baby's freedom.' She turned to Mrs May. 'I'm sorry, you do put across an interesting offer, but you have just confirmed that you are out of your fucking mind.' Back to Irving. 'Come. Now.' She grabbed his hand. They had been comfortable physically since their first meeting. He followed her to the front door.

They stopped at the threshold.

'I've got my keys. We get in the car and drive. You take your laptop, your work. It's still with you. The dream is still alive.' She was emphatic, convincing.

'Be careful, now.'

Mrs May had never said that somebody had to be killed, they were always allowed to leave. Part of her wanted Abe to get out, she could see his end. There was nothing she could do to stop Gail and she certainly would not be able to stop Irving.

'You've had your say, old lady,' Gail was getting feistier by the moment, 'I am not against grabbing something and smacking it around the side of your head again. Let the man think.'

Gail looked at Irving. He hoiked his laptop up onto his shoulder and she pulled at his hand to take him outside.

Mrs May was in the doorway. Silent.

'Come on. Let's do it. Let's go. The Beresford is Hell. Not the planet.'

They were walking away.

Irving stopped.

'What are you doing?'

At first he said nothing.

'Don't. You don't need to. Come on. You're talented. You work hard.'

'You go.' He spoke softly and certainly.

He never said that he was going to stay, that he was going to sign that contract and risk it all. Sell his wonderful soul. He just started walking backwards, keeping his eye on that brave, pregnant woman who was going to chance her arm. She had been told that she was in Hell and she was going to make the best of it.

Drive right through.

Keep going through Hell.

Irving was, too, in his own way.

He stepped back into The Beresford. Mrs May sidled up next to him. She didn't look smug that she had won, but you could see that she knew she had.

What do you want, Jordan Irving?

Everything.

Gail cried for Irving.

Mrs May closed the door of her building.

So it was done.

SIXTEEN

Gail continued to weep in the driver's seat of the car she had arrived in all those months ago, when she ran away from a situation she thought was hell. She looked into her rearview mirror. Irving was in the apartment with the Mrs Mays and was signing his life away.

Or his death.

His remaining time would undoubtedly be filled with artistic blockbusters and awards and sex and money. What the old lady hadn't explained was what happened after. Irving may not become another soul collector. He may be whipped for eternity in a pit of fire while being raped by demons.

She hoped he was reading the small print.

It had been nearly a minute. She could see a young man in his twenties with a large duffle bag over his shoulder, walking up the drive to the house he thought was an absolute steal. He had a dream and thought that the low rent would afford him the opportunity to pursue that.

She could wind down her window and warn him.

She could put him out of his misery by running him down on her way out.

But she was done with The Beresford.

It wasn't her problem.

She threw the car into gear. Somehow, she had less than she had arrived with, but she didn't care. She was out of there. Once again, driving in one direction. She didn't know if it was north or southeast. It didn't matter. It was away.

The roads were winding. It was dark. Gail was in her head.

Hell on Earth? Hell is Earth? Earth is Hell?

She tried to think back to her childhood. Nothing.

College. Nothing.

A time when her husband was not a piece of shit. Something, but perhaps it wasn't real. Maybe that was another of her dreams. She was creating a person that she wanted rather than a person that she had.

Driving. Winding. Darkness.

Could she have guaranteed her child's future? Increasingly she was certain the life inside her was a boy. He was going to be born. Born into Hell, if what the old lady had said was true.

Driving. Steering. Stopping.

She was home. Her old house. Like a carrier pigeon, she had automatically returned to the place she was from.

Was it any worse than The Beresford?

She pulled into the drive, got out and walked up to the front door. Gail didn't know what to do. Should she let herself in or ring the bell? Did it matter? Did anything matter anymore? She was feeling increasingly nihilistic. Not that life was predetermined, but that it didn't matter what we chose.

She let herself in.

It was quiet.

'Hello?' The first part of the word came out with a nervous croak. She asked again. 'Hello?'

Cautiously, Gail stepped into her old home. Into the hall, past the empty lounge and into the kitchen. She was so nervous she didn't realise she had left the front door open behind her.

The kitchen was a mess, but it looked as though her husband had been cooking for himself. There was a chopping board on the side with a dirty knife resting on top and some dried tomato seeds and garlic skin.

Her husband was not there but he wasn't far away. And he had, predictably, been drinking. When he got back and saw that the door was open, he clenched his fists and entered. Naturally, he clenched his teeth, too. He was ready for whatever was going to come at him, he thought.

He wasn't ready for Gail.

'Fuck. Gail. You're home. You're back.' The tension in his hands released.

'Don't you dare tell me you want a sandwich.'

She found herself somewhat pleased to see him. The familiarity, perhaps. The difference to her time at The Beresford.

Nobody wants their life anymore.

She hated herself for feeling that way.

'Are you home?' he asked, looking like a little kid.

'I don't know.'

He was hopeful. Then he spotted her bump.

'What the fuck? Where have you been? What is that?'

'It's yours. Don't worry.'

'Oh my God. A kid. A dad. I...'

Gail watched him. He went from elation to loathing in no time at all. That's when she knew that Mrs May had been telling the truth. It didn't matter where she went, she would still always be in Hell.

'You knew you were fucking pregnant. With MY kid and you ran away. You weren't even going to tell me, were you?'

Ordinarily, Gail would have submitted to him. She would have apologised for what she did, taken a backhand or three. But not with that innocent boy growing inside her. He was going to be the size of a rutabaga soon. Whatever that was.

'Shh,' she told him.

'What?'

'Shhhhh,' she repeated.

'Don't you come back here and tell me to—'

The knife was in his stomach. The blood was mingling with those dried-on tomato seeds from whatever he had made himself. Something more than a drunken sandwich.

She pulled the knife out, and he grabbed at the wound.

That first stab was for him. The next ones were for her. Two into the chest. One into his shoulder. A slit across both biceps. He was drunk and losing blood and couldn't move. She had complete control over his life and how he would die.

Castle dropped to his knees.

Gail pressed her heel into his chest and pushed him back.

He was weak and heavy, but Gail managed to flip him over. She laid herself down on top of him and whispered into his ear, 'You like it when I put my weight down on you like this? It's fucking awful isn't it? How about this?' She stabbed the tip of the knife deep between his legs.

'You like that, huh? You fucking like that?'

He was crying. This was his end. The tears were tinged with a sense of relief.

She spoke into his ear one last time. 'You're already in Hell, you fucking drunk. Where you're going is worse than this.'

Gail gripped his hair in her left hand and ran the tomatoey blade across his throat then stabbed it into the back of his neck for good measure.

She did not have to sell her soul. Nobody was going to hurt her son.

Gail went to the front door and shut it. Her husband was dying. Not long, now. And she was going to watch him.

The Beresford was behind her. Whatever happened there, whatever rules and routines occurred in that strange place with its eccentric owner, would happen only there. That's what she told herself, what she had to tell herself.

Castle's breathing was laboured, and his pulse was weakening. Gail could see him slipping away. He would have grabbed at his throat if Gail hadn't cut through the tendon attaching his bicep to the bone. He could no longer flex his arm.

He would never again raise his hand.

This is not The Beresford, Gail told herself. *Nobody else is coming.*

Castle stopped moving.

Gail slid her back down the kitchen cupboard, sat on the floor and smiled as she exhaled her relief.

The knife was still in her hand. She started to count.

Sixty...

Fifty-nine...

Fifty-eight...

Just to be sure.

In a minute, she would be free. Free of her abusive husband. Free from Mrs May's offer. Free of The Beresford.

The building had changed her, made her weaker, made her act out of character, irrationally at times. It had tried to trick her and make her believe that she was starting a new life when she was, actually, being broken down further. Too weak to say no to the bargain.

Take the deal.

Get what you want.

Give me your soul.

Gail knew that the bell would not ring, she knew that Mrs May only operated within the walls of The Beresford; that giant purgatory. Gail would be free, she would have her child, she would protect it with everything.

She didn't take the deal but had still got the thing she wanted most. Gail was strong. And whatever place she found herself to be would be a Hell of her own making.

ACKNOWLEDGEMENTS

This has been a strange year. I haven't seen that many people. I don't usually see that many people, anyway, but it has been fewer than even I am used to. I haven't been ill. I've kept writing and working and not sleeping.

I have to acknowledge my wonderful publisher, Karen, who has been hit hard in these unprecedented times. Yet she still managed to publish my last book and sign me up to write more and support me in my efforts to up my output and publish this stand-alone alongside the series we have worked on for the past few years. I don't know how she does it. I'm thankful for the editorial feedback, the encouragement and the daily texts.

The rest of the Orenda team have been brilliant in taking up the slack, too. West: classic, brutal edits. We locked horns on this one over a few things but it came out better – of course. And Cole, who had to be more on the ball than ever. Your creativity and focus went beyond expectations. Anne, thank you for keeping my book out there and organising a huge blog tour, I thought the book would get lost.

My agent, Kate, who reads my stuff first and says that it's weird and quirky, and still gets behind it – I'm starting to think she likes it. We managed to grab a breakfast between lockdowns, and talk about books and films and how much we love *This Is Us*. Then I say I want to write two books a year and she's like, 'Yeah. Done.'

Some awesome people in the book world who continued to shout about my writing even when I thought everybody had stopped listening: Liz, I want to make number one AND two this year. Pinborough, of course. Tom the advice-giver. Chris Hooley, Chris McDonald, Kriss Akabusi, Kris Kristofferson ... any other Chris you can think of.

And the real people. My mum and Brendan, who had to deal with Covid and a stroke and the worst sixtieth-birthday celebrations. Zoom quizzes and bingo died out long before you gave up on them, but it was nice to see you. And often nicer to mute you.

Phoebe and Coen, just when I thought I couldn't love you more, I had to homeschool you. You still make all the days better, and I hope I can leave you more than a pile of books nobody read. Hopefully you'll thank me, one day, for making you do the hard maths sheets that 'none of your friends had to do'.

Siena and Zoe and Will, I'm sure that I am a pain in your arse a lot of the time, too, but we have shared more of this year than any other and look at us … Stupid songs and hugs and dancing. Loads of love. But, Siena, I'm not sharing your Instagram until you are nicer to your mum. (Ha!)

That brings me to the mum. Kel. My Kel. So many people had the worst year ever. And it was shit, of course. But never with you. And if I'm languishing, there's nobody else I want to be languishing with. And if I'm struggling, I'm not struggling with you. We exercised our way through, and we drank our university body weights in booze most nights, but you keep me going, and you don't think writing isn't a real job, and you call it 'work' and, let's be honest, you buy most of the gin. I'm not a good enough writer to make you realise how amazing you are, but I'll keep trying.

I can't forget a supportive friend who stupidly opened an independent bookshop during a global epidemic. Please, find Fourbears Books online or visit in Caversham, Reading. Order one book. Now. Preferably one of mine.

Times are still weird, and I thank anyone who buys this book. We need decent stories and art and music more than ever. We need to take a step back, but we need to challenge. Instead of thinking about being kind, we need to try being kind. We need to talk to one another but, more importantly, we need to listen. Be present. Think. What do you want? Things are bad. But it can't be hell. It's not even warm.